C000148258

Cube Rube

Cube Rube

Scott Michael Decker

Copyright (C) 2014 Scott Michael Decker
Layout design and Copyright (C) 2021 by Next Chapter
Published 2021 by Next Chapter
Cover art by http://www.thecovercollection.com/
Back cover texture by David M. Schrader, used under license from Shutter-
stock.com
Typed by Joey Strainer
This book is a work of fiction. Names, characters, places, and incidents are the
product of the author's imagination or are used fictitiously. Any resemblance
to actual events, locales, or persons, living or dead, is purely coincidental.
All rights reserved. No part of this book may be reproduced or transmitted in
any form or by any means, electronic or mechanical, including photocopying,
recording, or by any information storage and retrieval system, without the
author's permission.

Titles by the Author

If you like this novel, please post a review on the website where you purchased it, and consider other novels from among these titles by Scott Michael Decker:

Science Fiction:
Bawdy Double
Cube Rube
Doorport
Drink the Water
Edifice Abandoned
Glad You're Born
Half-Breed
Inoculated
Legends of Lemuria
Organo-Topia
The Gael Gates
War Child

Fantasy:
Fall of the Swords (Series)
Gemstone Wyverns
Sword Scroll Stone

Look for these titles at your favorite book retailer.

Chapter 1

Jack stared at the cube, mesmerized by its iridescent color. One part of his mind calculated how long it would keep him in smoke while another part mocked him for thinking iridescence a color.

Two inches to a side, the cube stared back at him from the middle shelf of a contraption known as an oven.

He swore it stared, seeing deep into his soul, tracing his past through his three failed marriages, his four bankruptcies, his multiple encounters with the Imperial Patrol, and his constantly smoking himself into oblivion.

Ivory swirls sloshed across its surface, like laughter. The cube knew him.

Twenty minutes earlier, he'd dropped from orbit in his Salvager to sniff through the ruins of Canis Dogma Five, the old Circian homeworld, for something he might hawk to the junk lords for a few hundred galacti. He'd found someplace to park the Scavenger out of sight from the constant patrols, his ship almost as derelict as the ruins he explored. Then he'd worked himself between the decrepit doors of an apartment building, one of the few still standing amidst the ruins of a city that had once housed a million people, minimum. Two floors up, he'd cracked a flat whose stale air bespoke its millennial inoccupancy. The oven was a perfect find, as valuable in its current state as it would be after being dropped out a window. I'm not carryin' it down two flights of stairs, he'd thought indignantly, bending to look inside. The dusty glass pane obscured the interior, so he'd opened the door.

And stared at the cube inside.

Before he could think, he snatched it from the oven.

* * *

A scene filled his sight and a voice rang in his ears.

He was in a cavern, and a man stood before him, dressed in sequined silks of multiple colors, upon his head a slim, simple circlet, in one hand a two-inch silvery cube.

"I am Lochium Circi the Ninth, Emperor of Circi, a civilization that once reached to the outer arms of the galaxy." Behind the figure was a small table, on it a vial filled with orange fluid, and a large stone slab atop one-foot pillars. "Welcome to my final resting place, Traveler. You have now been selected for a sacred duty. You see me because you have been chosen to wield the Ghost cube." Lochium Circi the Ninth ceremoniously held up the silvery, two-inch cube. "With this modest device, the Circians spread their influence throughout the galaxy."

A remote rumble shook the chamber, and dust drifted down from the ceiling. "And now our influence is dying. Barbarians bombard Canis Dogma Five into oblivion as I speak.

"You, Traveler, have been chosen to become the next Emperor of the Circian Empire, with all the privileges, responsibilities, and obligations thereto implied, and to bring together again all the remnants of our once-great Empire under the auspices of one government, to live peacefully until the end of time under you and your successors.

"The cube has chosen you, Traveler, because you are worthy and noble and pure. May the billion suns of the galactic core light your path with brilliance."

* * *

His head spun and his face stung.

"Hold it by its edges," the girl told him.

Jack did as she bade him, the cube threatening to suck him elsewhere again.

He stared at her, she who had slapped him. She who knew what he held.

Because it was hers.

He wondered where she'd come from. The apartment had had the feel of having been vacant for a very long time. He also wondered why she hadn't just taken it from him. One part of him already knew, and another part ridiculed him from not considering for a moment handing it back to her. He'd be stupid to give up something that might keep him in smoke for the rest of his life.

She stared back at him, much as the cube had.

Jack saw what she was thinking. Me, Emperor?

The thought was beyond ludicrous and passing farcical.

She laughed softly, shaking her head.

He was a wretch, through and through. No amount of wealth, schooling, or breeding could remedy that. All a charm school might do is teach him how to insult people without their knowing it, something he now did without intending to.

He frowned at her. "I'm Jack, but you knew that, didn't you?"

She nodded. "Misty." She didn't extend her hand.

He might have been a leper. "Pleased."

"Likewise." Clearly she wasn't.

"This is yours, isn't it?"

"It was," she said, shrugging. "Or more accurately, I used to be its."

"And now I'm its?" He frowned at it in his hand.

"You catch on fast."

"What is it?"

"A Gaussian Holistic Oscillating Subliminal Tesseract, a ghost cube." She suddenly stood and beckoned him to follow. "Now that you're here, I need your help."

He climbed to his feet slowly, as though he'd been sitting for several hours. The quality of light through dusty panes hadn't changed appreciably.

She led him up several floors, some of the stairwells difficult to navigate, their steps mangled by time and inattention. He wondered as he followed her up what an eight- or nine-year-old girl was doing in a decrepit ruin like this by herself.

"It's been a couple weeks," she said, stopping outside a door at the end of a hall. "So he doesn't smell very good."

Not smelling very good was an understatement. He could barely hold his gorge. "What do you want me to do?"

Grief wrecked her face. "Help me bury him."

He knew without asking that just leaving the corpse wasn't a choice. He also knew that just leaving the girl wasn't a choice. A tantalizing lifetime of smoke-filled nights receded inexorably from his grasp. And right now, he really needed to smoke.

The blanket helped to hold together what decay was rapidly dismantling, but couldn't shield him completely from the ooze he should've expected.

She led him to a wildly overgrown park, two blocks away, where a pit had already been dug.

"I just couldn't figure out how to get him down here."

Once he'd finished, organic was the only word he could summon to describe his smell. In addition to the odors of necrosis and its associated fluids, a thick layer of freshly-turned soil now stuck to those stains. The cube was tucked in his pocket.

He'd just chunked the last shovelful to fill the pit when a distant whine alerted him. "Quick! The patrol!" He loped for the nearest building, the girl outpacing him easily and leading him toward a culvert.

They dove into it just as the craft roared overhead. Straining engines whined in complaint as it circled back.

"Stars above, they saw us. We can't stay here." He looked at her, despairing that they'd be trapped in the culvert.

Misty seemed unconcerned.

Jack tracked the incoming ship by sound as he looked her over. The backwash of the landing retros buffeted her thin, threadbare clothing, its many rents and tears each carefully stitched. Her hair fell in stringy, ungainly swatches to uneven, hacked-off lengths near her shoulders. Her cheeks were hollow with malnutrition or shock.

Maybe both, he thought. "Why won't they find us?"

Her eyes glistened with ethereal light. "You'll persuade them not to." She didn't glance toward his jacket pocket, but she might have.

Voices outside approached. "Over here. I told you I picked up a signal of an incoming ship. Probably some scavenger."

He brought out the cube.

* * *

Jack looked at the culvert. The drainpipe was three feet in diameter, barely room for anyone to have gone in. "We've picked up native signals before. Remnants of the old Circian Empire, eking out a meager life among the ruins. If it was a scavenger, where's the ship?" He turned to look at his shipmate.

The guy shrugged, his uniform immaculate.

Jack knew his own was perfect as well. "You goin' in after 'em?" He gestured at the culvert, and then picked an imaginary speck of dust off his sleeve.

The other guy shook his head. "They ain't payin' to replace uniforms, remember?"

"We'll set up monitors in a perimeter. If there's a scavenger, we'll catch 'em on the way out."

* * *

Jack snapped back into the culvert, his hand coming off the cube. The voices outside faded.

He'd felt as if he'd been dreaming, on the one hand hearing them talk outside the pipe, on the other doing the talking. Somehow, he'd maintained an awareness of his hand on the cube.

Misty watched him, her eyes on his face.

"What *is* this thing?"

She shrugged. "Grandpa never said, but he did tell me it's old, very old. My ancestors used it to control the galaxy."

He brought his gaze up from the cube. "What ancestors?"

"The Circians."

Archeologists had long wondered at the source of Circian power. A meek, unpretentious peoples, they had somehow spread their influence from a modest-size planet with few mineral resources across the galaxy, dominating multiple constellations with far more natural resources and far larger navies. Even their home system had been insignificant, a two-planet single-star system with a young blue primary sitting astride the narrow neck of empty space between Canis Major and Canis Minor. The Dog Bone, it'd been called by the early spacers who'd colonized the area some ten thousand years ago.

But somehow, Circi had come to dominate first the adjoining Majora and Minora constellations, then the Perseus Arm itself, and then the entire galaxy. Not by conquering anything, either.

All by persuasion.

Jack shook his head at her. "That your grandpa we buried?"

She nodded, looking sad.

"We'll go say a few words, once it's safe."

She smiled at him, looking grateful.

"Where are your relatives?"

Her gaze narrowed in bewilderment.

"You don't have any relatives?

"Grandpa never mentioned any."

"Your parents?"

"Died five years ago when the building two blocks over collapsed."

"There have to be other people around here."

She shrugged. "Grandpa always told me to stay away. There's a tribe six blocks to the west, another twelve blocks north. See them once in awhile, but they always run when I approach."

"What did he tell you to expect once he'd died?"

She brightened unexpectedly. "He told me, 'Expect the Universe. You're the Princess.'"

He was dumbfounded. What kind of upbringing was that? "Princess of what?"

"Circi," she said matter of factly.

He threw his head back in laughter and hit his head on the inside of the culvert. Laughing even as he rubbed his head, he shook it in wonder, bemused and bewildered.

She looked as bemused as he felt.

"And just how were you supposed to become the Princess of Circi?"

"Become?" She looked even more befuddled. "I already am!"

He roared with laughter all the more.

Misty looked annoyed.

Outside, the roar of engines signaled the patrol's departure.

He sleeved the tears from his eyes, his hands still grimy with fresh earth. "What the stars am I going to do with you?" He laughed some more at his own predicament, the sudden caretaker of a delightful nine-year-old.

A crusty, renegade salvage-hound too self-centered to make four marriages work, not diligent enough to avoid three bankruptcies, having tangled more times than both combined with the law, and an inveterate smoker, now the guardian of this orphan.

And owner of a cube that had ludicrously chosen him to become Emperor.

"Are you all right?"

He nodded and caught his breath, sure he looked a wreck, his face red and tear-strewn. "Too ironic, is all," he said, glancing down at the cube. "Well, if this was truly the source of the Circian's power, it's clear why their Empire fell." And he laughed some more.

* * *

"I think they're gone now," Misty said, peering from the culvert.

He could barely see her outline, night having long since fallen.

They'd likely set up infrared monitors in a perimeter, but they weren't interested in the native peoples. The Imperial Patrol would be looking for him and his Salvager.

He followed her out, trusting that she knew the area and where they could flee if the patrol returned.

They made their way to the gravesite and stood beside the unmarked mound of freshly-turned soil.

Her face swung up to his, a pale shadow amidst darker shadows.

What am I supposed to say? he wondered; I didn't know the man.

The moon of her face beamed at him brightly.

He took her hand and sighed. "We gather here at the final resting place of—"

"Augustus Circi, Emperor," she supplied in the pause.

"—to honor his passing from a life of devotion. Those of us who remain behind will never forget him."

The girl beside him wept softly in the darkness.

* * *

He climbed into a clean set of formalls, fresh from a shower, wondering the whole time how they were going to get off planet without the Imperial Patrol's intercepting them.

At least I'll be clean when they arrest me, he thought.

He'd parked Misty in the galley in front of a protein mush, his synth having sized up a meal for her.

Although famished, he had more of an appetite to get out of his soiled clothing and get cleaned up.

She licked the last off the spoon and glanced at him, her eyes taking in the fresh formalls.

"Your turn," he said, hiking his thumb toward the stall.

She half-frowned in that direction. "I've never been in one before. Does it hurt?"

He chuckled, shaking his head. "It's voice-operated, so if you scream, it'll shut itself off." He glanced around. Everything looked all right. "Did you touch anything?"

"Not a thing, just like you told me." She beamed at him. "The mush was terrible."

"You get used to it. In," he said, hiking the thumb.

He took her seat, the cube where he'd set it, after admonishing her not to touch it.

"It's not mine anymore, so I can't," she'd told him.

The galley was small, with barely room for two at the table. The seamless walls hid all the kitchen gadgets, but Jack needed just two: the synth and a spoon.

"Synth on," he said, and a whirring noise trundled out a bowl of mush. "My favorite."

He devoured it mindlessly, his gaze on the cube.

Two inches to a side, its edges slightly beveled, its sides completely reflective, the cube gazed back at him.

Belching, he pushed aside the empty bowl and put his hands on the cube.

* * *

The opulence stunned him, and the feel of the silk against his body felt like a mother's womb.

The two bulges at his breast bewildered him, as did the cavity between his legs. Mammaries and a vagina! he thought, looking around.

In his hand was a hairbrush. The marble columns framed a view of manicured palace grounds, topiary-tangled gardens, sprawling outbuildings.

He knew where he was, but not how he'd got here.

Or who he'd become.

Dismayed, he looked up from his ample breasts to see a servant approach.

"My Lady looks distressed, pardon my noticing," the handmaid said.

* * *

"What am I supposed to wear?" Her voice came from the shower, bringing him back to the ship.

He hadn't noticed she was finished. Ordering up a pair of small formalls, he took them from the sizer and thrust it into the showercube, his eyes on the kitchen, averted.

"Thank you."

He stepped back to the table.

She emerged, clad in formalls, looking down at herself in evident distaste. "I'll need better clothes than this before I can be presented at the Palace."

He roared with laughter and the bewildered look on her face caused him to laugh all the harder.

"You shouldn't have laughed like that," she said a long time later.

"I'm sorry," Jack replied, kissing the top of her head. She was curled against him in the Pilot's chair, one of three places to sit aboard the Scavenger.

He'd laughed so hard he'd begun to cry, and her face had crumpled as she'd slid to the floor and gathered herself into a fetal position to weep.

He'd picked her up and sat her on his lap and wept with her until they'd both wept themselves dry.

The girl quiescent in his arms, he wondered how he'd known what to do. An orphan, reared in a brothel on Alpha Tuscana, he'd run away to work on a garbage scow at age twelve. Jack had never known a mother's embrace. The brash buxom breasts of courtesans had been a paltry substitute, the boy cast away the moment a paying customer walked in the door.

"I'll get you finer clothes than Princess Andromeda, and she'll be so envious that she'll ask who your designer is."

Misty giggled. "Liar."

He giggled too, enjoying the moment and the smell of freshly-washed child and being close to another human being.

Far too little of the latter throughout my life, he thought.

* * *

Emperor Phaeton Torgas stared at Princess Andromeda. "There's been a change in the alignments, I tell you!"

She sat on an ottoman slightly to the right of his throne, the heiress in attendance upon the troubled Emperor. "Someone dares oppose the Empire?" she asked lightly, looking as dainty as a daisy. They were alone in the throne room, or as alone as they'd ever get, servants omnipresent and perpetually underfoot. *Like rats,* she thought.

He scowled at her over his scepter, a gold-plated staff two-and-a-half feet long, capped with a platinum-filigreed halo, which served to house a somewhat-plain looking two-inch silver cube. "No, it's not open defiance, as if we didn't have enough of that already." His gaze was on his own satin-clad foot.

Her satin slippers, embroidered with gold and silver thread in the shapes of roses, glinted in the evening light.

"It's more an undercurrent, but a strong one, a shift in the pillars that hold the Empire aloft."

"Sounds grave, Father. No doubt a concern easily addressed." She smoothed an imaginary wrinkle from the sleeve of her silk blouse.

"If only I knew where to look! I'd place the Armada on alert, but I haven't an inkling of what to tell Admiral Camelus to look for." A shudder shook him. "When I look around the room, I see the legacy of my forebears, and I'm invigorated to build upon their achievements," Emperor Phaeton intoned. "And when I look upon you, my dear daughter, I desire to extirpate any hint of resistance, that you may rule unhindered when I'm gone."

She glanced around the room, busts of her forebears lining the walls. For twelve hundred years, the Torgas lineage had held sway over half the galaxy, occasional rebellions flaring at the edges but nearly all put asunder quickly.

"I hear you had something akin to a fit this morning?"

She drew a sharp breath. Of course he knew about that, she reminded herself. The cube tells him everything.

"The cube tells me everything."

It was an open secret that this alien cube was the source of Torgassan power.

"I don't know what happened, Father. I was brushing my hair out in my dressing room and ..." She looked at him bewildered. "Remember that time you ghosted me? That's almost what this felt like. I was in a ship galley, small and cramped, a bowl with the leavings of some mush beside me, and a girl's voice called from around the corner ..." She shook her head, unable to recall what the girl had said.

They both looked at the cube mounted on the scepter.

The alien artifact functioned by reading the minute variations in electrical fields introduced by human thought. At its wielder's behest, it also injected electrical field perturbations in resonance with the brain's neuro-electrical activity, able to do so irrespective of distance.

Which was how her father had known.

These electrical fields were known as Gaussian fields, and the device was called a Gaussian Holistic Oscillating Subliminal Tesseract, but it was usually referred to by the acronym, GHOST. Thus the origin of the term. Whenever the Emperor wanted to know something or to influence someone, he simply ghosted them.

Their gazes met over the top of the scepter.

"Is there another cube, Father?"

Chapter 2

The next morning, Jack got Misty and himself some breakfast, and then Jack looked into the cube to find out what the Imperial Patrol was doing.

Slowly, its sides lost their reflectivity and an image formed.

The cabin of the Imperial Patrol vessel.

"—no sign of activity. Maybe he's laying low until we get distracted," one said.

"With that long a criminal record, I'd say he doesn't know when to lay low. What about that girl, the one he was with on the monitors?"

"What about her?"

"Think we should report her to Captain Jenks? He did say to report any suspicious planetside activity immediately."

"What's suspicious about a girl? Especially a native brat?"

The other patrol officer was silent a moment, looking pensive. "This scavenger is a loner. She's clearly a ground-dog. Doesn't make sense, their pairing up like that."

"There you go thinking again."

"What do you suppose happened that he'd want immediate reports? He's never expressed the slightest interest in this sector, much less the planet itself."

The other man extended a hand toward a tactiface, moved a few manipules until data spilled down the screen. " 'Canis Dogma Five, former Capital of the Circian Empire, whose last remnants collapsed in three hundred BTE'—over fifteen hundred years ago—'after ruling the galaxy for nearly a millennium.' " His eyes scanned the fountain of text.

"Maybe it's Torgassan Paranoia," said the other man. Clearly from one of the subjugated worlds, he wore a Torgassan Patrol uniform, swore fealty to the Torgassan Emperor, got paid out of the Torgassan coffers, but was no more Torgassan than his shipmate.

"Listen to this: 'Despite numerous attacks by rival empires, the Circians fought very few wars. The fifty or so naval engagements they are known to have had all ended in the surrender or negotiated capitulation of their opponents. They were never the victor by means of the outright defeat of their enemies.' " He turned to his companion. "Now, that's influence!"

Influence that Emperor Torgas wished he had, Jack was thinking.

"Influence that Emperor Torgas wished he had," said the other man, his face empty of expression.

Jack jumped, and the cube turned silver again.

* * *

"They don't look very friendly."

Jack wasn't about to let that stop him. They stood on a cracked and pitted major boulevard six blocks north of Misty's tower apartment, surrounded by rag-clad natives, each bearing a weapon, every weapon aimed at them.

After they'd eavesdropped on the Imperial Patrol, they had set out to find the other natives of Canis Dogma Five. They'd followed the wide boulevard, an occasional skeleton of toppled skyscraper blocking their path. They'd have made better time if they hadn't had to climb through the detritus. The boulevard itself was a veritable forest but a pygmy one, the thin, scraggly trees barely eking out nutrients from the rock-hard surface, most of them sprouting from seams.

Jack held out his hands to show they were empty. "I come to ask a favor. My name is Jack."

A large man with a heavy spear and even heavier gut replied, "You fell from the stars two nights ago, and the Imperial Patrol looks for you. Why shouldn't we sell you to them?"

"Because I helped this girl bury her grandfather, Augustus Circi."

The man lowered the spear. "The old man finally died?"

"About two weeks ago," Misty told him.

"I'm sorry for you loss," the heavy man said. "We honor those who help with our dead. Thank you, stranger Jack who fell from the stars. Come, and ask you favor in private. Away from the Patrol's prying eyes." He looked overhead as if expecting a patrol craft any moment, then signaled to the group.

Warriors melted into the surroundings like wraiths.

"I'm Xerxes, and my home is this way." He gestured to an alley between derelict buildings that looked none too inviting.

As his eyes adjusted to the darkness, Jack realized it was free of the detritus that littered the rest of the ruins. The smells of dank and dusty decay were absent too. Misty followed obediently at his elbow. The alley turned into a tunnel, then a corridor, and beyond a heavy curtain, an abode, the scents of home and food unmistakable.

"There she is," said a woman's voice. "Didn't I tell you, Xerk, that we'd be seeing the waif? How are you, my girl? Misty, isn't it? I'm your great aunt once removed, Gertrude. You can just call me Trude." Her manner was just as robust as her girth and her voice. If her man was large then she was larger.

Trude was a good name for her, Jack was thinking.

"That's *Princess* Misty," the girl said, a hand to her hip and her shoulder thrust forward. "And I'm anything but a waif!"

"Anything but is for certain, no question there. And who's the gentleman escort, your Highness?" From anyone else, it might have been mockery, but from Trude it actually sounded respectful.

"Captain Jack," Misty said, "this is my Great Aunt Trude, once removed."

"Enchanted," Jack said, inclining his head.

"Mutual, Captain, and welcome."

"And you were right," Xerxes said to his wife. "Augustus is dead."

"Now wasn't that what I was sayin'?" she asked in an "I-told-you-so" voice. "Knew it was comin', Princess, as he hadn't been well."

"Jack helped me put him to rest," Misty said, "and then brought me here."

"And a right thing, too," Trude said, looking Jack over again. "A good deed sometimes gets rewarded. Anything we can do, just you name it."

"Um ... " Jack looked around the lodgings, the walls clean if dingy with smoke from ill-ventilated fires, the carpets threadbare if in good repair, the furniture crude but looking comfortable even so, the walls riddled with cubbies full of useful items. "There is something I'd like to ask of you both. I brought Misty here not knowing of her relation, just knowing she needs care—care I can't give just yet. If I may ask—"

"But Jack," Misty cried, "you said you'd take me to the palace!" She looked as if about to weep.

"And I will," he protested, "if your aunt and uncle are willing, but I need a few days." He saw she wasn't believing him. "You know—to make arrangements."

"For what? We don't need arrangements! I'm the Princess!"

"But even the Princess needs the proper attire, Misty. You said so yourself. And it's much more proper and fitting if you received an invitation to the palace. Getting one will take a little time." Not bad, Jack thought to himself. I should confabulate more often, I'm pretty good at it.

Her face scrunched in disbelief. "But why should I stay here? How are you going to know if the clothes will fit if I don't go with you?"

"Well, I've got some trading to do before I'll have any money to buy the clothes. I'll be back in a few days." She still looked doubtful, so he added, "I promise."

She seemed to relent, then looked sad. "You sure you'll come back?"

"I'm sure," he said with quiet confidence.

"Oh good," she said, suddenly brightening, and then threw herself into his arms.

He couldn't help but embrace her. He didn't quite know how else to respond, but the warmth he felt deep inside made the whole trip worthwhile.

"He'll still have to get our permission, your Highness," Trude said softly.

"Of course," Misty said lightly, looking up at Jack with a smile that melted away all doubt he had about returning.

* * *

In retrospect, lodging the girl with her relative Circians had gone far more smoothly than he could have imagined.

Making his departure far more difficult than he could have imagined.

As Jack trudged doggedly back to the way he'd come, doubts gnawed at him.

I should go back for her, he thought a hundred times en route to his ship.

I'll miss her too much, he thought.

How can I do this to her? he wondered, his guilt adding to his indecision and regret.

Once you leave, you'll never return for her, he remonstrated himself. You never planned to return for her in the first place, he thought in self-recrimination.

The thought of her being left in the care of strangers was so reminiscent of how he had once felt as an abandoned orphan that Jack burst into tears and almost turned around on the spot.

He tore his gaze from over his shoulder and forced himself to continue southward, his surroundings blurry. A bystander might have thought him injured he wailed so disconsolately.

Back at his ship, hidden under a building at the base of a chute leading up the boulevard, Jack checked for signs of tampering or attempts at forced entry. Seeing none, he disarmed the gene-lock.

The ship did a quick gene analysis, then opened the hatch.

In the copilot's chair sat Misty.

"How...?" Between his befuddlement, relief, joy, and dismay, Jack didn't know what to say.

She looked abashed, as thought he might punish her.

Instead, he knelt at her feet and buried his head in her lap, weeping uncontrollably and protesting how terribly grateful he was that she'd disobeyed him and begging abjectly for her forgiveness.

"We'd better get going," she said sometime later.

He nodded mutely, wondering how he'd become enamored of her so quickly and why she had such faith in a terrible scoundrel like him. He also wondered how he could act such a fool and engage in such lugubrious buffoonery.

He looked over at her from the pilot's chair. "I'm not a very good person sometimes."

She looked ancient in her nine, elongated years. "You're always a good person, but your choices aren't always good."

He dropped his gaze to the controls, remembering what awaited them. He still didn't know how they were going to evade the Imperial Patrol, but he sensed he'd probably use the cube.

Setting it on the console, he gazed at it silvery sides, which promptly dissolved into iridescent rainbows. The patrol cabin materialized, the two officers scanning their instruments.

"Why do you suppose the Captain wants these ground-dog travels documented? What a waste of resources!"

"There you go thinking too much," the other one replied.

"And why electromagnetic activity? They don't have electricity. All we'll get on that is background static."

Jack looked at Misty.

"Concentrate on disappearing," she said.

He wrinkled his brow, remembering how he'd influenced them before as they stood outside the culvert, debating whether to go in after the two evaders.

"I wonder where that scavenger went. You think he's still ground-side?"

"We'd know if he wasn't. A ship that size leaves a trail visible from the primary. Don't worry, we'll see it easily from geosynch."

You think I'm gone already, Jack thought.

"You know what I think? Gone already."

You think I have a cloak, Jack thought.

"If I were him, I'd have a ship-cloak. Probably has contraband aboard right now. I don't think we'll see him at all."

"I think you're right. I think he's long since gone."

Jack powered up the ship. The hum of finely-tuned engineering vibrated the seat beneath him. Hold that thought! he thought, you won't see me at all!

He steered the ship out of its subterranean parkway space and pointed it at the stars.

Aboard the Imperial Patrol, sensors alarms began to flash, blaring their warnings at the two slack-jawed, empty-eyed patrolmen.

Jack engaged the main engine and launched the ship skyward. Two incognizant patrolmen watched without a twitch as their monitors tracked the Salvager.

Just get us off planet, he told the cube. Once in space, he could evade with a series of random hops.

Misty watched placidly, if attentively, from the co-pilot's chair.

As they hit the ionosphere, a thought occurred to Jack: "How did you get past the gene-lock?" He turned to stare at Misty.

Wide-eyed, she blinked at him.

"Bogey, bearing eight-one-nine, engage!" The patrolmen came to life.

"We've been spotted!" Jack picked the Vulpecula system at random and dropped the ship into an evasion pattern.

Just before the first hop, the ship slewed.

"Tractor beam" flashed on the screen, and Jack cursed.

The stars blanked out and a new set replaced them, but the patrol clung tenaciously.

"Come on, baby, shake 'em!"

The stars blanked again, and a fiery sun appeared a parsec away. "Tractor beam" continued to flash.

"You're under arrest," blared their speakers, the patrol using an override to commandeer the Scavenger's com system.

"Kiss my black hole!" Jack said, reversing the polarity to the hull in the hopes of breaking the tractor beam's hold.

The ship hopped again, and they appeared inside a nebula briefly, the thick plasmas nearly sending the shields into overload, but also weakening the tractor beam further.

The next hop took them to the Seven Sisters, and the "tractor beam" warning died.

"We did it!" Jack said, exulting, but he let the ship complete three more random hops before he was sure.

On the fourth hop, the Tuscana constellation appeared around them, and Jack powered down the ship, leaving on only the passive sensors. Without engines or other active systems, they would look like a derelict floating aimlessly in space.

Jack looked at the cube.

The silver surface stared back at him blankly.

Just in case, he willed them to be transparent.

The cube surface turned black.

"I knew you could do it, Jack!" Misty said with a squeal.

"*We* did it, or at least I think we did. Just to make sure, we'll wait awhile. Let's get something to eat while we wait," he told Misty, "and then we gotta sell that hold full of junk before I can take you to Torgas Prime."

Chapter 3

They walked the long avenue leading into the city of Perth on the garbage planet Corolla Tertius in the constellation Coronis Australis. On either side of the avenue stood slatted fences, little obscuring what lay beyond them. Mountains of junk soared in haphazard profusion, eclipsing any sight of the horizon. The gray, sultry sky seemed inadequate to contain the voluminous discard, the detritus of a hundred thousand occupied worlds.

Corolla Tertius had been Jack's first stop after stowing away on the garbage scow from Alpha Tuscana when he was twelve years old. Undeniably, the garbage planet held a comforting familiarity for him.

The mountains of refuse on either side of the avenue appeared to be moving. Upon closer inspection, the refuse itself wasn't actually moving, but hordes of scavengers were. The gleaners, they were called, picking through recently-dumped scow-loads of garbage for materials that might be recycled or reused.

Jack had been among them when he'd first arrived on Corolla Tertius, happy to explore what had been dumped here as garbage. One person's junk ...

"How come we're walking?" Misty asked, flitters whizzing past both ways on the avenue.

"'Cause Jack can't even afford a taxi, much less all the gowns, jewels, staff, and what-not that an arriving princess will be expected to wear, not to mention the fuel needed to get to Torgas Prime." The stench of garbage on either side was nearly overpowering.

She glared at him from under her brow.

"I said I'd get you there, right?" he asked, annoyed.

"Yeah?" Her voice looped upward, the question audible.

"So you can trust me to do that, Princess Misty Circi, or you can ask someone else." He didn't expect her to understand all the variables and hurdles, but he did expect her to have some patience.

"All right, I just might."

He raised an eyebrow at her, stepping around what was clearly a gear casing for a landing strut. Must've fallen over the fence, he thought, the fence bulging precariously from the weight of junk it tried to contain. "Just might what?"

"Trust you," she said, smiling with that perfect, classic face.

A face that opened the joy in his heart. He didn't know why, but just looking at her gave him hope and instilled in him a sense of redemption and purpose.

He'd had little enough of all three in his life.

Ahead was a warefront—the front of a warehouse—whose shoddy appearance lent itself to the idea that it might have grown out of the junk behind it. The smell wasn't any better inside than out.

A weather-beaten, toothless derelict looked up from a glasma counter in better shape that he was. "That you, Jack?"

"Sure is, Busby. Look at you, workin' the counter. Moving up in the galaxy!"

The two men embraced. "What brings you back, boy?" He threw his working eye toward the girl, the glasma one remaining fixed to Jack's face.

Jack was surprised he had a prosthetic. Only then did he notice that the iris was a vertical almond-shape, probably from a stuffed, big-game cat. "This here's Misty."

"I'm a princess!" she piped up.

Busby giggled openly. "What'd you do, Jack, marry a Queen?" He threw his head back and laughed, blackened stubs where teeth should have been. His face had the puckered lemon look of the chronic edentulous.

"Not quite," Jack replied. "Hey, I got a half-a-load I need to sell. What's your rate today?"

Busby's hand shot up toward the sign, the forefinger missing its last joint.

"A quarter galacti per ton? Last I was here it was four bits, twice that."

"It's the market, Jack. You know the song and dance."

Every choreographed step of it. At that price, he wouldn't even fill his tank. He didn't have much hope of cajoling Busby to up his payout.

Misty tugged on his sleeve.

He looked down at her, saw her glance toward his pocket. Could I use the cube and have him triple his price? he wondered excitedly.

The swirling misery inside Busby's head flooded through Jack.

He stopped himself. Busby had taken Jack under his wing when the twelve-year-old orphan had been dumped from the garbage scow with the rest of its refuse, had shown him how to spot valuable glean, how to keep from being sucked into giving away what he'd collected, how to outsmart the other gleaners, who were as likely to steal his pickings as to find their own.

"Show old Busby your teeth," Jack whispered, nodding toward the trash collector and hoping he didn't get jealous.

Misty looked at Busby, smiling slowly, widening it until a full rictus had plastered her face.

Busby laughed again, joy in his eyes. "I can't tell you how good it is to see you, boy, how much I enjoyed having you at my side. How about four tenths per ton, Jack? I could do that for you."

"What a charmer," Jack told Misty as they were climbing into the taxi outside. To celebrate, they went to the fanciest restaurant on Perth.

Shredded banners hung limp in the stench-filled breeze, a stench replaced by the smell of roast beast, when the wind was right. The warped and stained wooden benches barely held their weight as they wolfed down real food, probably made from the pig-sized rodents who fought with the gleaners over loads newly dumped from the bellies of scows, the roast beast a far sight better than the flavored mush synthed aboard the ship and served in their own edible bowls.

Downtown Perth looked little different from the outskirts. The buildings were taller and the streets were cleaner, but the architecture was similar if more chic. Fancy dilapidation, the motif was called, a high-class garbage dump.

Under a statue of Captain James Stirling, who'd named Perth in the 110th century following the Diaspora, Jack and Misty fed the birds their leftovers, giggling and watching the antics as pigeons and seagulls fought over the scraps. These citified birds were far smaller version of the ones who flocked above the dumps in all directions around Perth, scattering only when a scow descended from the skies.

The inscription under the statue amused them both: "In the name of God, the Father, and his Majesty King George III, I do hereby consecrate this ground as the first free settlement in all of Coronis Australis, may its residents long enjoy clean living."

"Do you think he knew it'd be one big garbage dump?" Misty asked, and they both dissolved in laughter.

Jack stopped suddenly, sitting up, the feeling of being watched dropping dread like a lead weight into his bowels.

Half a dozen people strolled leisurely through the square. Streets bordered all four sides, their sidewalks somewhat crowded.

There, at one corner, a man looking away. At another corner, a woman browsing something in her hand a bit too intently. Jack didn't need to look toward the other two corners.

"We're being watched," Misty said.

He still found it disconcerting how well she knew his thoughts.

"Who are they?"

"Oh, variety of possibilities. Maybe the collection company hired by my first wife to get her spousal support. Half a dozen worlds think I owe them various fines—I've never been arrested on Corolla Tertius, I swear—so it can't be here. And well, I am a few months late on my Salvager payments. Come on." He stood and strode aggressively toward the man who'd looked away.

They despised confrontation, these collection agents. It was what they least expected and most feared. A hostile target was a dangerous target. Oh, yeah, they call them recipients, Jack thought. Euphemistic confabulation.

Misty a step behind him, Jack strode resolutely at the man.

He half-turned as though interested in something else.

Jack collided with him, knocking him to the ground. "Sorry," he said. He wasn't and kept on walking, crossing the street and turning west toward the spaceport.

He ventured a look back.

The man and two collection companions stood watching him from the corner, brushing the dirt off him.

Jack took the next turn, walked half a block, loped up an alley, then stepped to the curb and hailed a taxi.

"That happen often?" Misty asked, settling in the back seat beside Jack.

"Makes life interesting," he said. "They'll probably have agents at the spaceport. Only way they could have tracked me here was my landing. They're all public information."

"All landings?"

"Listen, kid, I don't make enough money to bribe every space traffic controller who happens to handle my landing requests. We'll have to think of some way to avoid them. I know you don't have much experience in this type of thing but if you've got ideas, I'd like to hear them." *If this is that same collection agency,* he thought, *they probably know most of my tricks.*

"Since they probably know most of your tricks, it'll have to be something original."

He snorted, bemused by her. "You a mind-reader, kid?"

"My name's Misty, and it's Princess Misty to you, Mister."

Jack roared with laughter, loving her cheek.

"You want any help or not?" she asked in mock pique.

"Of course, my Lady Princess Misty." He inclined his head toward her.

"That's what I thought, so check the cheek, pal."

"Yes, m'lady."

They shared a laugh as the taxi pulled to a stop across from the spaceport entrance, as instructed.

Duty free shops selling mostly memorabilia crowded the area outside the spaceport entrance. Why memorabilia might be marketable on a planet as forgettable as Corolla Tertius was a mystery to Jack. He ducked into a shop to browse.

He checked his palmcom to see if the Scavenger had been refueled yet. In a hurry to leave, he hadn't had the chance to alert the dockmaster. He keyed in the request, and an autoreply alerted him to a twenty-minute wait.

"How does this look?" Misty had draped a boa over her shoulders. It trailed to her feet in a cascade of glittery tendrils, like a furry worm.

A display of mock official uniforms stood behind her.

Jack smiled. We've got a little time, he thought.

* * *

I hoped she can do this, Jack thought, following Misty at a respectful five paces, a manservant cap pulled low over his brow, a uniform-looking suit decking him from head to toe, sans insignia.

They'd fashioned a tiara from a bracelet, found a sequined evening gown to modify to her size, and snatched the red pumps from a girl-sized doll.

She erased his every doubt in the first encounter.

"Boy," she said to the youngish valet at one concourse door, "My fool servant—" she gestured vaguely over her shoulder in Jack's direction — "has not only lost my port pass and credentials, he didn't even have the wherewithal to alert my father, King Quantus of Fornacis Secondus, of my predicament. Can you show him what competence is and get me a shuttle out to my yacht, please?"

The valet perked right up. "Certainly, Lady—"

"Princess Misty Circi," she said, and then turned on Jack. "Fool!"

He cringed obediently.

The valet jumped to do her bidding.

As they were en route to the posh side of the spaceport, Misty asked the shuttle driver to take them to the opposite end, where all the independent traders were relegated. The driver glanced askance at her.

"The fool servant of mine even forgot where we parked!" She cuffed him for emphasis, sitting behind him in the back seat.

The driver threw a pitying glance in Jack's direction and banked the flitter.

"Right here is fine, driver."

They'd seen a shadowy figure slouched against a landing strut two spaces over from the Salvager. Their paltry disguises weren't likely to work on people who had a profile on Jack. Their disguises might be thick, but that profile was pretty thick, too.

"All right, miss genius, what now?" Jack asked, peering toward the Scavenger from behind a cargo transport five spaces over. They'd spotted two additional collectors surveilling the Scavenger.

"Why don't we walk right up to the ship and say it's under contract to King Quintus?"

"They'll recognize me, even in this suit," he replied.

"Not if you exert a little influence."

"Eh? What do you mean?" He saw her glance at his pocket. He kept forgetting about the cube. And he didn't owe these hired pests an electron's worth of anything, unlike Busby, who'd helped him out when he was young. "All right, let's try it."

She led the way.

He admired how good she was. Stars above, what am I thinking? She should be practicing her social graces, not trying to finagle her way past a debt collector!

Cap down, gaze on her feet five paces ahead, he followed.

The nearest surveiller intercepted them at the Scavenger hatch.

"Jack who? You must have the wrong ship. The one's under contract to King Quintus of Fornacis Secondus. There are at least three other ships here named 'the Scavenger.' And at least two others by the name of 'Salvager.' Get out of my way!"

You don't see me, Jack thought, feeling the bewilderment. You must be mistaken. Check your records.

"Uh, pardon, your Ladyship, I must be mistaken. I'll check my records. You would mind waiting white I do so?"

"Sorry, I'm already late. If this idiot servant of mine hadn't lost my port pass and credentials, I'd have left long ago. A princess can't get decent help these days, I swear!" She kicked Jack in the shin. "Dolt!"

He cringed and cowered, holding his leg, and hopped over to the gene-lock to palm it.

The surveiller stepped aside. "Pardon, Lady Princess."

They stepped into the ship, and the hatch slid closed.

They fell into their seats, laughing to the point of tears, and Jack started the preflight checklist.

"You were wonderful, Misty!" he said, guiding the ship into orbit, still giggling.

"I was, wasn't I?" she said, grinning at him. "I'll make a damn fine princess!"

He wondered where she'd learned to curse like a sailor.

Chapter 4

The first place they stopped after leaving the garbage planet was Denebi in the Summer Triangle, near the red giant Vulpeculae. Sometimes known as Alpha Cygni, Denebi was a blue-white supergiant that bathed its fifteen planets with such bright light that humans lived under polarized domes only on the outer three planets. Denebi III, their destination, was a cold if well-lit ball of rock and ice with barely enough oxygen to sustain life. At a half-grav, it was an easy landing for even the bulkiest and most awkward of craft.

"Why are we stopping here?" Misty asked.

"I got an old associate who might be interested in some merchandise. Low gravity planets make better transshipment points, so this is a commerce center for almost all settlements in the Summer Triangle."

"Doesn't feel much like summer," she muttered.

"You stay here and mind yourself," Jack told her. "Keep yourself locked in the ship and don't open the door for strangers."

"Why can't I go with you?"

"This old associate of mine likes kids—dipped in chocolate for dessert. I won't be long."

She made a face at him and returned up the gangway at his bidding.

Jack retracted it remotely and locked the hatch with the gene lock. He was still puzzled how she'd gotten past it on Canis Dogma Five.

He closed the cargo hatch and shouldered the bundle of exotic goods he'd put together to sell, the bulging satchel easily five times his weight. Without the satchel, he'd have had a difficult time walking in the low gravity.

The spaceport tarmac was littered with variegated ships, from yachts to deep-space cruisers, the bulk of them freighters. Salvagers like his were scarce, the densely-populated Summer Triangle having been consistently occupied, even in the long interregnum between the Circi and Torgassan Empires. There wasn't much junk around to salvage.

He found a carrier at the spaceport edge and rented it with nearly his last galacti.

"Where you gonna sell that load o' junk?" the clerk asked him.

Jack frowned at the jibe. "I get a discount for letting you insult me?"

The carrier groaned and wheezed under the weight but followed him obediently, its rear blades sliding smoothly across the perma-frost ground. Cornering was difficult, the momentum wanting to carry off the carrier.

He wound his way through the markets, puffs of icy air above hucksters who offered up their wares to the crisp atmosphere, each breath freezing instantly to a glitter, lit by the bright blue primary like jewels.

Passing smoke shops and shoot shops, snort stops and shot stops, Jack felt the yearning for a lungful of comfort. Not until I make the sale, he told himself doggedly. And what about her? he asked himself yet again.

What about her? he replied to his own question, daring himself to think the unthinkable.

I can't think about her right now, he told himself. While he didn't think about her, another part of his brain plotted how he could rid himself of the pesky girl.

The unassuming storefront declared in inch-high letters the underwhelming presence who might be found beyond the door: "R. Delphin, Proprietor."

Leaving his carrier behind, Jack pushed into the shop.

The interior was immaculate. Glasma cases displaying fine antiques lined both sides of the shop. The walls displayed stills of other antiques that had once graced the premises. An old man with half a cybernetic head peered at fine stones through a high-precision oculus. He wore a sterile white coat and white satin gloves. Even his shoes were draped with sterile white cloth.

"Stop right there. You need decontamination."

Behind the door was a small decom stall. Jack stepped dutifully inside; the machine hummed and whined, and he tried not to think about the years it was taking off his life. When he stepped from the stall, the cube in his pocket felt warm. Why's it warm? he wondered.

"Jack Carson, Junkster Extraordinaire," Delphin said, looking him up and down, as if appraising his market value.

"Richard, how very good to see you," Jack said, his enthusiasm sounding forced even to him, he who lacked all nuance.

Delphin looked over Jack's shoulder. "What monstrosity are you attempting to off on me this time, Carson? I don't want any, by the looks of it from here." The proprietor turned his oculus on Jack.

"I'm not here to sell that. I got something else, requires privacy." He let his eyebrow rise a bit.

"What about that?" He stabbed a finger over Jack's shoulder. "You take your eyes off it, it'll be gone."

"Good riddance." He might have shrugged, his voice nonchalant. "It got me here."

Delphin's oculus scanned Jack from head to toe and gasped. "I've never seen one of those. This way, Carson." He spun and led the way to the rear, turned into a nearly hidden doorway. "Boy, mind the shop. In fact, put out the sign and lock the door."

A rag-haired urchin ducked past Jack, steering clear of both men nimbly.

"Caught him trying to purloin a trinket," Delphin said, leading Jack into a small laboratory. "He's working off his debt. Better that than being sentenced to three years hard labor on a garbage planet." The oculus riveted itself to a gadget that looked quite similar to the one that adorned Delphin's head. "Put the cube there, on that platter."

A mounted platter occupied the center island.

Jack put the cube on the platter, its iridescent sides swirling ominously.

Delphin swung the larger, ceiling-mounted oculus around and positioned its gargantuan lens just above the cube. The smaller oculus attached to his head also peered inquisitively at the alien device. The man's hands danced across the controls.

The lights dimmed and a bright beam pierced the dark, the cube emanating no light itself. A dull, distant whine originated somewhere.

Jack wondered whether the images he'd seen on its sides had been projected from somewhere inside the cube, or whether the cube had put the images into his visual cortex. Its sides began to swirl.

"Where'd you get it?"

"Canis Dogma Five." Jack didn't have the subtlety to prevaricate.

Delphin gasped and swiveled his oculus toward him. "How'd you evade the patrols? That place is locked down tighter than a casino vault. Latitude and longitude?"

Jack told him and added, "The former Capital of the Circian Empire."

The oculus swiveled back to the cube. "How much are you asking?"

Jack's initial thought, en route, had been to get it appraised, but Delphin was already asking how much, and clearly wanted to buy it. Jack thought of a price and doubled it, then doubled it again, then for good measure quintupled that. "Fifty million galacti, ten percent now, the remainder once you've verified its authenticity."

"Done," Richard Delphin, proprietor of fine antiquities, said immediately.

"Cash," Jack added.

The hesitation was brief. "Of course."

Five million galacti cash was an inordinate sum. The trinket that the boy had tried to steal couldn't have been worth ten galacti. The baubles at the front of Delphin's shop were rarely worth more.

"I'll need a few minutes to make arrangements, of course."

"Of course," Jack replied, his feet barely touching the ground. Five million galacti was five million galacti. Even if Delphin stiffed him for the balance, Jack was independently wealthy for the rest of his life.

Delphin left him there to secure the money, turning on the lights as he stepped from the room.

The profusion of equipment lining the walls held no interest for Jack. The cube under high magnification on the platter had grown quiescent, its sides a dull pewter.

I didn't want to be Emperor anyway, Jack thought, the idea still as ludicrous as any he'd entertained. He remembered as a child—orphaned early and begrudgingly cared for until he'd stowed away on a garbage scow at age twelve—how he'd dreamt of achieving a position of power and helping all orphaned children to find a home. Jack had shared his dream with only one person, Cherise, a fellow orphan, whose prepubescent beauty bespoke the breathtaking comeliness she would acquire as an adult. To his surprise, she hadn't laughed at his dreams and instead had told him how much she admired him. Her joining the other entertainers had ultimately led to Jack's departure.

Looking at the alien cube, which had promised him the power to change the universe, Jack felt a distant, muted sadness.

He attributed his sadness to having left Cherise in the clutches of the old harpy who'd run the Southern Birds, but something about the cube on the platter...

I'm independently wealthy, he told himself, why don't I feel ecstatic?

The sense of an opportunity lost wouldn't leave him, but it was done. He'd made the transaction. There was no turning back.

Jack looked again at the cube, at its ugly pewter color, at its flat sides, and at its slightly beveled edges. Dull and unattractive. Just like Jack.

Well, maybe I'm more than dull, he thought. It would be a disservice to all ordinary-looking people to call me unattractive. He didn't need a mirror to see the bulbous nose, the recessed chin, the beetle brow, the buck teeth, the sunken cheeks. The closest he might aspire to an Imperial position was court jester, but his wit was as dull as his looks. It would be generous to describe his intellect as a dearth of cognition.

Jack sighed. No, he thought, I could never be Emperor.

Delphin came bustling back in with a satchel. "You sure you want it in cash?"

Jack nodded. He had a knife in his boot and knew how to use it wicked fast. It wouldn't stop a blaster to his back, but he'd manage. He'd developed a sense for danger, an intuition for intrigue. "I'll be all right. Which way's that back door?" He grabbed the satchel.

"You don't want to count it?"

"No," Jack said flatly.

Delphin shrugged and led him down a cluttered corridor.

Beyond it was an alley. Jack went deeper into the alley, picked a door at random—the back door to a small, indoor shopping mall—and walked toward the front.

He stopped at a boutique for a change of clothes. Remembering to remove the tags, he donned them and left the boutique.

Lightheaded, and much lighter in spirit, Jack started back toward the spaceport, the frosty ground crunching beneath his feet.

A smoke shop called his name.

Not with all this cash in hand, he told himself.

Just one to celebrate, and then I'll take the cash to the ship, he thought.

No, not even one! he remonstrated himself.

Before he knew it, he found himself asking for a booth in the back, positioning himself so he could see the front door. "Your finest, please," Jack said.

While the waiter went to fetch it, Jack dug into the satchel. The smallest domination was a thousand-galacti chit.

It'll do, Jack thought.

The waiter returned with a bowl of smoke. The pipe was a blue glasma tulip whose petals arced out gently and gracefully from a glowing center, its stem serving both as a platform and as the inhaling tube. In the center was a dusty, dun-brown ball of c-grade smoke.

"I said, 'your finest,'" Jack repeated, glancing at the chit.

In an instant, Jack was staring at the best smoke he'd even seen. Tears of resin beaded on the cluster, and the sweet smell clotted his nostrils. Already the entire establishment knew, the aroma pervading the place. Jack felt their eyes; he was glad he'd put the satchel on the bench beside him, out of sight below the table.

Jack took a practice breath, and then put his lips to the stem. The young waiter held up the burner. Jack bade him to wait and drew a lungful.

Heavenly scents filled his lungs and euphoria settled upon him. And the stuff wasn't even lit!

Jack signaled and exhaled, and the waiter applied the burner. All it took was a half a breath. Jack capped the glowing bowl and waved to the waiter, who left the burner.

The smoke expanded, sending its soothing tendrils out to his fingers and toes. His scalp began to tingle, and the surroundings began to glitter. The ceiling peeled away to show him each successive floor above him, until they too rolled aside to reveal the sky, the blue-white pinprick of Denebi like a brilliant diamond so pure that its light washed the universe clean.

The booth disappeared from around him, and he floated, the distant Imperial Capital on Torgas Prime beckoning him oddly.

Below him, the palace sprawled across a picturesque valley on the lush, semi-tropical world. Palms sprouted in small courtyards located in unlikely places, buildings of fabulous façade interconnected with colonnaded walkways and soaring fountains. Rooftops glittered with crushed crystal, walls were inlaid with intricate mosaics, and walks were paved with marble flagstone.

The sight of the palace shook Jack, as though physically. He'd never yearned for the sedentary, leisure life of a prince, only for the power of one, with which he might make the lives of others better. Why am I seeing this? he wondered, little interested in the trappings of royalty.

Again the sensation of shaking, and Jack realized that someone was physically shaking him.

The bowl of smoke, a blue glasma tulip with gently arcing petals, wobbled dangerously on the table.

"Where's it at, Carson?"

He put out his hand to steady the bowl. Somewhere, his brain was saying danger was imminent, but Jack just laughed.

"I should have known. Wake him up."

A galaxy exploded on one side of his head, and his face spun the other. A curious thing seemed to be happening; he was feeling what could only be described in conversational terms as pain, but it had no relation to any event immediately preceding it that Jack had recognized as painful.

A galaxy exploded on the other side of his face and his head spun back the other way.

This was getting annoying. A person's drug-induced euphoria was sacred. Didn't they know it was extremely bad manners to interrupt such euphoria? And what person in his or her right mind would attempt to engage in a sensible discussion with someone who was by definition insensate?

He tried to focus on the three, six, or nine faces in front of him. He couldn't tell how many there were. One was familiar in that didn't-I-just-see-you-not-long-ago type familiarity. The other two faces weren't familiar at all, but the fact that both faces sat atop bodies whose physical proportion far exceeded the human norm—and were at least double Jack's own mass—lent credence to the message his brain had been trying to deliver for at least a minute or two.

"Where's the blasted cube, Carson?"

His eyes focused on the middle figure, the familiar one. His brain supplied him a name: Delphin. "I left it with you," he said—or tried to say. He was sure it was unintelligible. He was sure his brain was unintelligible.

"What'd he say?"

Jack tried to repeat it, his lips too loosened with drugs to form proper words. A fourth blow to his head finally penetrated to his limbic cortex, and the trickle down his cheek was sure to be blood. "I left it with you, Delphin," he growled, giving the apes on either side of the smaller man a nasty look.

The oculus focused on Jack's face. "It's gone, disappeared as I was examining it. I don't know what sleight of hand you performed, and I don't care. Hand me that bag."

One of the beef balls laid himself half across the table to grab the satchel containing the five million galacti.

Jack wished it gone, and it was.

"Where'd it go?!" muscle man asked.

"The cube or the money, Carson," Delphin said. "You don't want to know the third option. Choose!"

"Shove a quasar up your black hole, Delphin. If you can't hold onto a cube, it's time they put you in a nursing home." Jack realized he was furious.

"Third option it is, then, Jack. Sorry, I can't stay to watch the show, but I don't want to lose my plausible deniability." He turned to the muscle man to the left, the one with a brain cell. "Wait till I've left the building." He spun and walked off.

Jack eyed the two lumps. And the distance between them.

"Don't even think about it," the brain-cell said.

"Think about what? Have a puff on me, boys," Jack said.

"I'm workin'," one said, "but I'll be off in about five minutes. Can I—"

The other shoved an elbow in his gut. "That's consorting. You know what the boss says."

"He does it all the time."

"He's the boss." The brainy one turned to Jack. "I'll put it bluntly, Cockroach—the cube, the bag, or your life. Which is it?"

"You can put the first two into your black hole, buzzbrain, and I'll keep the third. Now, get out of my way." Jack stood, the satchel in his hand, and took a step toward the door.

A hand landed on his shoulder. It might have been a side of pork ribs. It spun Jack around.

A fist the size of a comet careened toward his face.

He pulled to one side, and the fist sailed wide.

Another plunged for his gut.

He turned sideways, and it whistled past.

Quadruple cannons launched a fusillade of blows, which Jack nimbly avoided. Even as he pulled away from one, he saw the next coming, each blow close enough he felt its wind, none able to make contact.

He wondered what he looked like to a bystander—some puppet being jerked around by its strings, he was sure. The spasm dance left him against a wall with nowhere to go. Somewhere, his brain was telling him he'd never had reflexes that good before.

Two panting, sweating lumps of lard looked at him against the wall. If they saw the satchel in his hand, they gave no indication of it. They each threw a glance at the other and charged him.

Jack was on the other side of them as they crashed into the wall and crumpled into a heap.

That's one heap of flesh, Jack thought, striding out the door.

The crowded street held no danger for him, not a single passerby seeing him. Hovercraft hummed past, and a few ground vehicles crunched across the perpetual frost. The shuffling masses somehow parted to let him by, as Jack strode, mystified, toward the spaceport.

The commotion behind him didn't alarm him. He knew they'd probably come after him, but he was oddly convinced they'd never find him.

He couldn't say exactly what had just happened. Rolling events through his mind, each moment after he emerged from his drug-induced stupor as clear as a glasma pane, Jack found that even he could not believe that he'd moved that fast.

Satchel in hand, five million galacti richer, Jack strode resolutely toward the spaceport, convinced that whatever had happened, he'd somehow acquired a new destiny.

Perpetual loser, orphan, salvage collector, thrice divorced and quadruple bankrupt, perennially getting tangled up with the authorities, and always saturated with smoke, Jack felt that somehow his life had changed.

Maybe he'd even turned it around.

The future opened to Jack like the spaceport between skyscrapers. Ships lifted off and dropped between multistory buildings on either side. The bright glare of engines reflected off building windows, some of them evidencing the blackening of carbon burn.

He'd always wondered why they'd put such tall buildings around the spaceport.

Port security didn't look up when he strode through the checkpoint. No buzzer went off when he waltzed through the scanners. No one asked for his ID or did a biometric, genescan, iris scan, retina type, bone image, E. coli match, or mitochondria sample.

As if he didn't exist.

"I was wondering why you were taking so long," Misty said as he came through the hatch. "Ran into some trouble, eh?" She touched the now scabbed-over split to his cheek.

He winced as she dressed the wound.

"I don't know why I'm doing this," she said, "You could just use the cube."

He raised an eyebrow at her. "I sold it for five million galacti."

The bewildered look on her face turned to amusement. "You're so funny, Jack. You know, the way you tell jokes without any change in expression, you ought to consider comedy."

He stared at her. "Actually, I sold it for fifty million galacti, but all I could get was ten percent in cash. It's in the satchel." He gestured at it. "Go on, look."

Doubt working its way across her face, Misty knelt. "Where did you get this, Jack?" She held up a bundle of thousand galacti chits.

"I told you, I sold the cube."

She giggled at him, her green eyes mischievous above her girlish grin. "Stop, Jack. You're incorrigible. You did no such thing."

"Yeah, I did. Why would I lie to you about something so important?" He wondered where she'd learned a word like that. Probably the ship's teacher machine, something he'd never had the discipline to use on long flights.

She giggled again. "No, you didn't. It's in your pocket."

He felt the lump before his hand got there. The cube felt inert—body temperature—and swirled placidly in his hand as he brought it out.

He stared at it, stunned.

* * *

"You're sure?" Emperor Phaeton Torgas stared at his prime Minister, stunned.

"I alerted you as soon as I could, your August Highness," Custos Messium said, dropping his forehead to the floor.

It was the fastest Torgas has seen him bow.

The Emperor held up his scepter.

Cradled in a circlet of platinum was a plain silver cube. If he stared at it, its sides became translucent and iridescent, as though secrets within bubbled to get out. It was a literal source of Torgassan power. With the Cube, his family had ruled half the galaxy for fifteen hundred years.

Half ruled the galaxy, or ruled half the galaxy.

"You're sure?" the Emperor asked, realizing he'd repeated himself.

"I am, your August Highness."

Whenever they'd attempted to extend their dominion to the far side of the galactic bar, an insurrection had erupted on this side. On one occasion, during the reign of Letus XI, the Empire had given a rebellion little attention while pursuing its expansion across the bar, and very nearly had lost Torgas Prime to the rebels.

The literal source of the Emperor's power, the cube facilitated their exercise of near-absolute dominion—to an extent.

How the Circians had ruled the entire galaxy with the cube was a mystery, unless there was another cube or a series of cubes, as several historians had speculated.

Rumors flared from time to time of another such cube, but none of the rumors had been substantiated.

Phaeton stared at the cube, its mysteries predominantly hidden, like a dormant plague awaiting the right conditions before spreading its contagion through a vulnerable populace. It allowed him to delve into others' minds, no matter what their distance. To see what they saw, hear what they heard, feel what they felt, taste what they tasted, and smell what they smelt. More importantly, it allowed him to become them, to take over their minds and direct their actions, a phenomenon called ghosting.

With ghosting, rebellions might be averted and sometimes subverted.

"Where?"

"Denebi III, your August Highness. An antiquities dealer of high repute, a Richard Delphin, was approached by a salvager of ill repute, a Jack Carson, who said he'd recovered it on Canis Dogma Five."

Emperor Phaeton went white.

The former Capital of the Circian Empire, Canis Dogma Five was a derelict world, its surface laced with the crumbling infrastructure of a once-thriving civilization. Nearly two millennium had passed since the Circian Empire's fall, and still the successor Empire, the Torgassan, kept the Circian homeworld under close surveillance.

For precisely this reason.

"And the Dogma Five patrols?" the Emperor asked.

"A curious thing, your August Highness. Not a single report of anomalous movements, unless one reviews the sensor recordings oneself. The sensors clearly indicate the descent, landing, two-day stay, and departure of this very same scavenger, but all the reports indicate only his arrival. They are glaringly mute regarding his departure. The sector commander is investigating the discrepancies. When asked, patrols and monitoring-station crews exhibit remarkable similar responses."

"That must be hundreds of personnel."

"Precisely, your August Highness."

"What are the responses?"

"They mumble, 'I didn't see anything, Sir —even from those crew members with female commanders. Their eyes lose focus, their voices become flat and emotionless, and their faces lose all expression."

"As though they're hypnotized."

"Precisely, your August Highness."

Ten years before, just after Phaeton assumed the throne from his just-deceased father, Tilbury II, the subsector adjacent to Canes Venatici had erupted in rebellion, and in the first major test of his power, the new Emperor had ruthlessly subjugated its peoples.

With the cube.

He had ghosted the planet with the compulsion to bow to the least sign of Imperial rule, including the Imperial banner, a stylized depiction of the scepter in his hand.

In the first few months after the ghosting, the populace of Venatici the Outer had spent so much time genuflecting to ubiquitous symbols of Torgassan power that their economy had ground to a halt, crops went to seed for lack of anyone to harvest them, assembly lines stood idle, transport ground to a halt, and the rebellion fizzled. Everyone spent so much time on their knees that nothing got done. The people had nearly starved.

Served them right, too, the Emperor thought. We should have let them starve. Young and inexperienced, he'd let his ministers overrule his decision to extend them no help. Reports from the planet surface had consistently reflected the same perception: "They all look hypnotized."

Emperor Phaeton frowned, the Prime Minister forgotten. "Eh? What'd you say?"

Custos Messium, a tall man who'd served Phaeton's father before him, bowed in slight apology. "Pardon, your August Highness, I meant not to disturb your thoughts," he said, a slight smile upon his slight face above a slight form, "but this scavenger, Carson, appears to have retained the cube after purportedly selling it to the antiquities dealer. It disappeared as the dealer was examining it, and his efforts to recover it were met with an unusual level of evasion. It seems Carson made off with both the cube and the five million galacti that the dealer paid for it."

"You said this Carson appears to be held in low esteem. Why would a reputable antiquities dealer even entertain such a scoundrel?"

"Why indeed, your August Highness?"

Unless the scavenger had ghosted the dealer.

"Where did he go?"

"No one knows, your August Highness. Spaceport personnel are being remarkably mute on..."

"Yes, Prime Minister?"

"Pardon, your August Highness. Clearly the sensor data needs to be examined, as it appears the salvager hypnotized his way off planet."

"Clearly." The dolt!

"Pardon, your August Highness, if I may be excused...?"

"Certainly." Phaeton watched with increasing impatience as his usually sharp-witted Prime Minister removed his dull-witted self from the Imperial presence, bowing three times as he backed from the throne room.

The scepter beckoning, Emperor Phaeton quickly forgot the man. He looked deeply at the cube's swirling sides, as though a storm brewed beneath the smooth surface. Held immobile by a platinum ring, the cube was rarely touched by human hands.

Carefully, Phaeton released the catch and pulled aside the hinged, platinum circlet. Four of eight mounts came away.

"Grasp it by the edges if you must handle it at all," he remembered his father saying.

Nearly three inches from corner to corner, the cube would easily fit between the thumb and forefinger of a normal adult human hand. What purpose or intent there'd been in its alien manufacture had long since been lost when the aliens themselves had departed from this universe.

He placed his thumb and forefinger at those opposite corners. "The cube root of the sum of the cube of its sides is the length between the corners," he'd been told. The slight beveling of its edges made the corners comfortable in his grip.

He lifted it out of its mounts.

The universe inverted, and the fabric of time warped and skewed. The weft stretched and yawed but did not break or rend. And then all of it snapped back into place.

Where is this scavenger Carson? he asked the cube.
Unresponsive silence was his only answer.

Chapter 5

The Southern Birds sat at the end of a wooded lane outside a small metropolis on the southern hemisphere of a swampish world orbiting Alpha Tuscana. Jack could never remember the names of the lane, the city, or the planet, but the name of the establishment was forever etched into his memory.

The brothel was where he'd grown up.

Abandoned as an infant, he'd been given succor if not much guidance throughout his childhood by a bevy of women (and a few men) whose constant chatter frequently veered toward the bawdy banter common to such environs, the boy often forgotten as simply a constant presence underfoot. As such, Jack's education was weighted toward the idiosyncrasies of sexual behavior, the fleeting nature of relationships, the inevitable anxieties of aging, and the occasional invasion of Imperial law enforcement.

Not comely enough to attract customers' interests—in fact, rather the opposite—Jack had been spared indoctrination into the lifestyle and had remained an observer, getting rare glimpses into a complex and often tragic world. Not alone in this unconventional upbringing, Jack was one of half a dozen such orphans, all the others female, and all of them acquired as potential apprentices.

Misty looked quizzically toward the building as they approached. "What do they do here?"

"They're in the entertainment business." He'd come back on occasion since leaving at age twelve, but the last time had been nearly eight years before.

The house was quiet as they entered, almost deathly so. Midmorning was the deepest part of their night, nearly everyone asleep. Jack wondered if his childhood friend, Cherise, were still here. He rather doubted it. She'd been exceptionally beautiful and accomplished, and that even before she arrived at the Southern Birds at four years old.

The foyer was all etched glass and brass, shiny wood-grain floors, and gilt-framed portraits of nudes sprawled in somnolent leisure. The chandelier hung heavy and dark from three floors up.

"May I help you?" a girl not much older than Misty asked, appearing at their elbow.

"Uh, yes, please. I'm Jack, Jack Carson," he said. "I'm here to see Madam Mariposa."

"Certainly. Please have a seat. She's not prepared for visitors, so she'll be a few minutes."

"Of course, and please extend my apologies for not comming ahead."

"Certainly. And may I know the name of our other guest?"

Before he could stop her, Misty said, "I'm Princess Misty Circi, of Canis Dogma Five."

"Thank you." The girl nodded, evincing no surprise, and retreated soundlessly the way she had come.

Carson was the name they'd come up for him, confabulated for no other reason than he'd needed another name. Jack stepped into the reception room, where the guests chose their liaisons. A corridor blocked off by a curtain led to the "nesting rooms," as they were known at the Southern Birds. Around the walls were couches and loveseats and chaise longues, all so overstuffed as to invite comparisons to corpulence. In the center, cordoned by velvet ropes, was the viewing area, now empty. In this area, the courtesans would parade themselves, displaying their charms and looking amongst the customers for their next assignation.

Jack remembered with a twinge seeing Cherise parade herself for the very first time at age thirteen. A year younger than she, Jack had nearly ruined her first night in the rotation as he'd watched from the second-floor balcony. Madame Mariposa had stopped him from rushing downstairs, grabbing Cherise, and carrying her off to safety. He'd left soon after.

"You probably shouldn't introduce yourself that way," Jack said.

Misty turned her big blue eyes on him. "Why not?"

As he pondered that, imagining the thousands of political prisoners whose only crime was to oppose Emperor Torgas, and the millions who'd been slaughtered when they'd rebelled against his rule, whose worlds had been reduced to smoking cinders when their occupants had refused to capitulate to his demands. "Well, it's not safe," he said, looking at her directly to impress upon her the gravity of what he was saying.

He was just getting comfortable in the corpulent chair when the woman walked in.

He knew instantly who it was and he felt flabbergasted just the same.

"Jack."

That one word captured the entirety of his latency. The six most formative years of his life and their terrible culmination in having to watch his best friend and most loved companion prance and preen before a voracious audience all came rushing back to him in that one word.

In the six months before he had left, he and Cherise had become lovers, their liaisons quick and hurried and away from the watchful eyes of Madame Mariposa.

Cherise hadn't been around the other three times he'd visited, and he hadn't asked about her, afraid to open that door, afraid of what lay beyond.

Jack stood to greet her, and she stepped into his arms as though twenty years hadn't passed. If only, he thought. He pulled back to look at her, blinking away tears, seeing the same youthful innocence and purity that had always taken his breath away, seeing the simple joy of life in her soul, that capacity to be here now, fully, without a thought for the past or the future, without a care but for the one she beheld.

He knew she loved him still, as they stared into each other's eyes.

He also knew she wasn't free to pursue that love, just as she hadn't been free twenty years ago, when they'd stolen precious moments from their owners to be with each other. "You look wonderful," he said, his voice inaudible.

She beamed with his admiration, blush creeping up her neckline. She wore a chemise robe over a silk camisole, both of them a deep burgundy. "It's so good to see you, Jack. I've missed you terribly."

He nodded. For twenty years, he'd regretted leaving. He also knew he couldn't have stayed. "You're so strong and brave. I'm sorry to have been such a coward. If I'd—"

She shushed him with a smile and a finger across his lips. "Regrets keep us from living our lives today. Your courage has kept me going for many years, that and the joy of your companionship. You taught me just to be myself and honored me when I was completely truthful with you. Thank you." She took his hand and cradled it to her breast.

The empty years of his life spilled down his face. Companionship had been difficult to find, two of his three wives vulpine harpies who'd sucked his bank accounts dry. Trust had been difficult to build, even in simple transactions with other traders, a deep abiding mistrust of everyone around him undermining every exchange of goods.

"Who's your friend?"

"Misty, her name is Misty," Jack said hurriedly, before the girl could respond. "We're waiting to see Madame Mariposa."

Cherise threw him a slight smile and turned to the girl. "Misty, I'm Cherise. Jack and I grew up together."

"You were really important to him, you know," she said matter-of-factly. "And you still are."

Cherise threw him another look, as if to ask, "What have you been telling her?"

Unless I've started talking in my sleep, Jack thought, wondering how she'd known.

"Well, Madame Mariposa died a few years ago, and now, I'm Madame Mariposa. But you can call me Cherise. Come this way."

She led them to a door simply marked "private," one very near the entrance. Inside, one half the room looked like the perfect sitting room, overstuffed chairs around a low table. The other half was the compound security center, multiple monitors giving glimpses of every corridor and every exit. The girl who had greeted them moved through the monitors by turn, as though physically doing rounds.

"Morning rounds," Cherise said.

He saw the front stoop. "You saw us coming."

"But I didn't recognize you. You've changed, Jack."

"You're as beautiful as ever."

She laughed lightly and bade them to sit.

Facing her, Jack found himself suddenly at a loss for words. He needed her help, but now all he wanted was to remain here with her. Sell the Salvager and settle down as her business and domestic partner, running the brothel and starting a family.

"Jack's going to take me to the palace," Misty said.

Cherise's light laughter was little different. "It's a place everyone should visit at least once, I'm told."

"I'm not going there to visit. I'm going there to live."

"Oh, that's fabulous! It's what I'd do if I had the opportunity. But that requires an invitation from the Emperor himself. I'm too far beneath his notice to get an invitation."

"Jack's going to get me one."

Cherise turned to look at him.

"And I will, as soon as I can."

"And how, might I ask, will you be doing that?" Cherise had that what-have-you-been-telling-her look again.

"Jack's very persuasive," Misty told her.

"Yes, he is, isn't he?" Cherise laughed that soft, disbelieving laugh again. "And how might I help?"

"I don't know where I'll get the wardrobe necessary to live in the palace. Whatever will I do?" Misty didn't put the back of her hand to her forehead, but she might have.

Jack and Cherise both laughed aloud. His heart warmed to hear genuine laugher from his childhood friend.

"Stand up," Cherise told the girl, who did so. Then she twirled her finger, and the girl spun in a circle. "Show me a waltz."

Misty looked bewildered. "What's a waltz?"

Without a blink, Cherise stood and demonstrated a few steps. "Ta, da, da, ta, da, da."

And Misty aped her perfectly.

"Well, I think I have a few outfits to start with. A young woman not much more substantial than you left us abruptly a few weeks ago. Unlikely to be returning. And you'll be needing a bit more than a wardrobe, if you don't know what a waltz is. The Cherise School of Charm has its first official student. Jack, will you be joining us?"

About all he could do was charm a cat out of a bath.

"He's got half-a-hold of junk to offload."

Jack was getting annoyed, the way Misty was answering questions directed at him. He shrugged at Cherise.

"At least stay a day, and get a little rest."

He saw the promise in her eyes.

* * *

Jack had two stops to make in town before going back to the Southern Birds. Both were within easy walking distance of the tarmac.

The alley he approached looked the same as it had when Jack was twelve.

His heart aching, Jack had come to this alley and had approached the proprietor of the hock shop, Ignatius Argonavis. The two of them had struck up a conversation on one of the man's visits to the Birds, and Jack had taken a liking to him.

His life-long friend, Cherise, had just taken her first turn parading herself around the Southern Birds parlor.

"Get me a berth on the next garbage scow out of here, Ig!"

"What do you be wanting to do a fool thing like that for?"

Young Jack had stared across the chipped glasma counter into the wrecked face of the former spacer. Both of them were a sight to sore any eye, and they'd become fast friends. Ig, as he'd insisted Jack call him, had lost part of his face and most of his left shoulder and arm to the blast of an attacking Imperial Patrol. The injury hadn't stopped the Empire from convicting him of piracy and sending him to prison for ten years, but it had ended his spacefaring days.

"Cherise, you say?" Ig asked, his one eye searching Jack's face. "Many the tale's been told of the folly of falling in love with a whore, but—"

"She's not a whore!" Jack insisted.

"Of course not! Forced into it because she's an orphan like yourself. Something you'd have done if you weren't so downright repulsive."

"I'm not repulsive!" Jack insisted.

"And I'm a beauty queen, too!" Ig threw his head back and roared with laughter. "But you've gone and done it in a way that's quite original," Ig continued, as if Jack hadn't interrupted. "A fine fix, it is!"

And Ig had gotten Jack aboard a garbage scow, but not before Jack had extracted a promise from Ig that he'd stop frequenting the Southern Birds.

Now, twenty years later, Jack approached the same alley shop, headed for the same ill-repaired door, the sign above it in grimy letters declaring, "Argonavis Hock and Lucre."

Jack reflected what a fool he'd been. The rough years had followed, Jack working ship to ship, keeping to himself, avoiding trouble, staying away from smokeshops, snortshops, shootshops, drinkshops, and bodyshops, and somehow working his way to pilot, getting his license (forged), and taking out a loan to buy his own Scavenger.

I made it work, he told himself, pushing the door open.

The lumpy wreck behind the chipped glasma counter just grunted and mumbled, "Whatcha got?"

"Get me a berth on the next garbage scow out of here, Ig!"

The remaining eye swiveled toward him. "Jack!" And the old man barreled out from behind the counter and wrapped Jack with one arm.

Quite a powerful arm. Jack gasped for breath, laughing and hugging the man back.

"What brings you to town, boy?" Ig asked, holding Jack at arm's length to look him over, a woman peering at them from the back room.

He could see Ig blinking back tears, and he blinked away his own. "Just comin' to see that you kept your promise about the Southern Birds. Looks to me like someone made an honest man out of you, impossible as that may seem."

Ig nodded vigorously, his head only coming to Jack's shoulder. "Meet the missus, Jack. Sweetie, come and meet the boy I was always tellin' you about. Jack, this is Gretchen."

The two greeted each other.

"I told Ig he'd have to stop going to the Southern Birds," Jack said, "so I guess he got married instead."

"That ain't stopped him," she said, laughing as loud as Ig, her face as much a wreck as his.

"I go to see Cherise, make sure she's all right," Ig said. "You been out there? Runs the place now."

"I arrived yesterday, and Cherise looks wonderful."

"Aye, doesn't she?" And Ig winked at him. He turned to his wife. "I'm takin' Jack to the smoke shop. Mind the store while I'm gone, would you?"

"Startin' early today, are you?"

"Quit your gritching, Gretchen. This is a special occasion."

"Get on with ya, and be back before nightfall or I'm comin' to find you again."

"All right, all right!" He winked again at Jack and escorted him to the door.

He and Ig went to Jack's second stop on the way to the spaceport.

The place was nearly empty, and the walls reeked of old smoke and old sweat, but they greeted Ig like a conquering hero and got them a booth in the far corner where they could watch the door and the spaceport across the street.

The smoke was harsh, dry, slightly musty, and poor quality, but Jack breathed deeply, and his stress fled him as he knew it would and a slight euphoria settled in.

Jack calmly put his cube on the table between them, his arm beside it, blocking any view of it. "What is this thing, Ig?"

Ig's eye went wide, and his mouth full of rotted stubs dropped open. He rubbed his perpetual three-day stubble and whistled softly. "Pre-Circian technology," he said. With one finger he gestured Jack to put it away, an eye throwing a glance toward the smoketender.

Jack put it in his pocket.

"I've heard tales of like objects, traders comin' through, bedazzled looks in their eyes. A tesseract, isn't it? I seen people brought low in their search for such, dreams of untold wealth in their gaze, not a thought for their safety, their reason obliterated in their lust for power. I'm told you can read people's mind with one of those."

Jack met the one-eyed gaze and didn't nod. Didn't need to.

"And change it, too." Ig just nodded. "Quite the find. Couldn't happen to a better man." His eye misted over, and he grasped Jack's hand cross the table. "But there's more, isn't there?"

Jack nodded. "A girl, an orphan."

Ig threw his head back and laughed. "Got a thing for orphans."

"Moth to a candle, I guess. Anyway, the little girl thinks she's a princess, wants me to take her to the palace on Torgas."

The eye dropped to the table, as though to see through it to the cube in Jack's pocket. "With that in hand? Might as well be filling the coffers of the mightiest thief we know."

"I tried leaving her, but I felt so guilty, orphan and all." He didn't tell Ig about her unexplained reappearance aboard his ship. "Anyway, Cherise is going to help with a wardrobe, but I got half-a-hold full of jack I need to unload."

"I'm a hock, not a fence," Ig said.

"It's not stolen, it's just junk. Salvage."

The eye peered at him without a waver.

"I swear." Jack held up a hand as if in a court of law. "Well, half-salvage."

Finally, the eye relented. "For you, Jack, for you, but only the salvage, all right?"

"Thanks, Ig."

Somehow, Jack had extracted himself from the smokeshop before he'd become completely obliterated, but the poor quality of the smoke had helped. He suspected the shop kept its finer stash for the tourists and served its regulars its second-hand smoke.

Silently, Jack blessed Ig for buying half his load sight unseen as he supervised its transfer from his cargo hold to the lorry, beside it a fueler pumping the Salvager's fuel tank full.

On leaving the spaceport, Jack decided to take a detour through town. "Take me past the best place in town to get women's clothes," he told the driver.

"Take you past it?" the beefy hovertaxi hack asked, his jowls jiggling as he spoke. "Where you goin' from there?"

"Southern Birds," Jack said. He buckled himself in as the flitter pulled away from the terminal.

"Yeah? Pickin' up a mink stole or a fine pair of earrings for one of the girls out there?"

Disinclined to discuss his business, Jack shrugged. "No, actually, something for my daughter. You take a lot of people out there?"

"Yeah, busy place. That new Madam really knows how to entertain. Don't let them see what you're gettin' your daughter. Many a customer has left without all his belongings."

"Well, I don't know enough about clothes to get her anything. You ever try to buy clothes for a nine-year-old girl? I'll probably take her to the boutique and turn her loose."

"Sounds like a great plan," the hack said, "if you got a bottomless wallet. She sounds like a real princess, your girl."

Jack snorted. "She's a real princess, all right."

Chapter 6

Jack looked longingly out the glass storefront.

No matter where he went, there they were. And if it weren't a smokeshop, it was a shoot shop, or a snort shop, or a slug shop. They were all over the place.

I'd swear they're stalking me, Jack thought.

Cherise and Misty were in the back of the boutique, trying on something or other. They'd been at it for hours, prancing out on occasion to preen themselves in front of him, demanding his opinion, generally miffed that he wasn't effusively delighted, and then sailing back to the dressing room for the next outfit.

He didn't know how long they could keep it up. All he knew was that he'd long since had his fill, and absolute utter boredom had set in.

Then he'd spotted the smokeshop.

Quit lying to yourself, he thought.

He'd seen it when the taxi had brought him past the boutique yesterday. Every single smokeshop in the city had been calling his name for days, since he and Misty had returned to Alpha Tuscana. Five million galacti worth of smoke danced through his dreams like sugar plum fairies (whatever those were).

His interrupted smoke session on Denebi III and the few brief puffs he'd had after seeing his old mentor, Ig, had done nothing more than whet his appetite. All he wanted now was to plunge himself into a smoke-induced oblivion.

Which he'd been plotting since leaving Canis Dogma Five.

Jack looked over his shoulder toward the dressing rooms.

Neither had come out to preen in front of him for the last few minutes. Probably trying on some undergarments, he thought, or other such unmentionables. He could hear them twittering to each other, a clerk nearby twittering happily back.

They'd forgotten completely about him.

His plan had been—yes, he'd planned his obliteration by smoke to the last detail—to leave the Southern Birds in the morning, telling the other two he was going shopping, and spend the day in a cloud of smoke, and return to the evening, no one the wiser. What was he going shopping for ... something, it didn't matter, anything would suffice. Why did he reek of smoke ... well, er, uh, you know ...

Almost to the last detail.

The difficulty, when he was thinking things through, was the girl, Misty. How could he tell her he just needed a little release? A little break from the constant pressure? After all, it was quite a shock to find himself suddenly burdened with the responsibility of keeping the girl safe and fed and clothed and housed. It wasn't as if she were his actual child, whose care had been his responsibility since she was born. He wasn't accustomed to this, and he needed time to adjust. A day of smoke-induced oblivion was the perfect way to make such adjustments.

Jack was convinced she wouldn't understand.

In his experience, few people did. None of his wives had understood.

He tried to recount how many divorces he'd had. Got them confused with his bankruptcies. Was it three divorces and four bankruptcies, or four divorces and three bankruptcies? Maybe three bankruptcies and four divorces. No, it was definitely four bankruptcies and three divorces.

He shook his head, all of it a blur.

Any wonder why it was a blur? he asked himself, gazing out the boutique window at the smokeshop across the street. Throughout it all, he'd either been intoxicated, coming down, or crawling with craving. No one understood the craving.

The door to the boutique was opening before he knew it, and Jack nimbly dodged a flitter as he crossed the street, flipping an obscene gesture that general direction when the horn bleated.

The interior was dark. "A table in back, please," he said.

A fancy, "please wait to be seated" sign declared how formal the establishment was.

Maybe they'll have some quality smoke to match, he thought, the aromas wafting through the air already hinting at the palette of fine varietals available.

Himself, Jack wouldn't have come to such a place. For Misty to find the couture she needed for her arrival at the palace, they'd had to find the finest boutique on Alpha Tuscana.

When they'd arrived at the shop, Misty had planted a hand on her hip, shoved her nose in the air, and stomped her foot. "I can't believe this is the best available."

Colonnaded faux-marble framed glasma so thick that the models behind it looked smaller from distortion. The one man and three women donning and shedding the finest clothing on the planet seemed oblivious to their near nudity. Their finely-sculpted bodies, eidolons of the human physique, seemed inadequate frames for the finely-crafted clothing they displayed.

At her comment, Jack had almost turned into the smokeshop. Strategically placed right across the street, of course. While the spouse was in one establishment being immersed in a forest of fine fabric and chic design, the distinguished patron might indulge himself in an analogous immersion into seas of exotic exhaust and voluptuous vapors.

Jack browsed the smokeshop menu, the booth's low lamp outshone by the handheld pad showing the shop's array of fine smoke. He swiped through the long list of choices, from Aldebaran delight to Zosma Zoom, then reorganized it by price, most expensive on top.

He whistled in disbelief at the top one, Torcularis Titillation, supposedly the best available.

Putting a thousand-galacti chit on the table, Jack signaled the waiter. "That one," he said, pointing.

"If you'll note, Sir, the menu clearly specifies that the Torcularis requires a deposit."

"What's that on the table, emu excrement?"

The waiter sniffed indignantly and found a spot on his sleeve that merited more attention.

Jack put another chit on the table.

The waiter brightened. "Right away, Sir."

The bowl arrived, an elaborate fleur-de-lis wrought in Vulpecula Salacia ceramic, a material that was both unbreakable and impervious to heat. At the base of the fleur-de-lis was a reservoir. "And what liqueur would the monsieur prefer?"

Jack found it amusing that the pronunciation of "liqueur," "monsieur," and "prefer," all ended the same as the word "sewer." In the finer establishments, one's choice of liqueur for the reservoir was what separated the wheat from the chaff. "Anise is de rigueur," Jack said, pronouncing it the same, "but I prefer water with a slice of lemon."

"The titillation is best experienced with the least of accents, Monsieur. Good choice." The waiter soon returned with the condiment, filled the reservoir, then poised himself, a dainty tongue just reaching the corner of the mouth, his hand holding the striker above the bowl.

Jack wondered what perverse individual had instituted the custom whereby the waiter was required to apply the first flame to a bowl of smoke. But only in the finer establishments.

Jack gave the waiter a nod, and a flame kindled to life at the end of the striker. Jack drew and half-filled his lungs. The waiter capped the bowl and set down the striker, then bowed to Jack.

Euphoria filled him, and his corporeal existence fell away.

* * *

Disembodied voices intruded upon his euphoric obliteration.

"What should we do with him?" A girl's voice.

Jack knew he'd had too much, and he couldn't understand how he heard anything.

"What *we* do," said the waiter's voice, "is put people like this out in the alley, with the rest of the trash."

"Certainly is tempting, isn't it?" A woman's voice. Cherise?

His brain was so saturated with drug that he wasn't able to walk.

"I can't believe he just left us there."

Or talk.

"What was he thinking?"

Or think.

"Only of himself, clearly."

It was heaven.

"Why would he put himself through such hell?"

It's not hell, he wanted to say.

"Why would he put us through such hell?"

Put who through what? he wondered.

"You're nine, you can't say that."

"You did."

"I'm an adult. Stars above, I felt like such a fool, standing there with thousands in purchases, looking around for Jack. If the clerk hadn't mentioned it, I wouldn't have thought to look here."

"Did you see her face? If we hadn't been right in front of her, she'd have been laughing herself silly."

"Happens all the time," she said, "but not to us! The scoundrel! What a complete waste of time! What a complete waste of space!"

"I wonder if he can hear us."

"He's so thoroughly intoxicated, he probably thinks we're aliens come to do biological experiments on him."

"Can that stuff hurt someone?"

"You mean if they smoke too much? Eventually, but I've never heard of someone overdosing on it, not by smoking it, anyway. Oh, Jack, what are we going to do with you?"

"We're closing, ma'am. He'll need to leave." The waiter again.

"Could you get us a taxi, please? Is that the back door? Have it pull up into the alley."

"Yes, ma'am." Steps receding.

"Here, help me. I want to make sure they didn't filch everything from his pockets."

"Would they do that here? A place like this?"

Silence. He didn't even feel them tugging on his clothes, although by the sounds of their efforts, his pockets were difficult to get to.

"You know, what we're not finding is the cube." Cherise voice was low and secretive.

"If it doesn't want to be found, we wouldn't find it anyway."

"Huh?"

"Here comes the waiter."

"The taxi will be here momentarily, ma'am."

Sounds faded and Jack sensed little else but the cosmic rays of drug-exaggerated neural activity. He felt some sensations of motion but assumed it was the momentum of his blissful flight across the galaxy.

"Southern Birds?" A man's voice. "First time I've taken someone there in *his* state. Picked up quite a few. Quite the reversal. You're Madam Mariposa, aren't you? The trip is on the dash. Huh? I mean it's free. No, no, least I could do. Thank you for all your business. No, don't worry about him. I get regular calls from that place, happens…"

"All the time," the two women chimed in.

* * *

The sensation of rolling, and then the floor struck his face hard enough to hurt. He tried to squint, but the light was too bright so he kept his eyes closed. He tried to talk but the dirty rags in his mouth stopped him from talking.

Was I kidnapped? he wondered, his thoughts sluggish.

No, not rags in his mouth, just a dry, swollen tongue. Might as well be a rag for all it obeyed him. His brain wouldn't either, and he wondered what he'd been doing.

And where he was.

More than once, he'd awakened in an alley, his pockets emptied, along with his bowel and bladder, plunged so deep into an abyss of withdrawal that he'd lost track of where he was or how he'd got there.

He recognized enough of the feeling now to know he'd been severely intoxicated to the point of being insensate.

Cold water doused him, cold enough to elicit a gasp. He spasmed in shock. The light still too bright, he turned again to speak, a hand out and up as though to ward off more dousing, which did nothing to stop the next bucket.

It filled his open mouth, set off a fit of coughing, washed the gum from his eyes, dissolved some of the resin coating his brain cells, and got his tongue working.

"Stop!" he said, and his face filled with water again.

Coughing and spluttering, he sat up, trying to distinguish his attacker from the bright blaze of light.

A darker blotch against a blazing patch of daytime sky set down a bucket. "All right, I think that'll do."

"Awe, come on, one more," Misty said. "He deserves a lot more."

"He certainly does," Cherise said, kneeling.

He saw they were out in the shed, the two women in the doorway, two more buckets at the ready. The morning sun blazed in through the open doors behind them, blotting out all else. He recognized enough of the shed at the Southern Birds brothel, having played in and around it as a kid.

Morning.

That meant he'd spent the night out here.

He saw a blanket beside one door, bits of debris still clinging to it. He guessed they'd at least covered him with it. "How'd I get here?" He couldn't tell if his speech were intelligible.

"Scraped you out of a booth at the smoke shop," Cherise said.

"After you abandoned us at the boutique!" Misty chimed in. "We didn't have any way to pay so we had to leave all those beautiful clothes!" And she began to weep with rage, fists clenched at her sides, face twisted up like a dust devil.

Oh, he thought, realizing only now that he'd been carrying all the money. A hand of his flopped toward the pockets of his formalls.

"I checked; they got it all, including the cube."

He felt it in his pocket, and he tried to show her, but his hand wasn't coordinated enough to extract it.

"We'll, at least you didn't lose that."

He blinked helplessly at them both.

"Maybe he should have," Misty snarled. "Maybe someone else would have found it, someone more responsible. How could you do that to me, Jack? How could you? At this rate, I'll be an old woman before I get to Torgas! Just lose the cube, Jack, 'cause anybody would be a better Emperor than you!" Weeping, she ran off, her wails interrupted by sobs, until her crying faded, and was cut off with the slamming of a door.

He flinched at the sound. Shame and contrition washed over him in hot waves, and he resolved never to smoke again, then instantly rebuked himself for telling such lies.

He was doomed. He'd always screwed up his life, and he didn't know how to fix it. Worse yet, his every attempt to make things better just screwed them up worse.

He glanced at Cherise for any sign of compassion.

"Nice work, Jack," she said, then stood and left him to his misery.

* * *

He sat in his squalor for days, numb.

Oh, he functioned, after a fashion. He ate, slept, showered, and changed, but he didn't talk to anyone or look at anyone.

Mostly, they just left him alone. He found a cot in an outbuilding and slept there, shaved at the crude, industrial sink nearby, slunk into the dining hall after everyone else had gone—finding a plate left for him—and cleaned up after everyone else, in spite of the staff whose job it was. They seemed to know and just moved aside when they saw him coming. It was a job he'd done as a kid, anyway, and it seemed a suitable punishment.

On the third day, he went to town and found the boutique.

The young female clerk who'd helped Cherise and Misty kept giggling while Jack paid for everything. He was sure she overcharged him, but he didn't care.

He set everything outside Misty's room, not daring to disturb her. There, the packages remained, untouched.

On the sixth day, he wrote Misty a note saying he was taking the Scavenger to Tertius Diamond look into getting some suitable jewelry, and that he'd return as soon as he could.

Just as he was climbing into the taxi, Misty tore out of the house, hurled his note at him, and yelled, "Don't bother coming back!"

En route to the spaceport, Jack couldn't keep the blur out of his eyes.

The taxi driver kept looking in his review mirror, paying far less attention to where he was flying than Jack thought he should. "Having a tough time with the smoke?" the driver asked, his voice oddly familiar.

"How'd you know?" Jack mumbled, looking out the window, and seeing none of it.

"Seen a lot of good people wreck their lives with that stuff," the driver said.

"Don't tell me: Happens all the time."

"How'd you know what I was gonna say? Talent like that, you ought to play the lottery."

Jack snorted, thinking he'd really hit the jackpot this time—all the misery he'd ever want or need in one foul roll of the dice.

* * *

Jack peered through the glasma pane, the lettering etched into it distorting his view somewhat, but it was easy to see that the proprietor was in.

Scott Michael Decker

He tightened his grip on the satchel and took a deep breath. With his other hand, he reached into his pocket and grabbed the cube.

Better get it over with, he thought, his vision replaced with that of the proprietor.

The binocularity of Delphin's sight was disconcerting. Through one eye was the normal view of the workspace, tools strewn across the workbench, his hands on a mount which held the precious stone he examined. Through the oculus, mountains of blue crystals marched into a blurry distance, the short focal length giving him a crisp view of the subject area.

Crisp and close. Jack knew this was the surface of the smooth, blue stone mounted in front of Delphin. Smooth to the naked eye, mountainous jags to the powerful oculus.

You will not see or hear me, Jack thought, slipping into the antiquities shop.

Delphin instantly looked up. "Who's there?"

Ghosting him, Jack knew he couldn't see anything. There are entire universes around us, Jack recalled someone saying once, if we only have the eyes to see or the instruments to measure.

Jack moved into the shop, careful to remain silent.

"I know you're there, and I know you know I can't see you. If that's you, Carson, I want you to know you'll never do business in the Southern Triangle again. You're finished. I've reported your theft to the Imperial Patrol, and they're not averse to taking a few bribes. You're ruined and hunted, Carson. I've been this business too long to let a hoodlum like you defraud me. Your little prestidigitation may have cost me some money, but your loss and my gain in the way of reputation will show who came out ahead on that deal." The oculus moved around the room while he spoke but turned up nothing, despite the enhanced visual acuity.

Jack almost turned around and left. This man had come after him with two gargantuan trolls and had ordered them to kill him. This man had bribed Imperial Patrol officers, most likely to shoot Jack on sight.

This man had ruined Jack's reputation, preventing him from returning to his previous if meager employment.

It wasn't Jack's fault that the cube had refused to be sold. Why can't I sell it? he wondered, knowing he had as little use for it as it had for him.

Me, Emperor? Jack thought, scoffing mentally at such a ludicrous thought.

But in his efforts to turn an unfortunate event into a slight advantage, Jack had found the obstinate cube in his pocket, instead of its remaining in the possession of the person he'd sold it to. Was that my fault? he wondered, bitter at the trouble it had caused him.

No, it's not my fault, Jack thought decisively.

But it wasn't Delphin's fault, either, the antiquities dealer just responding the best he knew how to circumstances that had placed his livelihood—if not his life itself—at risk.

Which was why, at the heart of it, Jack had come back.

Quietly, Jack set the satchel on the floor. A satchel incrementally lighter and a few thousand galacti slimmer than when he'd left the shop with it a week ago.

Delphin in the meantime had turned back to his work, his thoughts far away, Jack already dismissed from his mind.

Jack stopped himself with his mouth half-open. The damage was done, and an apology wouldn't undo it. I can't make him forgive me, he thought. I guess I probably knew that the cube wouldn't let me sell it. I don't know why I tried.

Quietly, Jack backed out of the shop.

Delphin paused at one point, but didn't swing his oculus in Jack's direction.

Once he was outside, Jack continued to concentrate on keeping the satchel concealed until he'd nearly reached the spaceport.

There, the Scavenger sat, seeming to watching him as he made his way through customs.

He climbed into the pilot's seat and requested liftoff clearance from the tower.

"You took the money back, didn't you?" Misty asked, coming out of the galley.

"How'd you get aboard? I left you on Alpha Tuscana!"

She grinned at him and eased herself into the copilot's seat. "I'm glad you took the money back."

A little while later, the ship clearing the atmosphere, Jack gave her a small smile, mystified but still glad she was here.

"That must have been difficult," Misty said.

He shook his head at her. "That was the easy part." He didn't know how long he'd be able to hold his craving at bay.

Chapter 7

"Where are we going now?"

He glanced over at Misty in the copilot's chaise, her feet in fuzzy shipboard slippers, her hair pulled straight back at the temples.

Cherise had told them to go on ahead, their preparations for Misty's arrival on Torgas Prime likely to take some weeks. "In the meantime, the Southern Birds still needs my guidance, at least until I train my understudy."

And so, reluctantly, Jack had left his childhood friend behind. He knew he'd be returning for her. He'd always known.

"You and Cherise make really good companions, you know," Misty said. The classic Athenian lines of her face held an ancient wisdom, and her clear blue eyes evoked the limitless sky.

Well, the Terran Sky, he thought. Jack had never seen the sky on humankind's homeworld. Supposedly, it was breathtaking. The skies Jack had grown up under had been variously dull green, pale gray, amber, and lemon yellow. The other thing her eyes suggested was innocence. "You're too young to know the half of it," Jack said. Well, she'll soon be disabused of that, he thought, especially if she really wants to be Princess.

"I really want to be Princess, so I hope wherever you're taking me has something to do with that."

"A Princess has to have a set of crown jewels, right?"

"Damn straight she does!"

Who taught her to cuss like that? he wondered. "So we're going to the Jewel Box, otherwise known as Kappa Crucis. Inside the constellation are forty occupied worlds, each specializing in one type of precious stone or metal. We're headed for Tertius Diamond, the third planet orbiting the Diamond star, a blue-white variety super giant. I, uh—" he peered at her to gauge her reaction—"have an ex-wife who's a broker."

Misty shot him a look. "Do you owe her money, too?"

"Now, why would you even think that? I don't owe everyone I know, you know."

She giggled. "So she didn't loan you any money and didn't sue for spousal support during the divorce?"

Jack frowned. "Ever consider interrogation for a career?"

"I'm pretty good at it, aren't I?"

"You'd have to develop that wicked gleam in your eye. Since you'll never have the bulk to be physically intimidating, you'll have to rely on something else."

"I'd rather be princess, which is intimidating enough."

He conceded the point and brought the Scavenger out of uberspace.

The Jewel Box filled the screen, and Misty gasped.

A hope chest filled to overflowing with precious and semi-precious stones with multiple kliegs lights shining upon it might look thus.

Jack upped the filters, the stars so bright that it hurt to look at them, the heat coming off the screen causing him to sweat. He browsed the profusion, one of the most magnificent that the Milky Way had to offer. No matter how many times he came here, he never tired of the sight.

"Where are we headed?"

"Tertius Diamond is that one." He pointed to a blue-white supergiant, a star that one Earth writer from Russia had compared to the Orlov Diamond, the preeminent jewel in the Royal Scepter of the Romanov Crown Jewels.

"What's that one?" She pointed to a star. "Why's it changing colors rapidly, like some casino marque?"

"It *is* a casino marque. That's the Vega Strip," Jack told her, shaking his head. "We won't be going there." He'd already been there, and it'd nearly ruined him.

"What happened to you there?"

How did she know? he wondered. "The inquiry queen, they'll call you. Vega is one big gambling joint, whole worlds with nothing but casinos. Nothing there for us."

The third planet orbiting the Diamond Sun was a cold, blue ball capped on either end with ice two-thirds of the way toward the equator. The planet itself sat nearly in the Oort cloud of the massive blue-white primary, a supergiant so bright and hot that it had seared away the atmospheres of its two other planets, both of them now reduced to big, smoking cinders.

Jack brought the Salvager into orbit and commed for permission to land.

They took the shuttle from the spaceport into the Capital, Pretoria, Jack too cheap to spring for a taxi. A few blocks from the Capitol rotunda were the markets.

Shops like jewels lined the perimeter of a vast square. Crowds meandered past scintillating displays of diamonds, each display more breathtaking than the last.

Jack stopped at a kiosk decked entirely in red velvet and shaped like a crown, each inch displaying a blue-white diamond of "flawless" or "internally flawless" variety.

Jack could tell Misty was impressed.

"May I help you?"

The woman at the kiosk was looking intently at Misty, as though not seeing Jack at all.

He smiled at the sight of her, realizing he still loved her.

Daria Osborn stood six-two, was blond and fair-skinned as a Norwegian, with similarly honed features as Misty but heart-shaped. "You look like a Princess in search of a tiara," Daria said to Misty.

"How did you know?"

"I'm Daria, Jack's ex-wife. And if you're here with him, it means you've asked for his help. And there's only one thing a girl your age would ever want to be: Princess."

Misty shot him a glance. "You didn't say she was smart, too."

"Did I forget to mention that?" Jack grinned and turned to his ex. "How's business?"

"It's good. Those disturbances on a border are causing a spike in diamond sales. A little insecurity usually spurs investment. You look well, Jack. Let me guess. Orphan, found on one at those utterly derelict worlds you're always finding junk on, and you're needing some help with her, yes?"

Jack nodded sheepishly. He wouldn't just turn up for a social visit.

"Come with me." She called to a coworker to staff the kiosk, then led Jack and Misty around the red velvet crown to a door set in its back.

A small jeweler's workbench occupied one wall, a lever-mounted oculus suspended from the ceiling. Daria pulled up a stool. "Here you go, my dear, only chair in the house. Jack and I will stand." She then raised an eyebrow at him.

"Well, it's like this—" Jack began.

"If I'm going to be princess, I'll need a set of crown jewels," Misty interrupted, climbing onto the stool. "By the way, since Jack lacks the social sophistication to introduce us, I'm Princess Misty Circi, and Jack's taking me to Torgas Prime so he can claim the crown and be the Emperor."

Daria, he could see, was trying not to laugh.

"I don't want to be Emperor."

"The cube says you'll be Emperor, so you'll be Emperor," Misty said matter-of-factly. "And I'll be your princess."

"And how, if I may ask, your highness," Daria asked, "will you pay for all the clothes, jewelry, servants, and other necessities of being a princess?"

"Jack will figure it out. He's good at that."

Daria looked at Jack as if he'd lost his mind. "Did you tell her about your three bankruptcies?"

"Four," he corrected, and shook his head.

"And about your little problem on Vega?"

Jack cleared his throat and swallowed. He'd nearly ruined Daria's business by gambling away all their money. It wasn't a mystery to him why she'd divorced him. "Sorry about that."

"Foolish of me to trust you with the company's books."

"Even so, you didn't deserve that. I was wrong." Jack shuffled his feet, sure he looked like a child being admonished by a parent.

"We saw Vega on our way here," Misty said, glancing between them. "Get into trouble there, Jack?" She grinned.

"The inquisition queen, they'll call you," Jack told her. He was already flagellating himself. He didn't need her to salt his wounds. "Anyway, I was wondering if you could help us out."

Daria glanced between them. "Well, since you're unable to purchase a set of crown jewels, you'll have to lease them."

"Lease?" Jack hadn't thought of that. "Great idea!"

"Which is still a substantial amount, with a surety deposit, of course."

"Of course."

"For which some type of collateral might be accepted—"

"Like my ship?"

"Which the bank already owns, so Osborn Diamond would be a secondary lienholder, not adequate for a lease of this magnitude. No, Jack, I'm afraid I have to insist on cash. And I'm guessing your credit's not very good. How far behind are you on your ship payments?"

"Just two or three months." Jack shrugged.

Daria smiled. It might have been a wince.

"But I could catch up with my next load. Just sold half-a-load to Busby—"

"That toothless old man on Corolla Tertius? Jack, he's a bloodsucker. I can't believe you're still doing business with him!"

"He, uh, paid a premium," Jack said, glancing at Misty.

On cue, the girl looked at Daria and began to smile a slow creeping smile that spread like molasses across her sweet face.

Daria seemed to soften and relax.

"So, how much for a two-hundred piece set of crown jewels?"

Daria didn't look away from Misty. "Fifty thousand galacti per month with a five hundred thousand galacti deposit."

"Usurious!" Jack said instantly. "Don't I get a discount?"

"That *is* the discount rate, Jack. A set of crown jewels is easily worth half a billion galacti, pieced out. Together, as a collection, one billion."

"Done," Jack said, wondering where he'd get the money.

"I should be able to assemble the set in six weeks, maybe a month. I'll com you the contract." Finally, Daria looked away from Misty. "Jack?"

Jack perked up and met her gaze, hearing a note of concern in his ex-wife's voice.

"Be careful."

* * *

"What did she mean?" Misty asked as they boarded the shuttle back to the spaceport.

Jack shook his head as the glittering city of Pretoria slipped away, the tundra surrounding it like an ice cube. Jack felt a hollow place inside him grow larger, as though something precious slipped away, the ice cube surrounding his heart like tundra.

He realized Daria loved him just as much as he loved her, even now, five years after their divorce.

For the first year, before they'd married, they'd had a wonderful romance. All her friends of course had questioned her choice—a pinch-faced troglodyte with nothing to his name, a nasty divorce and a harrowing bankruptcy already behind him, four previous arrests for trafficking in illicit trade, and no family to speak of except a brothel Madame who'd relegated him to the kitchen because of his repulsive countenance, forbidding him show his face in the parlor if customers were present. Jack wasn't exactly marriageable.

But he'd adored Daria from the moment he'd met her, and he'd successfully given up smoke the entire time he was with her. For two years, they'd had a wonderful marriage, a fairly prosperous one, his salvaging business taking a brief hiatus. He'd taken over managing the back office of Osborn Diamond, while Daria—beautiful to the point of breathtaking and statuesque besides—managed the front office.

But the back office had been a small affair and he'd sold the Scavenger a year into the marriage and boredom had set in, travel rare, new sights and new worlds now replaced with new invoices and new transactions.

The wagers had started small, always from his own pocket, his company salary generous, and Jack found he was fairly good at sports betting. Reviewing a field of contenders in an Ostrick race—the forty-foot arcans from the Rara Avis constellation not terribly different from the large flightless birds from Earth known as ostriches—or assessing two opposing teams in murderball, Jack seemed to have a knack for picking the winner.

Only later, as he found himself in court, first for the divorce and then for bankruptcy, did Jack realized he'd been targeted.

He still kicked himself that he hadn't seen it then. The regular stream of shysters casually bumping into him at trade shows and shopping malls, grocery stores and immersi-theaters, all striking up conversations about some sporting event being held in the Vega Sector, hinting at the bets they were laying money on, and Jack finding himself lucky at the beginning, making huge wins on outlier competitors.

Initially.

* * *

His first visit to Vega should have alerted him to the scam.

They met him at the spaceport and greeted him like a conquering hero. He'd thought to himself at the time, I don't know these people; what are they doing here?

His escort, Whitey, had met him on occasion before, but now, on Vega, Whitey seemed stuck to his side like a Siamese twin, taking him to the most lavish casinos, whose overwhelming glitz left their employees with permanent suntans, where earplugs were de rigueur and sunglasses required at night. Whitey guided him to the high-stakes tables, the sluttiest slots with the putah putouts, the keynote keno games.

And everywhere that Jack went, he was sure to win.

Two days later he went home to a furious Daria. Until she saw all the money he'd won.

"It's too good to be true, Jack. Promise me you won't go back."

He'd promised, but the off-Vega bets on races, sports games, and powerballs continued, Jack having an infallible sense to his picks.

Then Whitey showed up on his doorstep.

The lurch in the pit of Jack's stomach should have alerted him as he stood just inside the threshold, looking at bedraggled figure before him, Daria right behind him.

Known as Whitey for his pure-white ice-cream suits, which glowed even in the darkest, most sultry of casinos, he looked rumpled and un-shaven, his hair unkempt, a hollow I-can't-believe-this-is-happening look in his eyes.

"Jack, you gotta help. Here's the deal." He claimed to have been swindled into placing all his assets in a surefire, too-big-to-fail, one-time-only wager being staged by the biggest and most prestigious gaming house on the Vega Strip, Ballsy Palace.

"And you lost."

Whitey broke down and wept, hurling epithets in the general direc-tion of the Vega Strip, swearing revenge. "But I got it all figured out, Jack. Here's how I can get it all back, doubled."

"Sounds illegal," Jack said, when he heard the plan over a cup of stim at the local breakfast bar. Daria had refused to let Whitey in the house.

"It's not, Jack. It's not only legal, it's exactly what they deserve."

"But you need my help."

Whitey spread his hands in silent plea, looking pathetic.

Jack forked over all his winnings in the past few months.

"Is this all you have?"

"Every cent," Jack told him.

Whitey disintegrated in front of him, melting to the floor in a blubbering puddle of warm ice cream. "It won't work, Jack, we need at least twice that." Whitey ranted and railed about the injustice of it all and how the universe was deliberately persecuting him and how Jack was part of the conspiracy to reduce Whitey to a pathetic, impoverished street derelict. "What about your business?" Whitey asked, suddenly perking up, completely composed.

"Huh? Osborn Diamond? Can't do it, Whitey, not mine to bet."

For the next six hours, Whitey harangued and pleaded and pontificated and moralized. "These bastard casinos have been bilking the likes of ordinary folks like you and me for ages, and if someone doesn't show 'em which side the butter is breaded on, they'll continue to lay it on thick!"

By the end, the metaphors were so mixed that they sounded to Jack like homogenized milk. Finally he relented, wondering if in this circumstance Daria might be acquitted of justifiable homicide.

"So here's what you gotta do, Jack."

" 'Me?' What do you mean, 'me'?"

"You think they're going to let me on the property, knowing they've already milked me dry? Look at me! Not a drop to be squeezed from my sponge. They'll have me arrested for trespassing. No, Jack, I'm too well known on the Vega Strip. They'll bounce me out on my skinny behind." Whitney was nothing if not skinny. "It's gotta be you, Jack. They gotta think you're a new mark. You've got to blind them with your innocence. You're the one, Jack. Make 'em suffer!"

And of course, Jack had lost it all.

Afterwards, Whitey was nowhere to be found.

All through the divorce proceedings and bankruptcy, Jack had berated himself. Why didn't I see it coming? How could I be such a fool?

Slowly, he'd realized that he'd been targeted from the very beginning, from that very first bet, all of it orchestrated toward convincing him he couldn't lose, building the drama until they could persuade him to place it all on a single wager, Whitey having engineered every last detail.

Now, five years later, riding the shuttle from Pretoria to the space-port, Jack still couldn't believe he'd let himself be swindled on such a grand scale.

He didn't blame Daria for driving such a hard bargain. Considering the worth of the Circian Crown Jewels, Jack really hadn't expected Daria to agree to anything. I don't exactly have a sterling track record, he thought, grateful to his ex-wife for her forbearance.

Jack looked at Misty, sitting across from him, sighing and wondering where he'd get five hundred thousand galacti.

Chapter 8

"Uh, looks like a bit of a problem, Jack."

A bright orange boot was bolted to the Salvager's landing strut.

Misty looked it over, as though inspecting how it worked. "What is it?"

"Repossession boot. I'm afraid I've been a little delinquent on my payments. First thing the bank does is have a boot put on so the ship can't be taken anywhere."

She looked over at Jack in disbelief. "But it's not attached to anything. Not even the ground! How will it stop us from lifting off?"

He really didn't expect her to understand the mechanics of such a device. Nor did he have the patience to explain it to her, not right then. "We can't take off with that thing attached, all right? Take my word for it."

"All right." She put her hands on her hips. "How are we getting to Vega?"

He'd told her about his idea on the shuttle. Frowning, Jack looked at the boot. Frustration and helplessness built inside of him, feelings that reminded him of when he was twelve.

At the brothel, he and Cherise had become constant companions. She was a year older than Jack as beautiful as the wind and just as dainty. While Jack worked in the kitchen and yard, Cherise had worked the parlor, serving the guests their drinks, and shadowing the working women when they took their gentlemen customers into the nesting rooms. Cherise typically would wait behind a screen in the room, ready to get help if the encounter should go awry.

Thrown together frequently because of their similarity in age, Jack and Cherise became close across their five years together at the Southern Birds Brothel, and he'd been her first, and she his, the both of them so young and inexperienced it was by turns amusing, anxiety-ridden, and awkward.

But then Madame Mariposa had insisted that Cherise join the other working women. And Jack, feeling overwhelmed with frustration and powerlessness, had stowed away on the garbage scow, vowing he'd make a million and return for Cherise someday.

The same frustration and powerlessness beset him at the bright orange boot bolted to the landing strut.

He couldn't even think.

Misty went over and kicked the boot. "I'm so mad!"

Down the sewer, all of it.

Without a ship, Jack couldn't do anything. They weren't going to the Vega Strip to reclaim Jack's losses from the Ballsy Palace Casino, they weren't getting Daria's surety deposit for the Circian Crown Jewels, and they certainly weren't getting to Torgas Prime.

The entire scheme collapsed around their ears.

Like the house of cards it was, Jack thought.

He remembered back to the moment he'd found the cube in the derelict building on Canis Dogma Five, when the ancient holojector had pitched onto the wall the image of the deceased Emperor Lochium Circi IX, telling him, pathetic Jack with the pinched Paleolithic face, ineluctable charm, and cursed life, that the Circian Empire was destined to rise from its ashes and be restored to its former glory, Jack as its next Emperor.

Jack looked at the bright orange boot and knew none of it could happen now.

The sight began to blur, and he began to weep.

Hope had been so bright recently. For most of his life, Jack had struggled to find a flicker of hope in the perennial dark, some hint that life might hold something better for him than persistent poverty and un-remediated suffering. The few periods of joy in his life—six months of awkward bliss with Cherise, somehow finding Cherise again and rekindling their romance, and two years of wonder with Daria—had been welcome respites in a life of penance, poverty, and privation. And to have spent these last two weeks with a girl who knew boundless hope in spite of her own nearly insurmountable circumstances, Jack felt privileged.

And now it was over.

"Uh, Jack?"

He wiped away his tears and focused on Misty. He was sitting cross-legged on the tarmac at the Pretoria spaceport on the planet Tertius Diamond, his ship booted by some repo thug, and no hope of ever getting back aboard and getting off this rock and getting on with his life.

I wish I'd never found this cube, he thought. "What?" he asked her listlessly, sniffling and pulling his jacket tight against the cold.

"If someone put the boot on, someone can surely take it off."

"Where am I gonna get the money to bring the payments current?"

"You can do that later, when we get back from the Vega Strip."

He gestured helplessly at the bright orange boot. "But—?"

"Whoever put it on can take it off, right?"

"I wish it worked that way." He shook his head at her, admiring her persistence, especially in the face of futility.

She frowned at him. "Maybe they're still close by." She stood and peered toward the tower, a phallus against the cold, white sky. "What's that?"

He peered the direction she pointed. Beside the main terminal stood a service building, its many bays half empty of vehicles, flitter craft flittering in and out, and a large, black vehicle sitting squat and menacing nearby, its portals deeply tinted. It was a Crown Dictoria, known among law enforcement agencies as simply the "Crown Dick," their predominate choice for transportation, even among clandestine units, one instantly recognizable as an undercover vehicle, and a pretty common pick among repo agents, too.

"That's the bank repo rep if I ever saw one," Misty said.

He refrained from asking where a nine-year-old orphan from the derelict planet Canis Dogma Five had ever seen a bank repo rep.

"Come on," she said, pulling him to his feet.

Indolently, listlessly, he followed her.

Besides the vehicle was a burly man with a butch haircut. If he'd been any more militarized, he'd have had epaulets on his shoulders. He was talking to security, oblivious to the two people walking up behind him "... booted this guy's ship two other times, always late on his payments. Never met the man, but his dossier headshot is ugly as sin. Looks like a caveman."

The security guard spotted Jack and Misty. "Uh..."

The repo man turned. "Sweet suffering stardust!"

The sights of Jack's face had been known to blow video circuits.

"Are you the gentleman who put the boot on my friend's ship?" Misty asked.

"Uh, yeah, I guess that's me."

"Would you be so kind as to remove it, please? We'd like to get going." Misty nudged him.

Jack turned to look at her, puzzled.

"Uh, sorry, can't do that." The big man spread his hands apologetically, one of them holding a doc-cube. "This here says the payments are in default, and the bank's gotta reclaim its property."

"And you've got triple-sided copies, I assume?"

The repo rep looked at her funny. "Uh ..."

"I'm sure you can make an exception, Sir." Misty elbowed Jack in the ribs.

"Ouch!" Jack said.

"Afraid I can't do that, miss," the man said.

She put a hand on her hip. "That's your Highness, Sir. Don't you know how to address a princess properly?" From the side of her mouth, she muttered to Jack, "The cube, blast it, use the cube!"

"Sorry, your Highness, but even if Mr. Carson were the Emperor, I'd still have to boot his ship."

"But he is the Emperor—or he soon will be—and I'm Princess Misty Circi, and you'll take the boot off his ship immediately!"

Jack put his hand into his pocket.

The beefy repo man grew a dazed look, his jaw going slack and his eyes becoming unfocused.

The man's thoughts flooded into Jack's mind, the catalogue of repos on his itinerary long enough to fill a small encyclopedia. Despite the number times he'd been on the receiving end of a bank's repo order, Jack was dismayed by the number of ships headed for repossession. Furthermore, their methods—logging payments late and adding excess "surcharges" for superfluous administrative tasks like taking a com from a customer—infuriated Jack. He didn't know how many times they'd weaseled in a balloon payment clause, and then invoked it if a payment was a single galacti short or a single minute late.

"Yes, your Highness, I'll attend to it immediately," the man said, and he staggered like a zombie toward the Scavenger.

While he was unbolting the boot from the landing strut, a robotow arrived and hovered expectantly, its caution lights flashing.

"Hey, Jack," Misty whispered. She pointed toward the repo man's Crown Dick.

He grinned, shooting a glance at the short-haired big man.

The repo guy carried the bright orange boot over his own ship and started to attach it.

"Hey, what are you doing?" the security guard asked.

Jack threw him a look, and his face went slack.

When the repo man finished, the robotow attached itself to the Crown Dick and lifted off, leaving its owner on the tarmac.

Jack grinned at Misty. "Let's go to Vega."

* * *

Misty was the perfect foil, particularly at the gaming tables.

Jack knew he couldn't win big. That'd be defeatist, since the casinos would likely deploy their recovery experts. And like their Whiteys—

their lead draws, the ones who preyed upon likely victims—their recovery experts had entire repertoires at their disposal. Jack knew he wouldn't leave unscathed with more than a hundred thousand galacti.

The casinos couldn't afford the kinds of wins that Jack needed.

They fell into a routine, Misty chatting up a dealer while Jack played fifty to a hundred hands. He set himself a pattern, enough in wins to make it worth his while, then on to a new table or new casino before the pit boss became too suspicious.

He was careful, but he knew he couldn't escape detection. His best strategy was to fly low enough that he didn't raise a lot of concerns. He felt them watching, and at the edge of their minds was a suspicion that he was gaming them, but Jack always made sure he lost some games, that he never had a streak of too many wins.

He also found he needed to have a human dealer. The robotic dealers didn't lend themselves well to ghosting, their circuitry sometimes indecipherable through the Gaussian interface. Like the human brain, cyborg bio neurology emitted electrical fields, but the Ghost cube wasn't well adapted to interpreting those fields. So when the management substituted a robotic dealer for the human one, Jack would often take that as a signal that he'd better move on to the next table.

Win, win, win, lose, win, win, lose. Again and again. Jack's winnings began to accumulate.

But as he worked the tables, he kept his eye on the prize, the one bet in which he could simultaneously recoup his losses from five years ago and exact his revenge on the iconic industry gorilla: The Ballsy Palace Casino.

Word of him spread, enough to have earned him a constant shadow, but no one could figure out how he was doing it. He never brought out the cube, of course, but he always had it with him. They tried separating him and Misty, by enticing her away to a kid's playground, but soon found that didn't alter his pattern of winning. When the surveillance grew too thick, he simply moved on.

Jack also learned from them, as well. He discovered that they even surveilled the slot machines, and that any overly generous machine could be tightened up at a few taps by the slot monitor, one operator typically supervising hundreds of machines. Further, they would sometimes loosen a machine to entice a customer into staying and then recoup those losses afterward. They also had shills, gamblers on the floor who were plants, put there by the casino to win and win big, and thereby sucker other nearby gamblers into putting more money into the slots.

Then there were the hawks.

These were interlocutors whose seeming-random, spontaneous exchanges with customers might entice one or two to up the ante—to play the games with better payouts but steeper odds. They were meant to look like ordinary customers, but they always gave themselves away. They'd sit down for a hand or two, tell Jack he was pretty good, say they'd just come over from the torqueball table where someone just won three quarter mil.

Even those games of seeming random chance—like torqueball or roulette—had nothing random about them. Magnetized cushions and micrograv nodes might subtly redirect a ball into a hole or deflect a die from landing a particular number. Those mechanized machinations weren't used overtly, since a casino might be fined if caught, but enforcement was difficult and complaints were lodged at far higher rates than they could be investigated. The casinos gamed their regulators too.

Jack bided his time, his wins slowly growing.

Misty didn't seem to tire of the routine, and since Jack never went back to the same casino, she never seemed to get bored. Her role was simply to ask questions about everything and provide that low-level irritant distraction that allowed Jack to do his work relatively freely.

The independent sharks inevitably got word of him. The house sharks were a clique to themselves, frequently sharing information from house to house, many of them moonlighting elsewhere. They knew who the current marks were and how much they could be milked; further, they'd often tag-team to wear customers down. There was some predatory, casino-to-casino sharking, where a shark from one casino would lure a mark from beneath the noses of another casino, but most of them tried to discourage this practice, abiding by the general dictum that if the mark was inside your doors, he or she was yours.

But the independent sharks weren't beholden to such rules. They worked only for themselves. That was Whitey, who'd sent numerous fishing boats into Jack's waters when he was married to Daria. He'd finally figured out that it wasn't him Whitey had been after; it'd been Osborn Diamond. Whitey harvested the big fish, luring them to swim in Ballsy's corner of the pond. He had a heart of larceny pumping avarice to his every thieving extremity.

Only this time, it was Jack who was fishing for Whitey.

About two weeks later and a hundred thousand galacti richer, Jack was working the floor at the Carnival, Carnival Casino, drifting from blackjack to poker, about five grand to the better for the day, when a ghost in a white suit sat next to him.

Whitey looked so gaunt that Jack's heart almost went out to him.

"You look terrible," Jack said, noting the disheveled suit, the thin cheeks, the deep-set eyes ringed in black, the straight, sheared-off teeth. And the pouch mounted on the shoulder.

A vein sack.

Whitey was an addict, a port now permanently in a vein, a sack of fluid mounted on his shoulder. "I've had it rough, Jack. Look, I, uh, I'm surprised frankly that you'd even speak to me after what happened. I'm truly sorry. We both got the sharp end of that stick. I couldn't get out of bed for two years after that—and well, I started on the injectable, too. Trying to wean myself off now, but it's so hard, Jack, so hard. How about you? You seem to have recovered somewhat. Who's the girl?"

"I'm his daughter, Misty, and I'm a princess!"

Whitney didn't even blink. "You certainly are! What a darling girl, Jack, she's a sweetie. Perfect for a place like this, help you milk a few thou out of em! More unscrupulous than I am! What a scoundrel."

Jack grinned, not sure whether to be proud or insulted.

"Sir, can I ask you not to bother the customers?" the dealer said.

"He's not a bother," Jack told her, shrugging.

Even so, she pointed her double cannons toward the pit boss and waved.

The pit boss sauntered her double barrels over.

Jack mused that he'd never seen a flat-chested female casino staffer. Probably made them wear twin prosthetics as a condition of employment. "I said he's with me," Jack told the twin-peaked pit boss.

"You don't understand, Mr. Carson," she said.

He hadn't introduced himself, his name known already along the strip.

"This man is forbidden by the management from associating with any of our guests. His unseemly activities are well known. Aren't they, Whitey?"

"They certainly are, Zelda. It's all right, Jack, I'll be going."

Jack held up a hand. "Zelda, I'm asking Whitey to stay. I know what he does, and it doesn't bother me. Thanks for the warning but it's unnecessary. Even if he wanted, he couldn't bilk me for a single slick galacti. And if you insist he leave, then I go too."

Zelda relented and faded into the background, but her eyes remained on them, Jack knew.

Whitey watched her retreat. "Awful nice of you, Jack. I don't deserve a free moment of your time, much less a defense like that."

Jack shrugged. "We were both fools once. I'd offer to buy you a bag—" he glanced at the one on Whitney's shoulder—"but I'm guessing you'd prefer not. How about joining me for a few hands, eh?"

"Oh, Jack, I couldn't."

"Sure you could," Misty piped up. "Daddy'll pay your bets, won't you?" She grinned at Jack.

"Little pipsqueak knows what I'm thinking," Jack told Whitey.

"No, I can't, Jack, not even a single hand. It gets to me, even worse than this." He threw a thumb at the shoulder pouch.

"Not even one? Come on, Whitey, for old time's sake." Jack patted the stool next to him. "I insist."

After a little more cajoling, Whitey sat.

Jack pushed a stack of chips in his direction. "Use only what you need."

Whitey's eyes glistened. "You're a kind man, Jack, more kind that I deserve."

"We all deserve a little kindness, no matter what."

They both bet against the house, and they both won, turning black-jacks. Jack grinned. "You keep the proceeds for spending money. No, no, I insist. Stay and watch if you want—it'd please me if you did—but don't bet anymore. Wouldn't be good for you."

To his surprise, Whitey stayed but only to observe.

Jack lost the next hand, but kept his bet small, then won the next three, each time ending his bets in a little higher. Three wins, one loss, two wins, one loss, four wins, one loss.

"Nice little routine, there, Jack," Whitey said. "You know they're onto you."

He nodded and glanced at Misty.

"Not enough to accuse him of counting cards," she said, "and not enough to persuade him to leave."

"Teaching her all my old tricks, eh, Jack?"

He grinned. "Two more hands here, and they'll replace the dealer with a borg, which is my cue I've outstayed my welcome."

Two more hands, and the dealer cleared her throat. "Excuse me, gentlemen, it's my break time. Bennie the borg will assist you while I'm gone. Not much of a conversationalist, but he can make a mean martini."

Jack gathered his chips to go. "Nice to meet you, Bennie, gotta go." He turned to look at Whitey. "Pleasure. See you tomorrow maybe?"

"Probably not, Jack. Not good for my moral redemption, these places. Been good seeing you. And quite nice meeting you, Misty." He shook hands with them both and faded into the darkened casino.

"He'll be back," Misty said.

* * *

The next day he was back.

Jack had moved on the Palms Palisades, a desert-themed, light-festooned palace whose floors were covered with sand, but somehow Whitey found him anyway.

"Thought I'd come to watch you work," he said to Jack, "and frankly, it was quite a pleasure yesterday to see you walk out of that place with fifty grand. Bilked the snot out of 'em before they knew what was happening."

At the Palms Palisades, Jack settled himself at a poker table, deuces wild, playing two house opponents and two human competitors. His strategy here was different, five-player hands subject to far more variation. The house in this case had rigged the game, the dealer having remembered the cards, a fact known to Jack by his ghosting the dealer. The house had been expecting him.

Patiently, Jack worked the game, letting the house win most the initial hands. Then Jack changed tactics, drawing one more or one less card than the dealer expected, and confounding the resulting hands, to make the dealer lose. His two competitors began to win to their delight, Jack exhibiting a slightly puzzled looked at his apparent luck-lessness. His bets small, he didn't lose much, but the house was losing significantly.

The pit boss pulled the dealer and put in another gentleman, who by his drab looks was probably sharper than a rocket scientist.

"This could get ugly, Jack," Whitey whispered to him.

"Daddy's already ugly," Misty whispered back.

The first thing Jack noticed about the new dealer was how furtive his thoughts were, as though in his efforts to keep his thoughts off his face, he actually kept them out of his mind. There was an economy to his movements which betrayed his intimate knowledge of the game. As though he'd seen every gambit ever played and had remembered its nuances. Further, the new dealer didn't appear to be counting cards.

Formidable, Jack thought. The house had upped the ante.

One of his competitors didn't like the change. "I'm out."

Jack shot Whitey a look, and the thin man took a seat beside Jack.

Two against the house, always better odds.

The pit boss appeared instantly, a man so thick through that he stretched the seams of his jacket. "Oh, no you don't, Whitey."

"He stays," Jack said, "or I go."

The pit boss glanced between them. "The cameras are rolling, gentlemen. Any hint of collusion, you both get the boot." He said something unintelligible into his wrist. "Capisce?"

The old languages die hard, Jack thought. "Capisce." He could see Whitey hesitating. "Just for today, old friend, just so these mother buggers don't win."

"You got it, Jack." Whitey grinned.

The other competitor bowed out, glancing appreciably at Jack and Whitey.

Now it was two to two. The dealer and the house player against Jack and Whitey.

As tempted as he was, Jack didn't let the upped ante get his goat. With the evened odds, two against two, Jack was able to work the house, he and Whitey winning two, three, and four in sequence, then losing one. He controlled their losses.

When next he looked up, two hours had passed. He was drenched in sweat. But he and Whitey each had impressive stacks of chips beside them.

They'd drawn an audience, he saw. Odd how he hadn't noticed before. Usually a sign he was winning too much.

Jack saw several pairs of knowing eyes in the spectators. He and Whitey together were far ahead of the progress Jack usually made on his own, and he didn't like the attention it was generating.

Se he began to lose.

Gradually, subtly, but still losing, working his stack down until it was barely larger than when he started.

"I gotta step out, gentleman," he told his opponents. "Salvage my dignity, at least." He was guessing he'd cleared only a thousand.

Whitey easily had seventy thou in front of him. "It's all icing to me, Jack, if you want to continue." He gestured at his stack to indicate that Jack could have whatever portion he wanted.

"You earned it fairly, Whitey, I couldn't." He grinned at Misty. "Daddy didn't do so well today, did he?"

"Quitting ahead, at least," she said brightly. "But you're right, it's time to stop."

Together, they walked to the cage to cashier out.

Hand in hand, Jack and Misty headed to the entrance, where they ran into Whitey, tucking a stash of chits into his pocket.

"Dinner on me?" Whitey asked. "It's the least I could do." The drip bag at his shoulder was nearly empty. "Gotta stop for a refill, but how about it? What's a little chow between chums?"

Morose, Jack agreed reluctantly, letting himself be talked into it.

"I'm hungry, Daddy."

That convinced him.

* * *

Over dinner, which Whitey dove into with gusto, they talked of old times, Jack barely touching his food.

"All right, Jack, you can lay it out for me now. No cams or mikes here." The nearest table was at a casino one block over. "What brings you back to the strip, really?"

Jack was taken back. "Brings me back? What do you mean?"

"What are you playing for? What's your stake, what's the goal, what's the wager you're wanting in on?"

He waved dismissively. "I'm just playin' it day by day, putting a little aside for a rainy day. I'm not trolling for any big fish, Whitey. I know better than that. We both know these big casinos have entire arsenals they can aim at us. There isn't a fish big enough to risk my life on, or my daughter's life."

Whitey shook his head. "Great job thus far, making them think so, especially by bringing her along. But I don't buy it, Jack. You're too good not to be working some angle. Don't tell me if you're not comfortable. It's all right. I understand. There's a streak of luck or skill or something that's kept you in the black for the last few weeks, and it just doesn't make any sense if you didn't have a plan."

Jack shrugged in bemusement. "But I don't, Whitey."

"At the poker table today, you lost deliberately. Why?"

"We were winning too much too fast, drawing too much attention."

"See? If you didn't have some long game in mind, you wouldn't have done that. But it's all right. I can see you're not comfortable telling me what it is. I don't begrudge you that for a moment. Whatever you've got in mind must surely have Ballsy Palace as its goal. Don't tell me you haven't plotted your revenge..."

Jack laughed aloud. "But I haven't, Whitey. Look, sure, I've thought about it. Of course, I was angry. But I'm not here for that and any grudges I might have harbored initially just don't interest me anymore. It's past, and I'm done with that." Jack smiled at the thin, older man. "I've got my daughter and I'm enjoying life. What more can a person ask?" He looked at Misty and winked.

"But if someone hatched a scheme to filch a few million from their vault," Misty said, an evil gleam in her eye, "you know you'd go along with it."

"No, I wouldn't, not if it would put you in danger."

"But you'd certainly consider it," she chided, grinning at him.

Jack smiled at her. "Of course I would, wouldn't you?"

* * *

"Listen, Jack, I've got a lead on something, but I gotta know what I'm working with."

Jack was mid-morning through a day at the Triple Trump, a card house sitting glumly amidst the glitz like a dour older sister, her décor all in clubs, hearts, spades, and diamonds. He'd been raking the tables in pinochle, the opportunities to win fewer and farther between, but far higher in payoff. He and Misty hadn't seen Whitey in a couple of days, so he was surprised when the ice-cream suited old man saun-tered in and sat beside him.

Intrigued, and guessing he wouldn't want to talk at a table, Jack glanced at the clock. "Join me for lunch in an hour or so?"

Whitey hesitated then agreed somewhat reluctantly.

The casino restaurant like the casino itself was decorated all in play-ing cards, some of them large than life. A talking suicide king took their order, while a pair of deuces cleared off a nearby table.

"What do you mean, 'you gotta know what you're working with'?" Misty asked Whitey point blank. "You think Jack is just gonna tell you how he's skimming thousands off these bastards?"

"Don't get cheeky with me, midget. All the casinos know you aren't his daughter. And you certainly aren't a Princess, so you can put your pretensions up your exhaust port."

"Listen, you fatuous fathead—"

"Hush," Jack said, his hand on her arm. To Whitey, he said, "She's right and didn't deserve to be addressed that way. She deserves an apology."

Whitey made a face.

"An apology doesn't cost you a dime, but the lack of one might lose you millions."

Whitey sighed, his gaze on Jack. "Sorry, Misty, I shouldn't have called you a midget."

"Apology accepted. And the question still stands." She smiled cutely. "But you're right. I was getting cheeky. Sorry about that. Jack keeps telling me I don't have a filter."

"Thank you, and no, I don't expect Jack to tell me anything. That'd be a breach of my professional ethics."

Jack kept his face expressionless, somehow.

"But whatever you've got, Jack, it might be useful." Whitey looked at Misty. "Maybe it's the same as what you got, girl. You mentioned filching a few mil from the Ballsy Vault the other day. Guess what came my way this morning? Word that someone has its blueprint."

Misty glanced between them, her blank look in high contrast to the eager expressions of both men.

"It means knowing how to get in and out, what the security devices are and where they're at, how the place is laid out." Jack looked at Whitey. "How do we know it isn't a set up?"

"I'll know." Whitey leaned close and whispered, "I've been there."

Jack sat back, the possibilities sending his heart into the heavens. "What if word gets back to Ballsy? They'll be expecting something, and they may lay some traps."

"It's an inside source, Jack. Someone with a knife to sharpen. You can't make billions without upsetting somebody. The other piece, Jack, is what you got. We've got to exploit every edge available to us, 'cause their security is the finest. They've got more layers of security than the royal palace on Torgas Prime. The vault is six stories underground, with more checkpoints than the Imperial Bureau of Investigation compound on Alpha Tuscana. We're talking geno-typing, iris-scanning, retina-typing, facia-metricking, bone-imaging, E. coli-matching, mitochondrial gene-sampling, strip-searching, and even anus-imaging."

"No two assholes alike," Misty quipped.

"Where'd you learn language like that? Jack, what have you been teaching her? Anyway, that's why I'm asking, Jack," Whitey said, shaking his head. "I wouldn't ask otherwise."

"A caper like this is a one-time thing," Jack said, hesitating. "We'll have contracts on our lives for the rest of eternity."

"We'll be so filthy rich, we'll be able to buy our own rogue planets." Whitey was grinning from ear to ear.

He hated to be the naysayer, but there just wasn't any help for it. "Sorry, Whitey. I can't." He grasped Misty's hand. "I don't want my little princess to be on the run for the rest of her life. It's just not worth it."

"Aw, come on, Jack, with your talent, we could score big. Just tell me you'll consider it, Jack. Don't let me down!"

Jack could see the pitched fit coming. He remembered the tearful breakdown he'd witnessed at his front door on Tertius Diamond, pitched with just enough finesse to beguile Jack into playing along with Whitey's scheme. "Save it for the mongrels, Whitey," Jack said bluntly. "You flamblasted me once with that routine, and it ain't gonna happen again. Unless you have a way to bring down Ballsy Gaming and put it out of business, I don't want any part of your scheme."

* * *

Whitey caught up to them the next day at the Galloping Galaxy Casino, themed upon a period in ancient Earth history called the Wild West. Staff wore boots and outrageously large hats called ten-gallon hats, sported a pair of projectile-emitting barrels of metal known as guns, and spoke with drawls so elaborate that your food grew cold while you waited for the end of the word.

Texas hold 'em seemed to be the house specialty game, with mock "gun" fights going on after accusations of marked cards or other cheats. Long mustaches and longer games, bowlegged and bow-armed posturing, made it all look so ridiculous that Jack and Misty spent their first hour just watching.

It was afternoon when Whitey spotted them at a table.

After the usual pit boss threats and Jack's insistence that Whitey stay, the white-decked man settled on a stool beside Jack.

"You look different, somehow," Misty said.

Jack had noticed it, too.

"What's it to you, midget?"

"No, I'm serious, Whitey," Misty said, stopping Jack by lifting her finger.

Jack waited, Misty sometimes full of surprises.

"You don't have a bag on your shoulder." Misty raised an eyebrow. "Have you stopped using the juice for good?"

Whitey looked half-bewildered, half-suspicious. "So?"

"So, congratulations," Misty said. "Quite an accomplishment."

Jack seconded that. "You're looking better all around."

Whitey glanced between them. "Why, thank you. That's quite kind of you. Guess I didn't really notice, so preoccupied with other things."

Jack gestured Whitey to join in a hand.

Whitey picked up his cards. "I found a way," he said, placing his bet.

Jack placed his, hold 'em even worse than pinochle, more difficult yet to win and more lucrative. He had a stack of almost a hundred thousand galacti beside him. "Found a way what?" Jack said. I'll probably have to lose some, he thought, the crowd in spurred boots and ten-gallon hats getting thick behind him.

"You know, what we talked about."

Having ghosted him, Jack did know. "What's the way?"

The dealer laid out the first of three community cards, the "flop," calling out each in turn.

"My insurance policy. Every shark has one." Whitey grinned.

"Didn't know you could find a policy for that sort of thing," Misty said.

Jack signaled her to zip it. "Tell me about it."

"Tell me about yours."

Jack didn't need to look around. Too many eyes and ears. "Over dinner, eh, old friend? I don't like talking business while doing business."

"Over dinner, then."

And for the next hour, Jack lost steadily, getting more and more upset as he did so. By the time he withdrew, he had only twenty thou beside him, and he was red-faced with rage. Most of his previous winnings seemed to have migrated to Whitey.

"Don't say I never did you a favor," Jack told him as they cashed in their chips.

The management approached Whitey at the door, a small dapper man with two bulky bulls behind him. "Don't come back, Whitey. It won't be pretty if you do."

"Put your Galloping Galaxy into your back black hole," Whitey said amiably.

Outside, on the busy, blazing-bright boulevard, Whitey threw his head back and laughed. "Gotta say, I'm sure been enjoying your company, Jack. Good times, friend!" He patted him on the back and laughed the whole way to the bank. From there, they went to a restaurant.

"So, when I started doin' this some thirty years ago, I made sure I had something on each employer. I've worked for just about every corporate gamer on the Vega Strip. Every conversation, all the nasty little schemes, and yes, even that entire episode with you and Osborn Diamond. All the marks I've brought in for Ballsy—recorded every single one of them. Must be a million hours of video and audio, half a billion coms, fifty million stills, all of it booby-trapped."

"You mean, set for release to the public if Ballsy should try to eliminate you?" Misty asked.

Whitey grinned, nodding. "Way too smart to be anything but a midget."

Misty stuck her tongue out at him.

"Dropped into the hands of a reporter or filed with the Vega Strip Gaming Commission—and Ballsy's out of business."

Jack smiled. "You'd risk implicating yourself?"

"I could turn state's evidence or disappear like a wraith. It's about time I retire anyway. Before Ballsy decides to retire me."

It all sounded too good to be true. But if it were true, then Ballsy could be crippled right after he and Whitey had cracked their vault.

"Where's the booby-trap?" Jack asked.

Whitey gave him a look of pure indignation. "What, and show you the goose that'll lay my golden egg? Not happenin'." Then Whitey brightened. "But I'd sure like to know how you're doing this, Jack."

The hook is baited, Jack thought. But who's handling the fishing pole? Me or Whitey?

"Tit for tat, Jack," Whitey sniggered.

"Sounds too good to be true, Jack," Misty said to Jack, sneering at Whitey. "For all we know, Whitey's workin' for the Gaming Association to try to put you out of business. We haven't seen any blueprints or this booby-trapped stash of dirty Vega Strip laundry. He's full of flambé."

"Suit yourself," Whitey said, and he stood to leave. "Very nice seeing both of you again." He bowed and turned to walk off.

"Uh, Whitey—?"

The thin, white-suited man turned, one eyebrow raised.

"Have a seat," Jack said, gesturing across from him.

"Jack, don't!" Misty protested. "You're giving away your edge, throwing away all your advantage."

He looked at her. "Ballsy came after me. I happened to be married to the owner of a lucrative diamond business, and they targeted me as an easy source of money. They systematically lured me into their web with the full intent of bilking me and my wife for very galacti they could. I've dreamt ever since of nothing more than finding some way of putting them down, permanently. So they can't do the same to anyone else. Now, finally, I have a change of doing that, and recovering the money they stole from me and Daria. I'll do everything I can to protect us both, Misty, but this is something I have to do.

"I have to." He looked her straight in the eye. "Are you with me?"

Misty smiled. "I'm with you."

They shook.

Jack told Whitey about being able to ghost someone's thought, but didn't tell him about the cube. "So I can read what's going on in their minds, and sometimes I'm even able to see what they're seeing."

"That's the stuff of science fiction, Jack. How are you doing that?"

He smiled and shook his head. "Leave me an ace or two in the hole, would you, Whitey?"

The older man shook his head. "I knew it was something. I knew you had some gimmick." Whitey sat back. "That's phenomenal, Jack. You could'a really cleaned house with that kind of skill. So why the low level wins? Why the gradual approach?"

"Ballsy," was all Jack said.

Chapter 9

Ballsy Palace stood solitaire in the desert, surrounded by dunes hundreds of feet high. Turrets ringed the resort compound like sentinels. The main casino tower soared above all else for hundreds of miles around, a gigantic inverted pyramid held aloft by antigrav units, its underside ablaze with multi-colored lights.

The thick column where the pyramid peak met the ground housed multiple elevators shafts.

On the grounds between the column and the ring of turrets were the outdoor sports: an ostrich track, a golf course, a murderball diamond, a crippleball gridiron. Underground, beneath these playing fields, were the administrative offices of Ballsy Gaming, themselves in the shape of an inverted pyramid. And at the peak of this pyramid, six stories underground, was the vault.

One elevator went there, an armored elevator. Six keys operated this elevator, one person at each level receiving the elevator from the floor above, inspecting its contents, and then sending it to the floor below. Each day's take was sent to the vault below for counting and storage, and then once per week, the week's take was loaded back onto the elevator in a sealed, secured container. The weekly deposit was sent up from the vault level by itself to the fifth level, where six suited thugs boarded. At each level, the sealed, secured container was reinspected for tampering and the six thugs reidentified for veracity before being sent up the next level. Atop the building, the container was loaded onto a freighter and sent under heavy guard and multi-ship armada to Metropli Bank on Dorado Quintus, where banking laws were so stringent that no one knew who banked there.

Once this container was safely delivered to Dorado Quintus, a journey that took only a day, the six thugs returned under continued blackout to the Vega Strip and the Ballsy resort, having done their job. Two days work out of seven, five days off, living expenses paid and leisure on the house. What more could a muscle-bound pea-brain ask for?

Entrance to the vault was restricted to four people, including Leticia Ballsy, the Chief Financial Officer and scion to founder Leonard Ballsy. The other three were virtual prisoners, going into the vault only to count the money and living Spartan lives on level five underground, right above the vault itself. Not even Leonard Ballsy was allowed into his own vault.

Leticia Ballsy lived in one corner of the above-ground pyramid, on the top level, her suite taking up the entire corner, rumored to be palatial, that corner of the roof given over to her personal golf course. She wagered on her own golf games, and nearly always won.

At one point in the not too distant past, Leticia Ballsy had developed an interest in one of those six thugs, a not-so-pea-brained fellow named Carmody Carruthers. For a time, when Leticia wasn't counting profits in the Ballsy vault, she could be found straddling Carmody's considerable bulk. Much as they tried to keep their impassioned liaisons under the covers, word soon spread throughout the resort staff. All might have remained copasetic, since the pair was discreet and didn't engage in public displays of passion, nor betray by look, word, or gesture that their nocturnal activities might have provided footage for the most salacious of adult films, but for the cupidity of Carmody Carruthers.

Which actually became the title of one such adult film.

An individual with an impressive physique, Carmody had worked all his life to defuse the myth that he was dumb. So in his carousing with the CFO of Ballsy Gaming, he mentioned after a particularly invigorating coupling one sweat-soaked night that his one ambition in life was to assume command of the six-thug unit that guarded the weekly deposit.

And Leticia's response was what ultimately put the chink into the armor that had thus far proved impenetrable to all schemers seeking to subvert the security surrounding the weekly Ballsy deposit. She laughed and said, "We already have the smartest possible man for the job."

She didn't intend to insult him. And few people would have taken either the laugh or the comment as insult. In fact, either by itself might have only pricked Carmody's delicate ego. But both together pierced the thin veneer of competence and burst the blister of his infectious insecurity. Carmody grew discontent and his long-festering inadequacy regarding his intellect became the suppurating boil upon the buttocks of Ballsy Gaming. After a time, Leticia tired of his titillation and acquired other boy toys but had not an inkling that beneath Carmody's stoic surface stirred the venom that ultimately proved deadly to her organization.

Whitey was well known among the Ballsy Gaming staff, the number and range of marks he'd managed to get in the door having enhanced Ballsy's bottom line significantly. He'd even been granted an honorary tour of the Ballsy vault.

And it was Whitey who'd been given first pick when Carmody sought to sell the vault blueprints.

When Jack, Misty, and Whitey arrived by shuttle on Vega 14, the "Biggest little Star System in the Galaxy," they caught the casino flitter at the spaceport and were whisked along with the hundreds of other gamers to the Ballsy Palace complex.

The flitter crested a towering dune and dropped toward the turrets, the inverted pyramid already dominating their view, the flitter top a single sheet of glasma.

Jack realized when they were still a quarter mile away just how large the Ballsy pyramid was.

It hovered directly over them.

The top floor, their brochure declared, was a full half-mile square, the roof large enough for a full nine-hole golf course, Leticia Ballsy's private course, and a swimming pool the size of a small lake.

It looked as if it would fall over and crush them at any moment.

The three of them were the Jones family, Mr. Jack Jones, Mr. Whitey Jones, and their daughter Misty Jones. Whitey for this operation had set aside his ice cream suit and now wore the de rigueur flower-print touristy formalls that everyone else wore.

He looked positively ghostly, his skin a nasty, nearly-translucent hue of colorless white. Jack guessed that only the ice cream suits gave him any relief from the near-death look.

"Cute outfit, Whitey," Misty had said at the outset.

"Cork it, midget."

They'd also brought all the requisite equipment that any tourist of middle class means would have: camera, sunblock, polarizers, audio-players, vidtexts, and of course the inevitable ignorance.

The moment they got off the flitter, they all three looked up at the edifice dangling precariously by a thread above them and exclaimed, "How does it stay up?" The central pillar which housed all the elevator shafts looked (and was) far too insubstantial to hold up its bulk.

Crowds of people just like them streamed in and out of cramped elevators, and Jack knew that the largest of them, the central elevator, the armored one which took the day's take to the vault and the week's take to the launch pad, was used exclusively for moving money and was never utilized to relieve the crush of patron.

One elevator had been set aside with velvet ropes and red satin carpet. A single, impeccably-dressed young man strolled leisurely toward the gold-plated elevator door, blithely ignoring the crowds of sheep-like people being funneled systematically into already cramped elevators.

"That's how we should have arrived," Misty said, looking up between Jack and Whitey, that princess pout plastered to her face.

"Exactly the kind of attention we don't want," Whitey said.

"Maybe you don't want it, but a princess demands it."

"Pipe down, pipsqueak."

The check-in process at the most popular gaming complex on the Vega Strip took hours, but the staff were most accommodating, making sure the guests' needs were attended to. The aromas of smoke, drink, snort, and shoot were all around them, waiters and waitresses floating among the guest with trays of all the best mind-altering drugs. Jack could smell the fine blends in the smoke they were serving, but as tempted as he was to obliterate himself with huge lungfuls of the stuff, he refrained.

Oddly enough, he identified with Whitey's sentiment that he simply had too much else to think about and had mostly forgotten or at least set aside his cravings.

Room key in hand, they toted their bags from an elevator to their room on the sixteenth floor, the numbers on the buttons going all the way to one hundred twenty, the most expensive suites at the top. Yes, they might have afforded one such suite, but would have garnered that unwanted attention.

Their modest suite was already labeled "Mr. and Mr. Jones," and a bouquet of flowers adorned the low, living room table, a welcome card stuck prominently among the stems.

Misty went immediately to the door with her name on it, looked into it, and promptly "oohed" and "ahhed."

Fir for a princess, apparently, Jack thought. The master bedroom across from Misty's room was certainly plush by any measure if somewhat shy of palatial. Then he looked at the bed.

A single king size bed.

He swore, knowing he'd rather sleep on the floor of Misty's room than leave himself vulnerable to Whitey's knife between his ribs. They'd asked for separate queens, a request they were sure had generated a good deal of sniggering on the part of the hotel staff. Jack was almost relieved that the request had either been ignored or had gone astray. Now, he wouldn't have to find an excuse to sleep on Misty's floor.

Whitey shrugged when he told him. "Better that way," he said.

They laid out the blueprints on the living room floor after scouring the suite for surveillance devices, then rehearsed their plan once again. Verbally, Carmody had alerted Whitey to a few security measures that had been added since the facility had been built, primarily cameras to monitor blind spots, motion detectors, and the like.

One feature of the security system—and its primary flaw, in Jack's opinion—was its reliance on human video monitoring. Each camera's signal was routed to four different monitoring stations, the quadruple surveillance intended to obviate any vulnerability. What they'd overlooked was that all four monitoring stations relied on the same ventilation system.

Their intent was to introduce a gaseous, odorless soporific and then shut down all the communications and security apparatuses including the laser-trip beams, the retinal- and iris-scanning, the geno-typing, and all the other identification checks.

"And especially that anal-imaging," Misty said. "I know no two assholes are alike, but stars above!"

"Midget," Whitey muttered.

"So we place canisters here, here, here, and here," Jack said. "Did Carmody get those maintenance orders in?" They'd badged and uniformed themselves as HVAC maintenance techs.

Whitney in his gray-striped suit looked like a prisoner. "Maintenance orders placed. Complaints of dust in the vents. Probably haven't been cleaned since the place was built."

"They go off at twenty-two hundred, two hours before shift change. We then have ninety minutes to disable communications and security apparatuses, gather the take, and get out the door. If all goes well, we'll have a thirty-minute lead to get to the escape yacht. Everything ready with that, Whitey?"

Whitey had secured a modified Mercury Orbit—touted as the family's family car—but all its emblems and registrations removed and its engine hypercharged. It awaited them at the Vega 14 spaceport. "The Orbit's ready," Whitey said, winking.

"Let's go," Jack said.

* * *

They changed in a utility closet, even putting a "company" skirt on their tool cart. Misty wore an outsize wig and head piece, taking Whitey's "midget" insult to that next level. They'd parked the "company" flitter near the service entrance.

Whitey led the way, the service elevator stopping at the first floor underground. "Work order to clean the ducts," he told the security guard. When the guard balked, Whitey pushed him. "We got four floors to do today, pal, and I ain't ready for a coffee break yet."

"Why the midget?"

"You ever try to crawl into a vent? Ain't easy. What's the hold up? That's your own blazin' work order."

The guard waved them through, and they wheeled the cart to their first stop. Jack helped Misty up into the vent, where she installed the canister, then they spent the next hour acting as though they were cleaning the duct.

"They've even got motion detectors farther along in the duct," Misty whispered, one of the modifications that Carmody had told them about.

Methodically, they worked their way down to the fourth level below ground, the security getting thicker at each level. By the fourth level, word had spread among the staff, and the sight of this crew in gray-striped formals with a cart and a midget was by then somewhat familiar.

On the fourth level, as Misty was installing the canister in the vent, Leticia Ballsy herself stepped off the elevator. "What are they doing here? I didn't approve any maintenance!"

Floor security babbled something inane.

Jack began to sweat, Leticia's gaze on his face. They'd done what they could to obscure Jack's features behind a scruffy beard, his visage a frequent feature of intergaming communiqués for the last few weeks. Any winner working the strip was profiled for the major gaming houses.

"Let me see that work order!" She didn't take her eyes off Jack.

He swallowed nervously, and he felt her scrutiny in the prickling up and down his spine.

She was as beautiful as she was deadly. She shoved the work order back at the security guard. "Get me Marcuse," she said.

Marcuse Narvone was the smart man whose position Carmody had coveted, a meticulous man with a face of stone. Carmody had warned them he was a prick, as likely to shoot someone as he was to smile.

Jack knew their flimsy work hadn't truly been approved but only filed in the right places by Carmody. It would never pass Narvone's inspection. Jack concentrated on the cube in his pocket, and the swirling thoughts of Leticia Ballsy surged into his mind. You've got better things to do, Jack thought, imagining the golf course atop the casino itself.

"Never mind, I've got better things to do," she told the guard. "Keep your eyes on them at all times until they're done!" And she was gone.

He and Whitey exchanged a glance, and Misty poked her head from the vent. "Bitch needs a good schtupping," she muttered.

Whitey's mouth formed the word, "midget."

"Let's wrap it up, guys," Jack said. "You done with that sweep up there?" he asked Misty.

They packed up and prepared to go.

"Hey, these dates don't match," the guard said, her brows drawing together.

Exactly the kind of thing that might give them away. "Let me see," Jack said. He hadn't really looked closely at the flims. He didn't look closely now. "Well, one's the day someone called for a quote, and the other when they placed the order."

The guard's thoughts were filled with images of Leticia's voluptuous figure.

Jack pushed her thoughts that direction. You can't wait until your shift ends, Jack told her, feeding her an image of Leticia unclothed.

The guard's nipples grew turgid even under the thick uniform. "Oh, yeah, I see." She ran her finger around the inside of her collar. "I can't wait to get off, today. You about ready to wrap up?"

"Yeah, we're done. Come on, you two, step it up." He gestured supervisorly in their direction, then looked at the guard, "Ain't she something?" He gestured at the ceiling.

The woman nodded, "She got it all!" They shared a laugh, and Jack gestured his crew toward the service elevator. Beside it, the armored elevator door opened, and he stepped that direction.

"No, no, no," the guard said, "don't want to take that one." She herded them into the service elevator and pushed "ground." "See you next time." The doors closed across her face.

All three of them heaved huge sighs.

* * *

The waiting was the worst.

Between four and ten—sixteen hundred and twenty two hundred, in the shipboard parlance of spacers—all they had to do was wait. No one felt much like talking, and none of them was hungry. All Jack could manage was a cup of stim, which just frayed his already-frazzled nerves.

The below-ground offices began to empty, the swing shift coming on only enough to staff the four monitoring stations, one on each floor.

The clock ticked off time with mindless precision, and defiantly refused to go any faster, despite their pleas.

"Five years," Jack muttered, looking out their solitary window at the brightly-lit sports fields below them, the dining-area floor a clear sheet of glasma.

"Eh? What?" Whitey said, blinking haughtily his direction.

"Five years since this place destroyed my marriage and my life," Jack said, the lights below making his face look ghostly.

Whitey in his pallor didn't need any such lights to look ghostly. "Ballsy will burn in hell," he said. "I'll be glad when they've finally gone down. It'll be a relief to be outa this business. You know, Jack, I do believe that this corrosive lifestyle might have eventually corrupted me."

"Might have," Jack said.

* * *

When ten o'clock arrived, it seemed they were completely unprepared.

They weren't, but it just seemed that way.

They returned to the service elevator, and instead of exiting on the ground floor, they climbed through the ceiling and boarded the armored elevator through the top.

By now, everyone at all four monitoring stations was unconscious. Donning gas masks, they overrode the elevator controls, retrieved their cart, and stopped at each station in turn to shut down all the security system on level six, in and around the vault.

They had to shove aside a few bodies laying across the control consoles, but otherwise it was quick work. Each monitoring station controlled separate and duplicative security systems on level six, so each had to be visited in turn.

After shutting down the last of those systems on level four, Jack punched up a system scan, which alarmingly alerted them that all systems had been disabled. Jack then ghosted all four levels to insure not a single staff person was still conscious.

Jack, Whitey, and Misty stepped off the armored elevator on level six and wheeled their cart into the vault without a hitch.

Satchels of cash in a pile reaching Jack's shoulder sat in the middle of the floor, receipts stapled to each satchel, awaiting tomorrow's accounting of today's take. Tucked into wall cubbies were previous day's takes, awaiting the weekly shipment to Dorado Quintus. Each satchel had a prominent Ballsy emblem on it.

Thirty million galacti, easy. They didn't gloat too much, not yet.

Swiftly, they loaded the cart, first with the satchels in the middle, then with those in the cubbies.

The cart loaded, they pushed it toward the elevator, so heavy they all three had to push. The elevator had no complaints about the weight, Jack guessing it was antigrav augmented. The inside was dead silent, insulated by two-inch thick steel plate. None of them spoke, nor even looked at each other.

They took the cart out the service entrance, their "company" flitter nearby. They'd rigged a winch inside the van and pulled the cart directly in, the winch whining under the strain.

About to close the van doors, Jack got a sudden thought. "Hey, Whitey," he said, "pose with this for me, would you?" He put a satchel with the Ballsy emblem into Whitey's arms and backed away to snap a still.

Whitey grinned at the camera, the open flitter hold behind him, several dozen Ballsy satchels visible.

Snapping the still, Jack reached into Whitey's mind with the cube and suspended Whitey's volition.

Whitey froze in place with catatonic rigor, the satchel still in his hands.

Misty hopped into the driver's seat and Jack climbed in beside her. The flitter complained but lifted reluctantly, carrying them past the silent turrets at the Ballsy Palace perimeter.

Behind them, a frozen Whitey stood vigil with a satchel of cash.

Twenty-five minutes out into the desert, and just five minutes from the spaceport, Jack watched through Whitey's eyes as lights blazed and alarms went off, the entire grounds flooded with a brilliance brighter than day, "Intruder alert, intruder alert," repeated inanely by robotic voices loud enough to deafen. Armed crews spread out to the perimeter, one squad quickly finding Whitey near the service ramp. A cadre surrounded him, their weapons raised.

"Drop the satchel," the commander said.

Jack released Whitey.

The thin, paste-white huckster in gray, pinstripe formalls dropped the satchel, shoved his hand into the air and defecated all over himself. "It was them," he screeched, "I had nothing to do with it!"

Jack withdrew and smiled at Misty. "How about the drop?" Whitey's damning information would release any moment.

Misty checked her palm com. "Data dump set for five, four, three, two, one—data transferring." She looked over at him. "Did Whitey really crap all over himself?"

Jack grinned and nodded, the lights of the spaceport ahead. "I almost pity the guy," he said. "But not for long."

"Data transfer complete," Misty said, pulling the flitter up to the checkpoint at the tarmac gate.

Jack briefly ghosted the security guard. All good, he thought.

"All good," the guard said, a dazed look on her face as she waved them through.

Jack remotely opened the Salvager's cargo hold, and Misty drove the flitter directly into it. He commed for permission to lift off even before he got to the pilot's seat, while Misty secured the cargo. That much mass loose in the hold might easily cause the Scavenger to wreck.

Misty climbed into the copilot's seat, and Jack engaged the engines. The Salvager leaped for the skies, he and Misty giggling inanely.

But the time they reached escape velocity, Jack and Misty were laughing so hard they couldn't see anymore.

Thank the stars for autopilot! he thought.

Chapter 10

"Where did you...?"

Jack shook his head at Daria. He'd just put down five hundred thousand galacti for the Circi Crown Jewels. "You don't want to know."

"That man I saw on the news yesterday!" The realization spread visibly across her face, her grin at Jack broadening. "Arrested for grand larceny—sixty-five million gone from the Ballsy Palace vault, and only one satchel of fifty thousand recovered. You didn't have anything to do with that, did you, Jack?"

"Not a thing."

"I thought I recognized him," Daria said, as though Jack had answered otherwise. "He came to our door, didn't he?"

He was glad the three of them were alone, Misty in front of a mirror trying on a tiara. "And here's something else for you." He handed her a flim.

"Certificate of Deposit," she read. "Metropli Bank, Dorado Quintus, the contents of one cubic yard, belonging to Daria Osborn of..." She looked up at Jack. "What's in the container?"

"Everything that you lost five years ago." Jack watched the blood drain out of her face.

Then tears welled up in her eyes. She shook her head and wiped them away. "I can't, Jack, you know that."

"Not right now," Misty said, rejoining them at Daria's desk. "And you shouldn't, not for five years, at least. But it's money that Ballsy stole from you by exploiting Jack. It belongs to you. It's yours."

How can you tell a princess no? Jack wondered.

"How can I say no to a princess?" Daria said, sniffling. She looked at Jack and smiled. "Thank you. You're as wonderful as I always thought you were." Daria embraced him.

"You're welcome," Jack said, an awful rent in his heart finally healing.

* * *

The first punch came out of nowhere and put out his lights almost instantly. He felt the Ballsy goons dragging him somewhere as the last shreds of consciousness left him. I hope Misty's safe, he thought as he plunged into darkness.

He and Misty had left Tertius Diamond in the Kappa Crucis constellation and had stopped at a diner in the middle of nowhere, one of those places that had sprung up from the ether simply because two heavily-traveled space lanes happened to intersect nearby.

The Erehwon Diner hung suspended from nothing like a holiday ornament that had lost its tree. Spines of glittering light shot out like flaming lances from the diner core, an asteroid that had been towed to the spot. Along these spines were docking bays, most of them occupied with ships in a myriad of sizes and varieties. The long-haul shippers, those tractor-trailer units too large to dock anywhere, stood in ranks a few points away, a diner shuttle ferrying their crew in for a meal and then out when they were done.

Jack had berthed the Scavenger near the end of one such spine, and he and Misty had walked the long glasma tube to the diner itself, occasionally dodging retro-clad waiters and waitresses taking dock-side meals directly to ships.

"Why didn't we order dock-side?" Misty asked.

"You ever been to a place like this? It's half the entertainment."

"When are we going to start using our new identities?" she'd asked.

Jack had purchased two pseudodents, one for her and one for him, but he hadn't quite figured out what to do about the Salvager. He'd had the ship for three years and really liked it. It was home, and he was reluctant to part with it. If he could somehow figure out how to transfer its ownership to his new pseudodent, he wouldn't have hesitated.

The diner itself was gravitationless, effectively, the asteroid's mass so small it exerted no pull at all. The dining tables were suspended in three dimensions along geodesic girders, the wait staff navigating the maze with a combination of guide rail, grav nodes, and retro blasts.

They cycled through an airlock to the maître d's desk, the restaurant chaos inundating them with noise. Jack signaled for a table for two, not even trying to outshout the cacophony.

The kitchen glowed with flickering flame, rivaling a steel foundry, and seated at the counter facing the kitchen were the usual suspects: bloated long-haul freighter pilots in grease-stained formalls, bleary-eyed and poorly-groomed, their portly forms perched precariously on stools so small they threatened to slip between the abundant buns they were intended to support. Had the gravity been any greater, they would have.

One bulky pilot, more brawn than fat, threw an eye toward the door.

Jack dismissed it as random. He considered ghosting the place, but decided that he'd probably find the cacophony of thought to be comparable to the auditory one.

The host seated them, helping them navigate the weightlessness. Nearby was a sign indicating the restrooms.

The vids placed ubiquitously throughout the restaurant caught his attention. "Breaking news from the Vega Strip in the multimillion-galacti heist of the Ballsy Palace vault," The bobbing head of a reporter said, "The Gaming Commission has received a virtual jackpot of information spanning twenty-five years of Ballsy Gaming operations, information so shocking that the commission has issued a preemptive order to halt all gaming at all Ballsy resorts throughout the Strip until its investigation is complete."

The mic was shoved into the face of a smartly-dressed woman, the caption identifying her as President of the Vega Strip Gaming Commission. "The tactics depicted in this documentation are so egregious as to warrant immediate action. That's all I can say right now."

The reporter returned. "Oddly, the information was gathered by the same individual who is charged in this break-in at the Ballsy Palace vault, Peter Whitey Van Schluss. When asked about criminal charges against Ballsy, the commission stated that the entire cache had been turned over to law enforcement."

Jack grinned at Misty as the vid broke for a commercial. Jack motioned that he was headed to the restroom, and Misty indicated the same for herself to the ladies' room.

He had just finished emptying his bladder into the suction urinal when he turned into the fist that turned off his lights.

* * *

Somewhere, pain pricked his consciousness, and Jack swam upward from the depths of oblivion.

Into hell.

Although not a stranger to pain, Jack hadn't known anything close to *this* level of pain. The left side of his face throbbed with the unending bass-drum beating of his heart. The wet stuff on his upper lip was sure to be blood.

He turned his head toward a light, and his nose flopped that way like a beached fish, a spike driving itself into his brain through his nostrils. He was convinced the facial reconstructions wouldn't do much to improve his appearance.

An attempt to speak caused a fresh gout of blood to burst from his nostrils.

"Where is it, Carson?" A low, menacing voice said from beyond the circle of light. A fist the size of a freight train leaped to his face and sent his head rocking back. "Where's the money?"

Focus! Jack told himself. I have to focus.

Focusing sharpened the pain and the pain consumed his thoughts and his brain wouldn't work. A tiny part of his mind pitched in some sarcastic remark about never having your brain when you needed it most.

But he knew they didn't want him to think. They just wanted their money. The Gaming Commission's shutting down Ballsy's gambling activities hadn't, apparently, extended to their enforcement or intimidation operations. Jack suspected that Whitey's info dump would slow down Ballsy, but not cause it to implode completely.

"What'd you do with it?"

The blow came from the other side and sent his head the opposite direction. Focus! he told himself, despite his overwhelming desire for the oblivion of unconsciousness.

His assailant was male and right-handed. Jack recalled the long-haul freighter pilot who'd glanced over from the restaurant counter as he and Misty had entered through the airlock, the one who was more brawn than fat. Jack tried to match that with the vague glimpse he'd gotten just as he was turning from the urinal and the fist collided with his face.

There must be others, Jack thought, unsure if the person pummeling him now was the same as the one who'd assaulted him in the restroom or the more brawn-than-fat long-haul freighter pilot at the counter.

It didn't matter.

What mattered was they'd captured him and now tortured him in an effort to recoup some of their losses.

How many are there? he wondered, another question and another blow distracting him momentarily. The sharp spikes in pain made it difficult to think, but he was becoming accustomed to the dull throbbing that he suspected he'd have as constant companion for at least the near future.

Where am I? he wondered. Another question and another blow spun his head the other direction.

The room came back into focus, and Jack guessed he'd lost consciousness momentarily. What was I doing? he wondered.

"No more blows to the head," said a distant, disembodied voice. "We want to know what's in it. Here, use these on his hands."

His hands, limp at the ends of arms tied in three places to a chair that felt bolted to a deck that vibrated with the deep thrumming of a starship engine.

"Where's the money?" A hand grasped one of his fingers, a pinky, and placed it in the jaws of some tool—pliers?—and squeezed.

A shock went up his arm, and his brain reported dispassionately that the knuckle on his left pinky had been reduced to a mangle of flesh and bone. The pain reached him a moment later, and he screamed.

"He has a voice," the disembodied voice said. "Let's see if he can talk." The face shoved itself into the light. "Jack, my name is Bill. I am your Dante—your guide through purgatory. Are you familiar with the ancient work? If not, I'll acquaint you, one torture after another. You know what we want—our money. What you get is your freedom. And what good is freedom, Jack, if you have to spend the rest of your life recovering from your injuries? Don't make us hurt you further, Jack! Just tell us where it's at. Where's the money, Jack?"

He stared at Bill through two eyes that refused to line up, one of them nearly swollen shut. The two images, one of them somewhat fuzzy, went different directions, and Jack dived into the gulf that opened between them.

Water full in the face brought him back to consciousness. The evaporation cooled him and relieved some suffering, although it stung his lacerations too.

"Where's the money, Jack?"

A hand grasped his right pinky carefully, as though performing some delicate operation that Jack was too disoriented to follow. He managed to focus his good eye on his pinky just as the fingernail disappeared, leaving behind bright pink flesh that turned quickly red. Like a thunderclap that followed a lightning strike, the pain ripped into Jack's brain a moment later, the pinky on fire.

"How many fingers would you like to lose, Jack? How many toes?" The face poked into the light again. "How about your manhood, Jack?"

The laughter was wicked and cut into Jack's soul like a shiv into his bowels. "It's so simple, Jack. Tell us where the money is, and we let you go. No harm, no foul."

It was tempting, simply because the pain was excruciating, but Jack knew they'd never let him go. He was dead meat, and the only thing that kept them from killing him was his knowledge. He wondered how he could have ever been so stupid. He should have begun using the alternate identity immediately after the robbery. Of course, Ballsy Gaming would send its agents after him, if not its entire private armada. What was he thinking?

Jack prayed that Misty was safe. He suspected she was, since his captors hadn't mentioned her. If they had captured her, they would have tortured her in front of him to extract the information they wanted.

"How could you have been so stupid, Jack? You should have used that alternate identity immediately."

So they'd captured the Scavenger as well, had searched it thoroughly, and had found the documentation.

What about the cube? Jack wondered. Why didn't I think of it a long time ago?

The bucket of water to his face must have cleared his thoughts.

He tried to channel his interlocutor's thoughts but all he was aware of was his own. And pain, of course. He didn't have the cube, apparently. He couldn't feel it in any of his pockets, and he could assume they'd searched him thoroughly.

A chill coursed through him, and all hope abandoned him.

If these unscrupulous criminals knew what the cube could do, he thought, they wouldn't hesitate to use it to take over the Empire.

Then he remembered what Misty had told him immediately after he'd found it: "I used to be its." The cube had chosen Jack.

To be the Emperor, besides.

A thought so ludicrous at the time that he'd dismissed it outright. A thought that grew more improbable yet as the interrogation proceeded. A thought so beyond the realm of possibility that Jack, in excruciating pain, deep in debt, pursued by the bank's repo agent, being chased for the alimony he owned his first wife, and now in the clutches of a criminal organization intent on extracting information before killing him, a thought so far beyond reason that Jack began to laugh.

Because it also meant they couldn't use the cube either.

The vibration from his laughter exacerbated his pain.

And incensed his captors.

"You dare laugh! I'll give you something to laugh about!" And Bill whipped out a blasma pistol and blew off Jack's foot.

And the chair leg and a foot-size piece of floor.

"Fool!" And someone knocked the blasma pistol from Bill's hand.

Jack stared at the place his foot had been, in his head an inane thought that he should be falling forward. The Criperor, they'll call me, he thought giddily. The Limperor! Then every nerve that had occupied the now-missing foot sent its pain into his brain. Fire now engulfing his stump, he wondered why it didn't emit a fireball.

He remembered with some long-forgotten part of his mind that the chair was bolted to the floor. The stench of fried flesh filled his nostrils. As the smoke cleared, he realized that a woman stood before him. He'd seen her face and knew he should recognize her, but the pain had pushed him past knowing and past caring.

He prayed to all the gods ever created to kill him now and relieved his torment.

"We're doing this all wrong," the woman said, her posture one of command, her focused gaze one of privilege. She shoved a palmcom into his face. "Tell us where the money is, or we kill your ex-wife." On the screen was Daria Osborn.

"Jack!" Daria writhed as though in pain.

He knew what she'd say if he were to ask: "Don't let the bastards win! Don't give in to them for my sake, Jack!" And he could see it in her eyes as well, but he also knew they'd do to her exactly what they were doing to him.

"Tell us!" Leticia Ballsy said, grabbing pliers from the table. She ripped off his little toe, the small one from his remaining foot, a fleabite to an elephant stomp.

"Tell us!" And she twisted the ring finger of his right hand into a neat little knot. He didn't know a finger could bend like that.

With each digit, Daria on the palmcom screamed as well, and he saw they were doing the same to her as to him. All he could think was, "I have to stop them."

It was also occurred to him with clinical precision that they wouldn't stop not matter what he told them, that his and Daria's mutilated bodies with their tortured faces would end up gracing the headlines of all the broadcast tabloids, their lurid deaths fodder for the masses and a memorable lesson to every shyster contemplating a caper similar to the one Jack had pulled on Ballsy Gaming.

Ballsy had no choice, and neither did the industry. They had to lay down in full graphic color what the consequences were for trying to bilk a casino—any casino.

So even if Leticia Ballsy were to release him now, the other gaming houses would finish the task out of principle, from the very moral fiber of their convictions.

"All right," he gasped, "I'll tell you." He could barely get a breath, his lungs seeming compressed by sheer pain.

"Jack, no!" Daria said, and a cry of pain was cut off when Leticia ended the com.

"Tell them to stop!" Jack spat. "I said I'd tell you!"

"So get on with it, Carson." Leticia hung a finger over her palmcom. "Only you can stop her torture."

"I have to use the bathroom." He'd noticed awhile ago that he'd already lost control of his bladder. Now his gut was cramping and a bowel movement was trying to force its way forth.

"You can sit in your own feces, Carson. You aren't going anywhere, so if you have to go, then you can go right where you're at." Then Leticia smiled. "And your ex-wife's torture continues until you tell me where the money's at."

Jack couldn't hold it any longer, and he began to weep as he voided all over himself. Warm chunky liquids spread around his behind and down his legs. The aroma of feces joined that of burning flesh. Shame and helplessness flooded through him as he sobbed at the indignity. "Not telling you now," he choked out between sobs, rage pouring down his face, his breath coming in huge gulping gasps.

Then put his head down and let his weeping take control.

Amidst his weeping, he felt a hand on his arm. And then someone put the cube in his hand.

"Here you go, Jack," said a voice, as ethereal as rain.

It sounded like Misty, and he wanted to yell at her to flee, but then he noticed that the only sound was his weeping. Through his tear-streaked vision, he saw Leticia, her expression fierce, ferocious, and frozen. Even the thrumming of engines through the floor had been silenced.

His hands and arms, he saw, had been freed. How did that happen? he wondered.

His legs, too. Both of them.

And they were intact.

So were his fingers. The chair leg was still a molten strip where it hung over a foot-wide hole in the floor, but his leg that had been vaporized by the blasma blast was intact again.

Glowing softly in his hand, the cube stared at him.

He was still covered in feces and urine, but his body was intact—completely intact.

Rising unsteadily, he pushed away the bright lamp they'd shoved into his face. The shadows emerged. Three others besides Bill and Leticia had been watching from the perimeter, and along one wall was a workbench with an arsenal of implements ready for use.

No one stopped him as he took a tentative step forward.

They all stood still as stone, unmoving.

He glanced over at the table of implements they'd been ready to use on him. He glanced among his erstwhile captors. The ghost of pain was still unimaginable, but the shame and humiliation sat on his chest like an alien parasite eating into him.

Jack very badly wanted to subject them to the same indignities.

And to what end? he asked himself.

Jack stepped around the statue Leticia and found his way into the corridor. In a daze, barely recognized what he was doing, he found a cleansall and a clean pair of formalls. The person who looked back at him in the mirror was a ghost of Jack Carson, haunted by the harrowing experience.

He made his way to the bridge, where a crew stood frozen at their posts. In one vid, his ship trailed the Ballsy vessel, the Scavenger attached with a tractor beam.

Jack deactivated the tractor beam, left the bridge, and maneuvered toward an escape pod. He flew it toward the Salvager. With his palmcom, he opened the Scavenger's hold and maneuvered the escape pod inside. He didn't wonder how he'd found his palmcom. He was so far beyond wonder that he couldn't question anymore what came his way.

Setting the cube on the console, Jack brought the Salvager to life and set a course for Tertius Diamond, thinking he needed to make sure Daria was safe.

During the day-long journey there, he stared sightlessly at the ship around him and the cube beside him, all of it so surreal that he couldn't take it in.

As though his sensory processing circuits had been blown.

All that remained was shame, humiliation, and pain.

He knew he needed to attend to these but he held them at bay somehow.

At one point en route, he slept the dreamless sleep of the dead, a deep restful sleep, refreshing and invigorating. He knew he'd have nightmares, but somehow they too were held at bay.

On Tertius Diamond, Jack took a flitter taxi from the spaceport, which stopped down the lane from Daria's home, the home he'd once shared with her. The place was surrounded by Crown Dicks, and the street was blockaded. A hover buzzed overhead, bristling with weapons.

"Who are you?" the officer at the checkpoint asked him.

"Her ex-husband," he said. "Jack Carson."

She looked at her palmcom. "You're not authorized, sorry."

He looked toward the house, about to ask the officer to check with Daria on that, when Misty emerged.

Jack brightened immediately. He'd somehow known she was safe but to see her brought him profound relief. He remembered the voice, ethereal as rain, telling him, "Here you go," and her putting the cube in his palm.

Misty stepped through the checkpoint into his arms.

"I'm so glad you're safe," he whispered, wonder and awe, bewilderment and bemusement, pain and relief all floating through him in chaotic catharsis. "How's Daria?"

"She's safe." Misty pulled away and looked up at him, a wisdom beyond her years in her eyes. "How are you?"

He nodded and looked along his arms to his fingers, down his legs to his toes. "I'm intact, thanks to you." He grinned at her.

She grinned back. "Sorry I couldn't get there sooner."

"I'm glad you got there. That's what's important. But how'd you do it? How did you find me, and then get here from there?"

She shrugged, the classic lines of her face heavy with gravity. "I'm still not sure, Jack. But I had to it, because you wanted me to."

He stared at her, not understanding, and knowing at some level that he probably wouldn't ever understand. There had been a lot of things he'd wanted as his captors had inflicted more painful and degrading tortures. He'd wanted, under duress, to do far worse to them in retaliation, to subject them to inhumane indignities beyond imagining. But we all want our deepest darkest desires fulfilled when we're under duress, he thought.

"Because you needed me to," Misty said.

Jack nodded, accepting that. "Thank you." He held her in his gaze, letting gratitude shine through his face. Her face became blurry with his tears. He wiped them away and looked across the barriers toward Daria's home. "I should go see her, but I'm not authorized."

"You made sure she was safe," Misty said, "and now she's in protective custody. Did you see the news this morning?"

Jack shook his head. "I can barely function, can't believe I'm alive, and intact, and free." He glanced again at his foot, then at his fingers.

The right ring finger had been tied into a knot, he remembered. And now, there it sat at the end of his right hand, functioning perfectly, as straight as it'd always been.

He wiggled it, giggling.

"They captured Leticia Ballsy, arrested her for a slew of offenses. Somehow, vids of her torturing someone were leaked to the police. They're still trying to find that person."

He blinked at her, and then looked at the officer not ten feet away at the checkpoint. "Shouldn't I turn myself in?"

Misty shrugged. "They also have a vid of Daria being tortured, and she'll testify at the trial. There's no shortage of evidence. Leticia and her crew have all been denied bail."

"What about Ballsy Gaming?"

"Confiscated as evidence. They'll never do business again."

Jack sighed and looked again toward Daria's home, on whose very doorstep Whitey had given the performance of his life, convincing Jack to risk all his and Daria's assets on a bet he was sure to lose. "I guess I really don't need to see her. But won't they find me eventually?" He looked again at the officer not ten feet away.

"They can't find any information on Jack Carson. It's as if he never existed."

Jack looked at Misty.

She looked at him innocently, once again a nine-year-old orphan sans awareness of galactic matters.

He didn't know how she'd done it, and he didn't care.

Because it meant he was free.

Chapter 11

Monique "The Bruiser" Brewster watched from Sedition Control Forty as the hapless junker loaded a set of pristine-looking crates aboard the Salvager. Much too pristine for a junker of his caliber. She was guessing it wasn't junk.

A Sedition Control Investigator with more than five thousand subjects under surveillance, the Bruiser had been alerted to the junker's activities when he'd slipped past a Galactic Patrol on Canis Dogma Five. The entire episode on the Vega Strip, and especially his bizarre escape from his Ballsy Palace captors, had convinced her he was the slimiest trickster she'd ever encountered.

The vids of his departure from Canis Dogma Five would have been hilarious had she had any disposition toward mirth. Two slack-jawed, drool-slathered patrol officers had watched insensate as the Scavenger belonging to Jack Carson had roared right past them, their alarms and buzzers going off unheeded. The officers had been suspended and were undergoing neuralizing, neither one remembering the incident, both swearing they hadn't taken their eyes off their monitors for a moment.

Maybe they should be tested for intelligence, Monique thought, or have some sense beaten into them. "What's going on at the Birds?!" she roared.

A tech jumped visibly in his chair. "The Southern Birds team has apprehended the proprietor, Cherise Mariposa, but they're still searching for the girl."

"Find her! We've got to tack this slippery junker to the tarmac, before he turns his persuasive energies on us."

Monique had had the Carson Junker under direct surveillance since his first visit to Alpha Tuscana. Who was the girl? Monique wondered for the thousandth time. She'd rechecked Jack's profile, but he'd never had a child by any of his three wives, nor had he shown the slightest skill in nor inclination toward rearing a child. The man can barely care for himself, she thought, let alone a child. Never had a home, she knew, the brothel the closest he'd ever come to actually living someplace permanent. Four bankruptcies, a ship about to be repossessed due to default, an empty bank account, petty charges pending on half-a-dozen worlds, and a cargo hold filled with girls' clothes sitting between him and starvation.

And why did the Torgassan Empire even consider this worthless Junker worth surveillance? It might have been a question for social critics, and it might someday be a question for historians, but it wasn't a question for Monique "The Bruiser" Brewster.

It was what she did.

After any act of sedition toward the Torgassan Empire—be it rolled eyes during an Imperial event or an obscene gesture toward the Imperial banner—her job was to pursue and detain the seditionist. And if the suspect somehow got hurt in her custody, well, that was just too bad. The same was true for any of her staff who flubbed the job.

"Birds team, report!" Monique was getting nervous.

On the tarmac, the fuel truck was pulling away. Unwilling to risk the bird flying away, she'd ordered the fuel replaced with water. Even if Jack Carson tried to lift off, the Salvager would take him nowhere.

"We can't find the girl anywhere," said Montgomery, the site lead.

"What do you mean, you can't find her? We had the house cordoned tighter than a black hole! Who's second in command? Is that Wallace? Put him on!"

A pink, scrubbed face popped up on the monitor. "Wallace here."

"You're in command. Get a camera on Mariposa and put a lazgun to her head. Make sure the lazgun's visible."

"Yes, Ma'am. Uh, what about Montgomery?"

"Fire that bitch!"

The former commander of the Birds team got on the horn. "You can't do that!"

"You're fired, Bitch!" And Brewster silenced Montgomery's com.

Monique couldn't actually fire anyone under her command, but everyone knew Montgomery would soon be out on medical leave. The Bruiser ground her fist into her palm in anticipation.

"All right, people! In we go!"

* * *

Jack palmed the gene-lock on the Salvager door, finished loading the last of Misty's wardrobe, which she'd enhanced significantly now that they were filthy rich. He'd left Misty and Cherise at the Southern Birds, hoping to be back quickly. Just a quick trip to see about a retinue for Misty, he thought, whistling tunelessly.

He'd given himself a week to recover from his escapade with Ballsy gaming, and he still felt a shock to his system whenever he thought of gambling, cards, dice, and ice-cream suits.

He'd had a week of the paradise in Cherise's company, Misty learning at her elbow as Cherise continued to train her understudy. Not exactly the kind of education he'd been hoping Misty would get. He wanted to turn the brothel into an orphanage, but he wasn't sure how to tell Cherise. With the money he'd filched from the Ballsy vault— the bulk of it going to Daria—Jack felt that he and Misty might have enough to finance an entourage fit for a princess.

"I can't arrive by myself!" she'd pouted two nights ago. "I have to have a full entourage of personnel, Jack. For stars' sake, what will Emperor Torgas think?!"

He'd looked at her, feeling so flustered he wasn't able to speak. "What are we talking, here?" he finally forced past his perplexed lips.

"Just the usual personnel any princess would have, Jack. You know, land steward, house steward, housekeeper, butler, chef, lady's maid, valet, first footman, second footman, head nurse, chamber maid, parlor maid, house maid, between maid, nurse, under cook, kitchen maid, laundry maid, page, tea boy, head groom, stable master, groom, stable boy, head gardener, game keeper, grounds keepers, governess, and gate keeper."

Misty took a deep breath. "But to truly impress his highness Emperor Torgas, I'll probably also need chauffeurs, kneemen, legwomen, coiffeuses, coutures, stockinglasses, chaperones, equestrians, scullery maids, enderlasses, chimney sweeps, fishmongers, nannies, tinkers, tailors, soldiers, spies, nincompoops, dunces, jesters, and jokers. And of course there's you, Jack. You'll go with me, won't you?"

His mind shuddering at the litany, he just nodded dumbly. "But what'll you call me?"

She scowled in consternation. "Hell, I don't know! You ask such hard questions! I'll try to think of something."

And he'd arranged a trip to an old Britannia estate on Cor Caroli in the northern constellation Canes Venatici. If anyone could assemble a menagerie of servants with such intricate gradations, it was the Britannians.

The Scavenger all fueled and ready to go, Jack pulled the hatch closed behind him. He stepped into the cockpit and stared.

Misty sat in the copilot's chair.

He blinked at her, as though she might disappear between blinks.

She blinked back at him, a hint of a smile on her face.

"You could have just said you wanted to come with me."

"I wanted to come with you."

"Better late than never." He glanced toward the Salvager hatch—the gene-lock secured hatch. "How'd you get past the gene-lock?" It was only the fifth time it'd happened.

"You know," Misty said, "you should really make a decision, Jack."

"Huh? About what?"

"Whether to call your ship Salvager or Scavenger. The way you're calling it both, sometimes in the same sentence makes you seem ... schizophrenic!"

Shrugging, he snorted at her, not having realized until she pointed it out. "Why should I? It's fine with me, whatever I call it. Are you going tell me how you get in and out through that gene-lock?"

Shrugging, she snorted at him. "Why should I?"

"Mutual, darling."

"Glad we agree on something."

The vidscreen filled with a bulldog's face, and a voice boomed from the ship's intercom. "Jack Carson, you're under arrest for sedition!"

Pounding commenced on the Scavenger hatch, a distant voice shouting, "Open up in the name of the Emperor!"

Sedition? Jack wondered. Trafficking in contraband, trespassing on secured archeological sites, absconding on spousal support orders, defaulting to his creditors, breaking and entering, grand theft, larceny, fraud. His list of offenses was lengthy, but sedition wasn't among them.

The bulldog on the screen growled at him. "We've got your woman, Carson! Don't even think about squirrelling out of this one!"

The bulldog face was replaced with Cherise, a handful of hair sprouting from between her captor's fingers, a lazgun to her head. "They swarmed the house after you left, Jack! And they can't find Misty!"

Dogface replaced Cherise. "Give up, or we shoot the woman, Carson!"

"You can't do that!"

"Look at me, Carson!"

He couldn't help but do so, her face filling the screen.

"I'm Sedition Control Investigator Monique 'The Bruiser' Brewster—" her badge flashed briefly on the screen—"and I do whatever it takes to capture my suspect. You give up or she gets hurt. Which is it?"

"I give up," Jack said quickly.

* * *

Sighing, Jack let himself fall back on the bunk, exhausted.

"What are you doing?" Misty asked him. "Now's your chance to escape!"

He looked at her in disbelief. Things had gone from ludicrous to bizarre in the last eight hours. He'd been hand-cuffed, strip-searched, geno-typed, iris-scanned, retina-typed, facia-metricked, bone-imaged, E. coli-matched, and even mitochondrial gene-sampled.

And for good measure, a still shot of his anus, for all the toilet cams they'd deployed throughout the Empire. "No two assholes alike," Misty'd quipped.

Jack looked around the cell where they'd just deposited him. Blank, featureless walls broken only by the door, the cot, and the all-in-one sanistation. His journey here had been through a labyrinth of gene-coded doors, iris-coded gates, badge-checked apertures, and even a foot-thick airlock. He couldn't imagine trying to get back out the way he'd come, the route alone enough to disorient a bloodhound. And through all the myriad checks, scans, imaging, and typography, Misty had followed, everyone around them blithely ignoring her.

Jack had been made to change clothes no less than three times, the two jumpsuits each a different color, but somehow he'd held onto the cube. No one asked him for it, nor had they tried to take it.

He frowned at Misty again. She'd seen him in his full, naked, slouchy glory thrice over, at no time evincing any change in expression. On the second full disrobing, he'd said, "Can't you look someplace else and spare a guy his dignity?"

One of the three officers doing the strip search looked at the other two and then back at Jack. "Who you talkin' to?"

Jack had glanced between Misty and the officer, but hadn't replied.

"Talkin' to unseen persons, they call that," one officer said to another. "We got a certifiable cuckoo." After that, they gave him a bit more room.

Looking at Misty, Jack shook his head. "Where am I going to escape to? And why didn't they see you?"

"Cause you willed them not to—with the cube."

He brought it out of his pocket, surprised the jumpsuit had a pocket. The opaque, silvery sides of the cube stared blankly back at him. "I'm doin' a good job of getting you invited to the palace, aren't I?"

"You're making progress," she said sans irony.

"So, if I can persuade them not to see you, why couldn't I persuade them not to capture me?"

"You gave yourself up," Misty replied.

He pondered that, knowing they had Cherise someplace. "And why would I try to escape, when they'll harm Cherise if I do?"

"We'll have to escape together, all three of us."

He thought about the multiple layers of security, the compound obviously meant to contain high-value detainees. It was impossible for a single person to escape, much less three.

"You can do it," she said. "Here, put your hands on the cube like this." She wrapped thumb and forefinger along opposite edges, then placed her other thumb and forefinger similarly but offset by ninety degrees.

He took it from her and did the same, and the world slammed into his brain. Cacophonies of sound and kaleidoscopes of light inundated him.

"Concentrate," she said, her voice impossibly far away.

He focused on her, and saw a scruffy drudge staring at him from a low slouch. Oh, that's me, he realized.

"All right, well done. You're ghosting me, now."

"Ghosting?" The lips of the drudge moved in time with the word.

"Yeah, it's a ghost cube, remember? Now, concentrate on the surrounding rooms."

Somehow, he knew what to do. In the adjoining rooms beyond two-foot thick walls were guards. Also above and below, more guards, all of them stationed in empty cells identical to the one he occupied. One featureless corridor served each set of cells, and the cell block itself was set six stories below ground. Odd, I don't remember descending that far, Jack thought. It occurred to him that they'd deliberately distracted him while delivering him to his destination.

He searched the compound, looking for Cherise and for the control monitoring station. If they were smart, they'd have two monitoring stations, each monitoring the prisoner and each other.

"If they're smart, they'll have two monitoring stations, each monitoring each other as well as you."

He could have told her that.

"And you have to find Cherise."

He stopped himself from telling her the obvious.

There! Four floors up and to the west end of the compound. Cherise lay on a bunk in a cell identical to his, weeping softly.

He sent her his comfort, and she sat up suddenly, looking around. Her gaze fixed on the door, where he observed her from, and her lips formed a silent word: "Jack?"

Quickly, he withdrew and scoured the compound for monitoring stations. He found three of them, one for the perimeter and two for the prisoners. Both were filled with stern-looking Imperial guards, eyes glued to vidscreens.

He'd have to keep his attention on all three of them, remembering his near-capture when leaving Canis Dogma Five. He focused on the main monitoring station, however, chiefly because of one occupant, a woman. A large woman with the face of a bulldog and a disposition to match.

"I got here as fast as I could," Bulldog said. "What are you grousing about? You brought him in, didn't you?" Brewster was saying to a silver-haired gentleman with a few more epaulets than everyone else. "First, I'll meet with Montgomery, and then I'll interrogate the prisoner."

"Montgomery," Jack discovered, was four cells over and one level up from his.

Brewster looked at the compound commander. "Absolutely no one in or out of the cell except me, under any circumstances. Got it?" She poked a finger into his chest.

The man tried his best not to recoil as she stomped from the room. "I think I have a broken rib," he said after she'd gone, rubbing where she'd poked him.

Jack ghosted Brewster through her escort, reluctant to infiltrate the woman directly, following her progress as she descended the stairs and passed through multiple checkpoints. Her escort changed several times, and Jack changed his ghosting to match.

At one point, Brewster stopped and cornered the escort he was ghosting. "What are you starin at, Newfuss?" She clocked him, and he slithered down the wall to the floor.

Jack was kicked back to his cell, but he soon reacquired the woman as she emerged onto level five.

"Why the hell am I being kept here?" Montgomery demanded as Brewster entered the cell.

The big woman glanced at her escorts. "We'll need a moment alone, thank you."

The two escorts fled.

Brewster looked up at the ceiling. "This is a private conversation, Captain."

In the monitoring stations, screens went blank at the Captain's nod.

Jack ghosted through Montgomery's eyes.

"And now *you're* looking at me funny," Brewster said with unconcealed disgust. "What's wrong with you people here? Does everybody on Tuscana have an IQ of two?"

"What's this about, Brewster? Arrest me for interfering with your investigation if you think you have to, but don't just hold me in a cell without explanation!"

"Explanation? You want explanation? You let that girl escape, is your explanation. You failed me."

The punch landed and Montgomery's lights went out before Jack knew what had hit him.

Back in his cell, Jack heard Misty saying something to him, but he was too disoriented after being knocked unconscious twice to understand what she was telling him.

He repositioned his hands on the cube and located the escorts out-side Montgomery's cell. The sounds coming through the foot-thick door weren't pleasant.

"Now's the time, while she's distracted," Misty said.

Jack zeroed in on the two internal monitoring stations and won-dered how he could do this. I have to get them to open the cell door, he thought. What better way than to have the prisoner disappear? He took himself off their visual cortexes.

"Captain, the prisoner!" Twenty people gawked at an empty cell.

"Escape in progress!" the Captain shouted. "Get in there and found out where he went! Lockdown on floors one through five! Quintuple the security at each checkpoint."

"Uh, Sir?" said a two-chevroned woman.

"Yes, Lieutenant?"

"Detective Brewster ordered no one in or out of the cell except her."

"Fuck that bitch! I run the place. Get in there!"

"Yes, Sir. Oh, uh, and lockdown means Brewster can't move either."

"About time someone put her in restraints!"

The two guards outside Jack's cell opened the door and rushed in. Jack nimbly stepped into the corridor, Misty at his elbow. They slith-ered down the corridor toward the two guards at the checkpoint. Both guards in fighting stances had their weapons in hand. Behind them was a clear glascreet door reinforced with poly-alloy bars.

A voice came from Jack's cell. "Not a trace, and not a mark on the walls. What about the vents?"

"Too small," said a voice from the monitoring station. "And vent shows clear."

He figured they probably had visual there. Probably in the crapper too.

"What about the toilet?"

"Crapper's clear!"

How are we going to get to the next level? Jack wondered.

Somewhere, a radio squawked.

"Open this blasted cell, Captain!" It was Brewster, who'd found some communicator. "What the hell is going on, anyway?"

The Captain signaled the door to be opened. "Escaped prisoner, Brewster. You're on level five. Get down to level six, maybe you'll see something no one else has. He just disappeared off the monitors."

"And you sent the guards in to inspect visually, didn't you?" Brewster sneered, her voice dripping with venom.

Jack saw her exit the cell, glimpsing the bloody pulp she'd left behind. He ghosted her escort to the checkpoint on level five, where they did a gene-scan, retinal scan, facial metric, iris check, and badge scan.

"What are you lookin' at?" Brewster snarled at the guard Jack was ghosting.

He withdrew before she punished the guard. "Here she comes," Jack whispered to Misty.

Brewster descended the stairs. Both guards at the checkpoint looked her direction.

One of them opened the door for her, and Misty skipped between Brewster and the door.

"What was that?" Brewster looked around, her nose knotting up, sniffing audibly.

You will not see us, Jack willed.

Brewster stepped forward, pulling the door closed quickly behind her. She took one step toward Jack's erstwhile cell and froze. "What's that?" Again her head swiveled on her neck, her gaze coming to rest right on Jack's face. "I'd swear if my eyes didn't tell me otherwise that he's right in front of me. Can't you smell the fear?"

"Right where?" a guard said, staring at the blank wall behind Jack.

"Right there." And Brewster unfurled a blunt bludgeon known on anyone else's physiognomy as a finger, and jabbed it at Jack's chest.

Somehow he sidestepped, and the finger dented the wall.

It's got to be solid block! Jack thought.

Brewster looked at her bent finger. "Ow, that hurts."

Jack could have told her it was broken.

"Let's look at the cell." And Brewster was gone.

The Captain came down the stairs and demanded entry.

Jack slipped into the stairwell before the door closed.

Misty looked at him with eyes bigger than moons. "That was close," she lipped at him.

They worked their way upward, slowly, having to wait at each checkpoint until someone came through, strobes flashing and alarms pinging the whole time. On the first level below ground, where Cherise was being held, a bevy of guards stood between the checkpoint and her cell.

Misty tapped his arm, and with a variety of pantomimes, indicated she would create a distraction. She descended a level and moved to the far end, away from the stairwell.

Watching her through the cube—and keeping her off everyone's visual cortices—and doing the same for himself—took a level of concentration quite at the limit of his power. Drips of sweat ran down his back. His arms and legs felt leaden.

He had to time this just right.

"Now, Jack!" Misty shouted.

Jack revealed her to the station personnel.

"It's the girl! Where'd she come from?" Brewster shouted, her voice echoing from the multiple pickups. "Get her!"

A series of instructions went out, including the order for the first floor contingent—the closest guard besides those at the second floor checkpoint—to investigate.

Misty raised her fist to the camera. "Come and get me, Bluster Brewster!"

And Jack slipped past checkpoint one as guards tumbled out and down the stairs.

Then he took Cherise out of the picture.

"Captain, now the woman's gone!"

One of the guards rushed into her cell, and Jack followed.

Cherise looked frightened, watching the guard, who dashed back into the corridor and yelled to his companions, "Vanished! And no sign of an exit!"

"Come with me," Jack said to her, his voice low.

Cherise jumped, her fright turning to terror. "Jack?"

He took her arm. "It's all right. Come on," he whispered, and pulled her into the corridor.

"The girl's a decoy!" Brewster shouted. "He's after the woman!"

Another series of instructions were issued, and guards bunched up at checkpoint one on both sides, Brewster ordering them to cut off Jack's escape.

On level two, a guard cornered Misty, and Jack made her vanish. Now holding himself, Cherise, and Misty invisible to the visual cortices of everyone in the compound, he began to feel faint, and sparkle began to cloud his peripheral vision.

"I can't hold it," he whispered to Cherise, knowing they were doomed.

"If you can make yourself disappear, you can make yourself appear elsewhere," she whispered back, her gaze not quite focused on him.

Jack saw Brewster pounding up the stairs, her bulk like a charging bull. He knew they'd never escape if she cornered them on the first floor. There was only one thing he could do.

He projected an image of himself in his sixth floor cell, and confusion erupted.

"It's a decoy!" Brewster shouted.

"No, it's not!" the Captain replied. "All the rest of it is an illusion!"

"All personnel to checkpoint one!" Brewster ordered, rounding the stairwell to checkpoint two.

"Belay that order!" the Captain roared. "I'm in command of this compound! Shut down checkpoints two and three, and shut off that bitch's mike!"

"That's my prisoner and if you let—"

Brewster went silent.

"All right, everyone," the Captain said, "Let's slow it down. First things first. We make the assumption that our prisoner has somehow compromised our video surveillance system. Second, we inspect every cell on every floor systematically by feel, and we access everything below level one through the maintenance tunnels."

Had Jack known about them, he might have escaped through the maintenance tunnels. I can see only what other people are seeing, he reminded himself. Backing to the end of the corridor, taking Cherise with him, Jack looked up.

A maintenance hatch.

How to get up there? he wondered, seeing no ladder, just blank, featureless walls. Must be mechanical, he thought, some switch somewhere that lowers a ladder from inside the hatch.

On level two and three hatches opened and ladders lowered, the guards already scrambling down them.

Jack searched the control room, found a bank of lighted switches, the ones numbered "two" and "three" blinking. He ghosted the technician, who punched the other four switches.

The hatch above his head opened, and a ladder descended.

"Who ordered those hatches opened?" the Captain roared.

But Cherise was already climbing, Jack right behind her. The piping-ribbed tube took them to a cramped landing, beside it a larger tube extending all the way down.

And up.

Freedom, Jack thought.

A quartet of soldiers dropped into the tube, and stopped just below the ground floor threshold. "All right, we hold here unless we're ordered elsewhere."

Below, on level two, Misty had crawled out into the larger tube, Jack saw.

And the girl began to climb downward. "Jack, if you can hear me, show me now," she whispered.

But if he did, and these four guards went after her, she would never escape.

He and Cherise would, but then Misty would be their prisoner. How could he let that happen?

"You have to, Jack," Misty whispered. "Let them capture me so you and Cherise can escape!"

He remembered leaving her with Xerk and Trude on Canis Dogma Five, and then with Cherise at the Southern Birds, how guilty he'd felt, especially that first time, how all he'd wanted was to turn around and fetch her with him and never part company with her again.

How can I leave her? he wondered.

"Because I'm asking you," Misty whispered.

She hadn't asked him to leave her those first two times, had only begrudgingly accepted it as necessary. This time she was asking him to leave her. Sighing, Jack made her appear.

"Sergeant, look! Isn't that the girl?"

Below them was a squeal, and she dropped rapidly down the ladder.

"Let's go," the sergeant said, and they all dropped past him and Cherise.

Jack poked his head out. The way was clear. They climbed up and quickly slipped behind some throbbing machinery as another guard headed into the maintenance chute.

From the maintenance room, Jack and Cherise made quick time out through the service entrance. The compound itself was surrounded by wire-topped cyclone fencing which hummed and crackled.

At the gate, a mesmerized guard opened it without a hint he was doing so, and Jack and Cherise ran across the road.

"Let's get out of here," Jack said, sweat pouring off him, his breathing rapid. "They've got her cornered on the sixth floor. She's giving herself up now."

"Can't you stop them?" She led Jack into an alley.

"I can barely stand," he said, his vision clouding. "She told me to leave her behind."

"So we could escape?" Cherise looked perplexed. "That's no help."

"Listen, we'll have to come back for her. There's no help for it. I'm not strong enough to get her out of there now. Just get us to the spaceport." Jack was barely aware of what she was doing, struggling to stay conscious. He knew she left for a few minutes, but that was all.

"Ok, come on," she said, helping him to his feet.

Jack didn't know whether he'd lost consciousness. He staggered from the alley and practically fell into the back of a flitter taxi. He heard the words she spoke to the driver, but he didn't understand what she was saying.

"Oh, I'm glad it's you, Mack. Listen, we need a bucket to get off this rock, and we'd better make it look like a hijacking, or the Imperials will start arresting people for conspiracy. And we'll need to change taxis a couple of times to make sure we're not being tailed. Me 'n' my friend just escaped from the compound back there—"

The driver mumbled something as they heaved around a corner.

"Yes, that compound, and there's a frightful agent named Brewster—"

Again the driver mumbled something.

"Well, I guess that's Brewster. Sounds like it anyway, and she's got a friend of ours, a girl!"

The unintelligible driver spoke.

"I don't know if she'll do anything to Misty."

More mumbling.

"All right, good plan, Mack. Thanks for your help. What? First stop already? Come on, Jack, changing taxis."

He had the sense that he'd put only one foot to the ground in between flitters. All he really knew was that the light was too bright and the colors were all wrong.

Then it all went away.

* * *

He had the sensation of being carried, twice, and then Cherise was shaking him.

"Jack, you've got to wake up!"

He struggled out of the darkness and noticed immediately how beautiful Cherise was.

He smiled beatifically. He was aboard a ship of some sort, he saw, like a freighter, perhaps. A small shape occupied the co-pilot's seat.

"You'll never guess who's already aboard."

"Misty?" he mumbled through his own thick mist.

"I'm here, Jack," the girl said, and her arms were around him and he felt her shaking and knew she was crying and he'd have cried too if he weren't so exhausted and he let consciousness slip away because he was with the two people he cared most deeply about and he was safe and he was free.

* * *

Emperor Phaeton Torgas stared at the two people kneeling before him, trying to control his features.

Another ghosting cube has been unleashed!

The strong undercurrent, that shift in the pillars upholding the Empire, the change in alignments he'd first felt about three months ago, now beset his rule.

The gold-filigree, platinum-haloed scepter holding his own ghosting cube lay hidden beside his thigh on the throne, his hand on the armrest just above it.

He hated not having his hand on the scepter. Many were the nights the Emperor awoke in panic, the cube fading from his sight, disappearing right out of the scepter, the dream dissipating as he awoke, scepter in hand, the cube securely ensconced in its setting, having gone nowhere.

His fingers twitched with the desire to grab it and blast these two supplicants into oblivion. *They're only the messengers,* he told himself.

But they'd bungled the capture of Jack Carson and his two companions, and for that they deserved oblivion. *Perhaps they're useful yet,* he thought, but he doubted it.

Emperor Phaeton had restrained himself during the interview from delving into their minds to sort through the true sequence of events, although the surveillance vids had given him a fairly complete picture. He thought it odd that the girl, Misty, hadn't appeared in a single vid.

"How do you think he did it, Captain Lang?"

"Your August Highness," Captain Caeneus Lang said, bowing deeply, "At first, I thought he had some device that disrupted our video surveillance system. After I reviewed the vids however, I'm convinced he used some sort of neural disruptor."

"Detective Brewster?"

Monique "the Bruiser" Brewster put her forehead completely to the floor. "Your August Highness, forgive me for declining to speculate. I don't know, but I do know the threat that such abilities pose to the Empire. And that Carson must be exterminated quickly, whatever the cost."

Yes, she would know that, the Emperor thought. She's a snake poised to strike. Emperor Phaeton glanced at Captain Lang, he who'd ordered Detective Brewster confined in a stairwell and had cut off her communications.

Perfectly within his rights to do that, the Emperor knew, but also the decision that had ultimately allowed the miscreants to escape.

Now or later? he wondered.

Phaeton glanced at Brewster. No, he thought, let her hear later how horribly the Captain dies. Not only that, but let her see it. "See Captain Lang to his quarters," he said to no one.

A servant appeared and waited until the two suppliants had exchanged pleasantries and the doomed-but-didn't-know-it Captain made his obeisance, then escorted him from the throne room.

Prime Minister Custos Messium, whose name translated from the ancient tongue as "keeper of Harvests," chose that inopportune moment to appear. "Your August Highness," Messium said, bowing with such grace and elegance that it might have been mocking for its obsequiousness.

I should have rid myself of him long ago, Phaeton thought yet again.

A holdover from his father's administration, Prime Minister Messium knew the Empire from its edge at the outer Scutum-Centaurus

Arm to the Galactic Bar. He'd made himself useful with that knowledge and so had spared himself a one-way ticket to oblivion.

The perfectly-proportioned Emperor scowled.

Messium stood six-foot-four and was thin as a pole. Silks draped the lanky frame, protrusions hinting at the gaunt, ethereal body beneath. The hair was a short, unruly halo of gray, the face pinched in constant pique. "Forgive my intrusion, your August Highness, but I thought it prudent to insert myself into the weighty matter that now confronts my liege, His August Highness, whom I'm sworn to protect."

"Really?" Phaeton asked bluntly, "They why didn't you capture Carson yourself?"

"His August Highness amuses himself by taunting a humble man. Like him, the humble man has only recently become aware of certain forces at work. And may I introduce myself to the supplicant, your August Highness?"

Viper meet Cobra, Phaeton thought idly, a single finger waving assent.

While the two greeted each other, he mused that neither species was an appropriate comparison for the Bruiser. No, a far more appropriate reptilian analogy would be Python. Yes, much better. Python.

"Eh? What?" He realized he'd missed something.

"Pardon, your August Highness, but I asked whether Detective Brewster was being considered for the task of capturing this rogue trash monger?"

Stupid to let your attention lapse, the Emperor admonished himself, especially in front of these two. "You have an opinion about that?" His tone was clear he'd asked for none.

"Pardon, your Highness, I meant no offense, only to acknowledge the reasonableness of such a course. The Detective's background is recommendation enough, and her knowledge of the suspect a bonus."

But you have something else you wish to point out, don't you? Phaeton thought.

"But I wish to point out, if I may, your Highness, that Detective Brewster has not been cleared."

Emperor Phaeton suspected she wouldn't pass clearance. "Superfluous, Lord Minister. Her background is enough recommendation, as you pointed out."

"There are procedures in the clearance process that are disregarded only at great risk to yourself, your August Highness."

"Risk that I'm perfectly capable of evaluating myself, Minister."

Messium dropped to a knee instantly, and even Brewster put her face to the floor.

Phaeton's jaw rippled, and he opened his hands from the fists he'd made. He pulled himself back from the brink of blasting the upstart into the next universe. "Now that you've inserted yourself where you weren't welcome, you may remain there. Detective Brewster, Prime Minister Custos Messium will be your Liaison. All requests for resources will go through him, and all will be granted, won't they, Prime Minister?"

"Indeed, your August Highness."

"Be gone, before I beridst myself of you."

"Indeed, your August Highness." Messium bowed and backed from the throne room, his gaze upon the floor.

"Disgraceful behavior," he muttered to himself. "I'd apologize to you, Detective, except that I don't apologize." He'd have called her "Lady," too, if her visage had contained the least vestige of feminism. "You'll report daily or more often as events require. Please see Admiral Camelus for a vehicle. He has a prototype fighter he's eager to field test."

"Yes, your August Highness," Brewster said, looking around as if sensing she'd been dismissed.

Then he looked at her directly.

"Yes, your August Highness?" Brewster asked, looking suddenly nervous.

I'd imagine if I'd just witnessed an Emperor admonishing his Prime Minister, I'd be nervous, he thought. He dropped his hand to the scepter.

Something fuscous, something furtive, something insidious, something feral. Her mind surrounded him like a carnival attraction—a funhouse filled with distortion mirrors. The world was warped and twisted. Innuendo and intrigue lurked behind every façade. Every person recited encyclopedic detail of his or her life. People poured out their hearts to her, their secret and most base desires, those yearnings found utterly abhorrent by society, the predilections to torture and dismember, the pure joy in seeing others suffer. These were the untold and unexpressed—and often unacknowledged—desires writ eternal upon people's souls, open for her vicarious viewing.

Phaeton snapped back into his body. "The faster you capture this miscreant, Detective, the greater your reward."

"Yes, your August Highness, and thank you." Detective Brewster bowed and backed from the room, her gaze on the floor.

The Emperor stared at the spot where she'd been sitting.

Depraved, was all he could think.

I'll have to rid myself of her the moment she captures this scavenger.

* * *

"But how did you escape?" Jack realized he'd asked the same questions now for the third time.

Misty shrugged. "They acted like they didn't see me."

"What I don't understand," Cherise said, "is how you found the ship. How could you have known I'd secured this freight tractor? I did it after we left the compound, while you were still trapped inside."

Misty shrugged at them both.

"And then you somehow got inside without anyone knowing," Cherise added.

The girl was beginning to look distressed.

Jack watched her from behind the controls of the freight tractor, their load of Tania Steele en route to Chamaeleon, to the planet orbiting Alpha Chamaeleontis, a planet encrusted with manufacturing, roboticized nearly to the point of no longer needing its human creators, and a virtual dead zone of human activity.

As such, it was the perfect place to lay low for a while, no one the wiser. The freight tractor would be put on auto-pilot for its next load—ten thousand widgets for the fashion-conscious widget-wearer, all the rage on the central worlds of the Torgassan Empire—and by happenstance absent its pilot and two passengers when it left Chamaeleon.

"Tell me about this," Jack said, putting the cube on the console between them.

The girl didn't even glance at it.

Cherise's eyes went wide. "Is that what I think it is?"

"A ghost cube," Misty said.

"You said the name stands for something?"

"Its full name is Gaussian Holistic Oscillating Subliminal Tesseract."

Jack glanced at Cherise.

"What's that mean?"

"Just that it reads, emulates, amplifies, and sublimates the electrical fields given off by a human brain."

"So it can tell what we're thinking and cause us to change our minds? Or persuade us to do things we wouldn't normally do?" Cherise looked at Jack suspiciously. "You didn't..."

"I swear, not for a moment," Jack said quickly. He saw she still harbored doubts. "And I wouldn't, not to you, my friend."

Her face softened, and she stepped to his chair to put her arm over his shoulder.

"Hell, I couldn't even ghost Busby, the old bugger." Jack looked under her breast at Misty. "When I met you on Canis Dogma Five, you told me it wasn't yours anymore."

"I wasn't its," she corrected.

"So why did it select me? Why did it select you?"

"After Grandfather died, there wasn't anyone but me." Misty looked pensive, her gaze on her hands in her lap. In their two days aboard the freighter, Cherise had given her a makeover, and then had declared she'd done all she could. Misty's hair was cut to a pageboy with a fashionable curl at the end and a single lock swirled back on her forehead. She wore a pretty pink jumpsuit with matching shoes, sequined lapels, and a pair of diamond-stud earrings.

"I don't know why it selected you," she told him finally, with a sigh.

"Maybe it knows that Jack's in the best position to care for you."

Jack and Misty looked at Cherise and said simultaneously, "I am?" and "He is?" respectively.

"Well, what's your one goal?" she asked, looking at Misty in a motherly way.

"To live in the palace on Torgas Prime as the Princess."

Jack smiled. They'd had an exhaustive conversation yesterday with Misty, trying to dissuade her from this course, but she hadn't been dissuaded.

"And your name is—?"

"Misty Circi, Princess Misty Circi."

"You said you're princess of the Circian Empire, didn't you?"

She nodded vigorously.

"Only the Torgassan Princess can live on Torgas Prime."

"I'll rename the empire when I become the Empress."

Misty wouldn't be deterred.

"And we know that the old Circian Empire dominated the Milky Way not by force but by persuasion."

Jack looked up at Cherise, wondering where she was going with this new line of reasoning.

"Inordinate persuasion, even of inveterate enemies bitterly opposed to their rule, even of entire constellations committed to secession. They never persuaded anyone to love them—stars forbid anyone try that with a human being—" Cherise gave Jack a poke—"but they did defuse animosity toward their rule and convinced nearly all of humanity to live placidly under them for a very long time."

Jack frowned at her.

"And maybe," she added, "maybe the cube selected Jack because he's your best hope, Princess Misty Circi, of reestablishing the Circian Empire."

Misty looked skeptically at Cherise. Jack looked skeptically at himself. "I don't think so," they both said.

"Well, maybe of getting you to Torgas Prime," she amended, looking deep in thought.

"Yeah, but what then?" Jack asked, having wanted not to breach the subject before. "You'll upset a lot of people when you show up on Torgas Prime and say you're the Circian Princess."

"Not if you're with me," Misty said.

"If I'm with you, even more people will be upset, especially that detective."

"But you'll persuade them to like me, won't you?"

"I'd have to go to charm school to do that." Jack snorted.

Cherise hid her smile behind her hand.

He raised an eyebrow at her. "Wouldn't help, would it?"

* * *

Later, after Misty and Cherise had gone to bed, Jack set the cube on the console.

Fuscous gray swirls roiled beneath its smooth surface, turgid with possibility.

"What can you do?"

Jack wasn't sure it was a question he'd asked aloud, but the cube didn't need it articulated.

He snapped into the body of a tall man, whom he knew was tall by the impossible distance to the ground. He wore fine silks and strolled through a garden whose topiary was just as immaculate as it was intricate. Even the sidewalk was etched with arabesques.

Jack pulled himself back, knowing there were subtleties to the cube he'd have to master. Getting them out of the Imperial compound on Alpha Tuscana had exhausted him, and without Cherise's resourcefulness, they'd have never gotten off-planet.

"How do I ghost someone without taking them over completely?"

The cube sides manifested a view of elaborate topiary and etched walkways. The tall one was having a conversation with a man bedecked with insignia.

"He's quite lost his reason, Admiral, putting that animal in charge of capturing this rebel."

"Hush! How do we know he isn't listening?"

"What if he is? Let him throw me into a singularity! Better that than having to watch the Empire unravel because the Emperor has lost his hold on his faculties. I'm not advocating rebellion, Lord Admiral, just a period of observation—to see what other areas his August Highness might be not so 'high' in." The tall man chuckled at his own pun.

"The Emperor's infallible," the Admiral insisted.

"Stardust! And you know it! You're saying it because you think he's listening. I'm sure someone's listening, but I'm not convinced it's the Emperor." The tall man peered into the cube. "You are listening, aren't you?"

Jacked looked away and the cube went dark. He was almost sure the tall man had seen him. But how could that be?

Remembering the detective at the Imperial compound, Jack wondered how Brewster had sensed Jack had been ghosting the person near her. And she'd done so not once, but thrice.

Then he realized what the tall man had said. "Putting that animal in charge of capturing this rebel."

Brewster? Capturing me?

Jack went cold, intuiting that indeed Detective Monique "The Bruiser" Brewster was out to capture him.

I'm not a rebel, Jack thought immediately.

Another part of his mind sneered, You're taking an upstart princess to the Imperial Capital, one who claims she'll be Empress, so that makes you a rebel.

He frowned. From what he'd seen of Brewster's methods, he was sure she'd never rest until he was a puddle of pulp in some hospital bed, or worse, some coroner's freezer.

Where's Brewster now? he wondered, and he looked at the cube.

Its sides grew dark and turbid, as though some storm gurgled beneath the smooth surface.

Jack waited, urging the cube to show him Brewster.

Striations appeared, as though a cyclone roared inside the cube, but no images formed.

Composing himself, Jack relaxed in the pilot's chair and reached for the cube, picking it up by its corners. He took a deep breath and placed his hands flat on its sides.

The galaxy spread below him like a whirlpool, the galactic bar like the filament of a halogen lamp, too bright to look at but irresistibly beautiful. Spiral arms pinwheeled outward, leaving tails of flame and dust, fading away the farther they got from the core, until mere wisps remained.

Show me Brewster, he thought, but nothing happened. As though Brewster doesn't exist, he thought idly.

Show me the Southern Birds, he thought. The brothel was in full swing, a lively tune playing, women strutting and men leering, drink and smoke abundant.

Jack pulled back, reminded that he hadn't had anything to smoke in nearly two months.

Show me Torgas Prime, he thought. The palace ballroom glittered brightly, almost as lively as the Southern Birds' parlor. Gentleman in spats or uniforms escorted ladies bedecked in sequins and diamonds. Jack looked toward the throne, catching a glimpse of the Emperor. Like the galactic bar, the figure at the rear of the ballroom was too bright to look at.

Jack pulled himself back into the freighter, puzzled. Why couldn't he see the Emperor? Why couldn't he ghost the Emperor?

He looked down at the cube. Show me the Emperor. Its side grew dark and turbid but showed him nothing.

Jack thought of Xerxes on Canis Dogma Five. Instantly, he was inside the dun, dingy abode, Trude across the table from him, remonstrating him for some imagined fault, declaring how faultless she was.

He thought of Cherise, and instantly he was looking at the inside of their cabin doorway, seeing the light from the cockpit seep underneath, wondering why Jack was taking so long to come to bed, and wanting him deeply, thoughts of him ...

Jack looked over at the door separating them.

One more, he thought reluctantly. Misty.

The cube stared back at him, unresponsive. The dark and turbid surface swirled aimlessly.

Odd, he thought.

Brewster, Emperor Torgas, Princess Misty.

Why wouldn't the cube allow him to ghost those three? he wondered.

I'll have to look into it tomorrow, Jack thought. Cherise was awaiting him now.

* * *

Before he went to bed, Jack checked the lifeboats from long habit. Whole crews had been lost on ships with poorly-maintained lifeboats.

This freight tractor had two lifeboats, one on either side of the bridge. The lifeboat to starboard, Jack saw, had a transponder offline. I'll have to fix that in the morning, he thought. The transponder was a beacon whose signal was automatically activated upon launch, so even if the occupants were injured or unconscious, rescuers could still find the survivors.

Yawning, he readied himself for bed.

"What were you doing?" Cherise murmured in his arms.

"Trying to figure out what the cube does," he replied, the feel of her against him like the touch of sunrise. "I can't ghost Misty. It's very odd. I wonder—"

She smothered his words with a kiss.

And he forgot what he'd been saying.

Chapter 12

The first blast was a glancing blow to port, but it still hurled Jack and Cherise from bed.

"Lifeboat," he screamed at her over the screech of wounded steel and injured ship. He shoved her that way and pulled himself toward the cubby where they'd made Misty a makeshift bunk.

"What is it?" she squealed over the noise.

"I don't know," he said, but he did know, and he expected a second blast any moment.

The gravgen failed, and Misty went tumbling.

"Just ball yourself up," he told her, demonstrating by pulling his knees to his chest.

Practiced at moving around in the absence of gravity, Jack maneuvered her quickly toward the lifeboat.

Cherise was already strapped in. She grabbed Misty and strapped her in the other seat. There were only two.

Jack braced himself as the second blast landed. He hit the launch, and they were flung away from the wreckage, tumbling.

Jack only got a glimpse, glimpse, glimpse of the disintegrating freighter as the lifeboat spun away uncontrollably.

But they were clear of the wreckage. And alive.

Jack relaxed against the lifeboat floor, confident their transponder would signal their position to any rescuer.

But would it also alert any attacker?

"What was that?" Cherise asked, glancing him up and down.

Jack realized he was completely naked. In his hand was the cube. He didn't remember picking it up, and he tried to recall if he'd had it when he went to get Misty from her cubby.

Cherise was naked, too. "There must be some formalls in this tub."

Misty giggled at them both, a knowing look on her face.

"I think we were attacked," Jack said, reaching for a kit beneath the seat. As expected, the kit contained two sets of formalls. Inside were emergency rations for two people for a week, first-aid supplies, and a back-up transponder.

Jack knew they were aboard the starboard lifeboat, the one with the inoperable transponder. He realized he'd known even before they boarded, the first blast to port having forced them to starboard.

He struggled into the formalls and switched places with Cherise so she could dress too. Their changing positions slowed the spinning somewhat, but the motion was still upsetting.

From the direction of the disintegrating freighter, a bright ball of light flared.

Cherise shot him a look. "That didn't happen on its own, did it?"

Jack shook his head. "Someone destroyed the freighter. Looks like a pocket nuke. We probably shouldn't stop our spinning until we're sure the area is clear. Let's hope this tub looks like another piece of debris." He traded a glance with Cherise, wondering what their fate would be if they were captured.

Their attacker had taken care not to leave any survivors.

"I don't feel very good," Misty said, looking wan and green.

Jack handed her a bag from the kit, in case she had to vomit. "Let me see what I can do." He positioned himself in the middle of the pod and did his best to gauge the direction of their spin. Bracing himself in a ball, he used his arms to spin himself the same direction.

After a few iterations, the lifeboat seemed to have slowed.

Jack eased himself to the floor.

Misty still looked miserable.

Without much else to do but wait, Jack encouraged them both to sleep.

He contemplated the cube in his hand.

Why couldn't he ghost Misty? Brewster? The Emperor?

He recalled their escape from the compound on Alpha Tuscana, and how he'd projected an image of his empty cell into the visual cortices of all the observers, including Brewster. How had he been able to do that, but still not have the ability to ghost her?

Perhaps it was a matter of degree.

What we need is someone to explain how this works, Jack thought.

An alien technology, a relic from before the dawn of Humanity, the cube operated on principles barely within the grasp of those who'd wielded it. The Circians had openly used the cubes to rule the galaxy, and the Torgassans were using the same cubes, even if there wasn't much evidence of it. They used their vast navies to put down rebellions and maintain control of their far-flung domains.

And what did it mean, Jack wondered, as he watched her sleeping face, that a young girl would come forward, declare herself a Circian Princess with the full intent of becoming Empress, wielding one of the very same cubes that her forebears had used to rule the galaxy?

And why had it chosen him?

A quadruple-divorced, thrice-bankrupt, and nearly always askirt-the-law junk collector, constantly on the run from creditors and courts, without a courageous bone in his body, nor a charitable thought in his head.

Why him?

Jack sighed, unable to say.

The slightly nauseating but somewhat soothing motion soon lulled him to sleep.

* * *

He dreamt he was hurtling through time, backward to the last vestiges of the Circian Empire. Barbarian navies prepared to bombard Canis Dogma Five into oblivion, the planet ravaged after nearly a century of war, the galaxy no longer a unified human civilization but a pastiche of a hundred thousand occupied constellations, each struggling to stay connected with each other as technology regressed and hostile ecologies rid themselves of this pestilential invasive species known as human.

Jack watched the last Circian Emperor descend deep unground into a bunker that would soon be his tomb, carrying the last known cube with him. Also with him was a microfusion projector containing a recording of his last will and testament and his proclamation that the finder of the cube was hereby conferred all the titles—and attendant duties, responsibilities and obligations—of the Circian Emperor, and exhorted that person to build anew the Circian Empire of old.

Suddenly, Jack was in the Emperor's mind.

Emperor Lochium Circi IX looked around the chamber, knowing what exactly he would need to do to escape detection and preserve this ark, this last Circian time capsule.

He would not fail.

Sensor field disruptors already encapsulated the ark, their microfusion batteries able to last five hundred years. But these disruptors would fail if he continued to occupy the bunker.

Lochium the Ninth would soon be Lochium the Last, as he laid out the implements he would need. The gasses he planned to use would dissipate over time, absorbed into the surrounding rock, and he wasn't concerned at the decades this would take. If by some chance, the barbarian hordes discovered this chamber in spite of the sensor field disruptors, they were in for a nasty and fatal surprise.

He laid out the copper band whose change in color would signal the release of hydrogen sulfide, and he prepared the divan where he would take his final repose.

Then he lay down and broke the ampule.

The smell of rotten eggs pervaded the chamber immediately, and the copper band turned green. His eyes watered, and he began to cough, his lungs quickly filling with fluid. The smell went away as his olfactory nerves were paralyzed, and he lost consciousness soon afterward.

Jack slipped from Emperor Circi's mind.

Within minutes, the necrosis to the basal ganglia was irreversible, and he died.

Emperor Lochium Circi the Last. The cube rolled from his hand and fell to the floor, where it awaited its next host for almost a millennium.

The sensor field disruptors failed at four hundred and fifty years post-collapse, but civilization had regressed locally to Paleolithic levels, and no means of remote sensing existed to find the underground chamber. Writing on stone with blunt instruments had once again become the primary means for recording events. For those who achieved some semblance of literacy.

At nine hundred ninety years post-collapse, an enterprising young woman dug up the hatch to the buried chamber. After she opened the hatch, the faint odor of rotten eggs dissipated, and she dropped into the tomb.

Her presence activated the microfusion projector. The holographic figure of Emperor Lochium Circi the Last appeared before her and conferred upon her the title of Emperor with all its attendant duties, responsibilities, and obligations.

She understood most of the speech in spite of its odd inflections and stilted pronunciation, although some of the words were quite beyond her comprehension. She carried the projector and the cube to the surface and declared herself the Empress of the Circian Empire.

She and her descendants were regarded for the next five hundred years as local lunatics cursed by their forebears to haul around a bulky projector and an odd-looking cube. Throughout that time, not a single craft dropped from the skies, and no contact was made with their near-Canis neighbors, either Majora or Minora. An occasional local convert or adherent might swear fealty to the self-declared Emperor, and an occasional miscreant might attempt to purloin either sacred object, but these erstwhile rulers of a long-bygone Empire most often lived out lives of lonely eccentricity and rarely ruled much more than the amount of land they themselves were able to cultivate.

In due course, the projector wore out, grew distorted and fuzzy, and finally stopped working altogether.

Then the strangers from the sky began to visit, saying they were from Torgas, a place impossibly far away. Initially, they were friendly, but soon began asking questions that indicated they were somehow afraid of the local lunatic.

Protective of their own, the people of Canis Dogma Five did their best to hide the crazy Emperor, and since the cube itself did not want to be found either, the Torgassans were never able to locate its bearer.

* * *

Jack woke with a start, the constant wobble having invaded his dream.

Cherise looked over at him from her seat, secured in it by her straps, she and Misty looking over the excretory hoses with horrified fascination. "Oh good, you're awake. We were hoping you could explain how we're supposed to use these."

He blinked several times and thumbed the sleep from his eyes. He glanced out a porthole, where stars wheeled past with undaunted regularity. Somehow, their escape pod hadn't been found by the attacking ship. Jack was certain if they'd been found, they'd have been destroyed.

He opened his mouth to explain how to use the tubes but realized he had no experience with one of them. And that he'd probably find it embarrassing to try and show them. He closed his mouth, not knowing what to say.

"Maybe if you could stop the spinning, we could sort this out," Cherise said.

Misty held up a curved trough like a banana with its inner half sliced off. "How's this supposed to work?"

Jack took it from her and started to position it, but then flushed with embarrassment and handed it back to her. "I'll try to stop the spinning."

"Quickly, please," Cherise said, squirming.

He realized he had to go too, and they'd been awake longer. Bracing himself, he rose slowly and found the covered control panel. There was barely room for him to lie down. Standing, he took up even more space.

The cover swung back and almost took out his eye. He recoiled from it and hit his head on the hull. Fixing the cover open, he activated the external retros, seeing he had thirty minutes of blast time.

Thirty minutes of thrust to get them to some destination.

Used efficiently, he'd probably need only a few minutes to stabilize the craft with the retrorockets.

But the crude controls and complete lack of sensors made his task difficult. He guessed the direction of their spin by the angle of the stars wheeling past, found the retro closest to the equator of their spin and repositioned it, only to have their slight wobble take that retro off their equator.

He muttered an imprecation.

As he tried to gauge the equator's position, he realized that their axis itself was variable. They were like a spinning top with a moving center of gravity.

"Uh, everyone has to hold as still as possible."

The wobble seemed to diminish when everyone was bracing themselves.

And now! He hit the blast briefly.

Stars still wheeled past, but more slowly.

"Once more," he said, waiting until the equator aligned once again with the retro.

Now! The retro flared, and the stars subsided to a slow cascade.

"That better?" he asked.

Both his companions nodded.

"I think that one fits like this," Cherise said, unbuckling herself to demonstrate.

"Oh, I see," Misty said. "Here let me try." Then she pointed a finger at Jack. "Eyes closed until I say so!"

He dutifully closed his eyes, his own bladder burning.

Once they were done and he'd taken his own turn—their eyes dutifully closed and Misty having a giggle fit—Jack wondered how they were going to be rescued. The lifeboat clearly didn't have enough fuel to get them anywhere near civilization, nor even the navigation equipment necessary to tell them where the nearest civilization might be.

"We'll having to assume whoever attacked us didn't stay to rescue any survivors," he told them. "An explosion like that is sure to be investigated, and the freighter's transponders surely activated at the first hull breach."

"Then there'll be rescuers in the area, searching for survivors."

"Imperial rescuers," he told Cherise. "And we were lucky." He told them about the inoperable transponder he'd found aboard the starboard lifeboat before he'd gone to bed, the lifeboat they were now on.

"So if it had been working, we'd probably be dead now," Cherise said, her gaze hollow. Then she frowned, "So what do we do? We can't just drift forever through space. There's only so much food, water, and air aboard this tub."

He nodded. "About five days of food and water." He looked up at the control panel, its hatch still fixed open, and made a quick calculation based on the amount of oxygen remaining versus the time they'd been aboard. "And about three days of air." Three occupants were consuming more oxygen than the lifeboat's usual capacity.

"So what do we do?" Misty asked.

Jack stared back at them blankly. "I say we risk capture by an Imperial patrol, take over their ship, and try to escape to the other side of the galactic core."

"And what are we going to do there?"

Jack shrugged at Misty. "Find a habitable world, or an inhabited one. Must be thousands of viable planets still populated after the Circian collapse."

Misty pouted. "Then how am I going to become Empress?"

Jack tried not to laugh or even smile.

Cherise was also suppressing a grin.

"You said you'd take me to Torgas." She looked miffed.

"Emperor Torgas just tried to kill us. You know going there means your death, don't you?"

"Some things are more important than life, Captain Salvager."

He winced, his life not exactly a paragon of ambition and achievement. He glanced at Cherise, hoping for reinforcements.

"You said you would," Misty insisted.

Cherise was silent.

Jack sighed, his choices limited. So much had changed since he'd first met her on Canis Dogma Five. Doing so aboard his Salvager—a ship with modest cloaking and maneuverability—had been a possibility. Taking her there aboard the freight tractor would have been extremely risky, but still doable. To try and land on Torgas Prime abound a hijacked Imperial Patrol vessel would get them instantly blown to bits in orbit, if they got that far. More likely, we'd be intercepted as we entered the system, Jack thought, and perhaps even as they entered the constellation, the Empire so paranoid of attack that the Capital was ringed with defense bases for a thousand parsecs around.

Don't fool yourself, pal, that other part of his brain told him. You know you had no intention whatsoever of taking her anywhere near Torgas Prime. Not for a moment.

"Well, we can't do it aboard a hijacked Imperial Patrol," he told her. "You tell me how we're going to get there."

"Why don't we ask them?" She pointed out the porthole.

Jack nearly broke his neck whipping his head around. The lifeboat's rotation took the object out of view. "Who?" he asked, waiting for it to appear again.

A black blot occluded the stars, and then was gone.

Jack reached for the controls and stopped the lifeboat's spinning. Then he adjusted their position to put the blot in the viewport.

"What is it?" Cherise asked.

The blot on the field of stars was a solid black featureless disc. It appeared completely inert, emitting no light nor reflecting any light. Its presence was notable only for the absence of everything behind it.

Jack watched carefully, his breath threatening to fog the inside of the glasma.

The blot was slowly getting larger.

"Why's it getting bigger?" Misty asked.

"It's not," Jack said. "We're headed directly toward it."

"But what is it?" Cherise asked again.

Jack shook his head. "A derelict space station, a rogue planet, I don't know. From this distance it looks perfectly spherical. We may be able to avoid it using our retro, but if it's too large, like a rogue planet, then we may not be able to avoid its gravity well."

"What's a rogue planet?" Misty asked.

"A planet that isn't orbiting a star. Sometimes planets are torn from their orbits, and they just drift through space until they're captured by another system, or destroyed."

"I've never heard of them," Cherise said.

Jack shrugged. "They're not very interesting. No atmosphere, or if there is one, it's locked up in ice. Without a primary, no heat or light or energy, unless you burrow hundreds of miles into the crust to reach the molten core."

He looked out the porthole and realized their approach was far faster then he'd initially thought. He reached for the retro controls. "Hang on, everybody!"

"Look!" Misty said.

Something flared from the disc rim, a flare or—

"A ship!" he and Misty said at the same time.

Cherise glanced between them, smiling.

The flare bent toward them, growing gradually larger. Twenty minutes later, it filled the porthole, and a tinted viewport slid past them. Jack and Misty waved excitedly, each trying to crowd out the other.

A cargo bay door opened on the ship's side, and it backed over them, the lifeboat sliding smoothly into the larger ship's cargo bay.

While Jack and Misty sang and danced, overjoyed to be rescued, Cherise watched them, looking somber.

"What's the matter?" Jack asked.

"How do you know they're friendly?"

Chapter 13

At first, the cargo hold of the larger ship was black, pitch black.

Then light flooded the hold.

Jack blinked rapidly until his eyes adjusted. What little he could see out the porthole looked like empty cargo bay walls. A hissing soon commenced—the cargo bay filling with air. Jack watched the external pressure reading increase gradually to one atmosphere.

"What if they're not even human?" Misty asked.

When humans had left their Earthly cradle some ten thousand years ago, they'd embarked on an exploration of the Milky Way, full of dread and excitement in equal measure—dread for the evil predatory races that would feed on humans until their stomachs were full and humankind was extinct, and excitement at the new and fascinating civilizations they were sure to find.

Neither had been the case.

Not that humanity hadn't found other creatures, but none of those species had been at an evolutionary par with these new interlopers. The closest they'd found was a semi-literate biped invertebrate on Yahoo Sextuplus who'd either hid from the visitors or had thrown their feces at them.

There was also evidence—Jack's cube part of that evidence—of a species who'd once occupied a three-dimensional, sub-light, body-based consciousness, but whose current whereabouts was unknown. It was speculated, and heavily debated in intellectual circles, that this species had transcended the bounds of corporeal existence and now floated in some ethereal ether ominously known as the Purity of Thought Itself.

"Well," Jack told Misty, "if they aren't human, I'd prefer feces-throwing invertebrate bipeds over the inventors of *this* cube."

He saw the puzzled exchange of glances between the other two, but ignored it.

A figure shuffled forward from a hatchway, Jack barely able to glimpse the person before he or she left his field of vision. "Anybody in there?" they heard.

Jack exchanged a glance and a shrug with the other two. "Three of us," Jack said. "Opening now." He cycled the lock, the pressure nearly equalized.

The hatch opened.

"Oh, hell," the young man said. "Three of you. In a space not fit for one. I'll bet there's a tale behind that dog." He laughed at his own pun. "Come on aboard. I'm Sammy, Sam Kinkaid. Mother will be glad to see the three of you!"

Jack climbed out and thanked the young man, Misty and Cherise right behind him.

"Looks like you've been in there a day or two at least," the boy said. He didn't wrinkle his nose.

Jack had overestimated the age, and now, based on development, he was thinking the other couldn't be more than fifteen years. "At least three days," Jack replied.

"Seems like longer," Cherise said, looking around the inside of the cargo bay.

"This way," Sammy said, "Let's get you to your quarters while Mom pilots us back to Chiron. You've time to freshen up if you'd like before we get there."

"What's Chiron?" Jack asked, not familiar with any local planet or outpost with that name.

"A dark planet, our home," Sammy said over his shoulder. "Other-wise known as a rogue planet—one that doesn't orbit a star. Here we are." He stopped an intersection. "Modest accommodations, to be sure, but then the last visitor we had was my father—but that was a few years ago."

About fifteen years, Jack guessed. Four doors at an intersection faced each other, three of them open.

Jack took the one across from the other two, throwing a glance at Cherise.

"Misty, you take that one," she said, "and I'll take this. Just tap on the wall if you need anything."

Jack felt a slight lurch under his feet. "Feels like we're underway. Thank you, Sammy." He couldn't wait to get into the cleansall, convinced he reeked of old sex, rank fear, and cramped quarters. He could barely stand his own smell.

He attended to his toilet, evacuating with immense relief, something he hadn't dared do aboard the lifeboat. It was one thing traveling alone to let one's hygiene go for several days. Aboard his Salvager, he might not shower for a week or shave for a month. But to do so aboard a cramped lifeboat with two others—repulsive!

The cabin was spare, just room for a sleeping net. Modest was an overstatement. He found formals where he thought he might and donned them, and had just slipped the cube in his pocket when he heard a tap on the door.

The woman stepped in without waiting for an invitation.

I'm glad I'm dressed, Jack thought.

"I'm glad you're dressed," she said. "Claudia, Claudia Kinkaid." She extended her hand.

He'd have had difficulty not shaking it, the cabin crowded with one occupant. "Jack Carson. Pleased."

"Thought I'd butt in since I didn't want to say this in front of Sammy. You're the passengers aboard that freighter, eh? Blew up three days ago? Thought as much. No survivors, according to the local authorities, but I'm guessing you had the transponder off for a reason." She held up a hand to stop Jack. "The less I know the better. That wasn't an accident, that freighter blowing up. Someone wanted you dead, and still would if they knew you were alive. The rest I don't want to know. Having you on Chiron puts me in a bind, so I'm getting you off as fast as possible. The main question, of course, is which way do you want to go? You're welcome to stay for a day, but not a moment longer. I can't put my home at risk any more than that."

Jack nodded appreciably. "Surprised you're able to risk that long." He estimated her age about ten, fifteen years his senior, and smart. Scientist smart. He noted the efficient clothes, precise haircut, clipped speech. Further, she was accustomed to doing everything herself. He saw she knew he was appraising her. All women knew, he knew. "It's very kind of you to offer any hospitality. And Sammy too. Sweet boy, by the way."

"Thank you."

"We'll discuss where we're going amongst ourselves and let you know well before tomorrow morning. Needless to say, but I'll say it anyway, thank you for rescuing us and especially for not turning us over to the Imperials. If there's anything we can do—beyond getting off Chiron as fast as possible—please let us know."

"Thank you. Landing in three minutes. For safety, please use the nets." And swiftly, she was gone.

Odd, he thought, how a person of the opposite sex can give off no signals of any kind, as though completely sexless. He strung up the net and climbed in, just as the ship began to descend toward Chiron.

* * *

"There are worlds around us on multiple levels if only we have the eyes to see or the instruments to measure," Professor Claudia Kincaid told her guests over dinner. Wines from Lorraine—a plain on ancient Earth in a region to the southeast of what was once known as France— and silver from Lepus Secundus, translucent ceramics from Vulpecula Salacia, and crystal forged deep in the Virgan gas giants, Claudia knew how to lay out a table.

The finely-sculpted sythemush couldn't be helped, however.

No matter how she dressed it up, it still tasted like mush.

She was annoyed she couldn't obtain anything better. She owned her own exoplanet. She ran her own business. She conducted her life with the utmost efficiency.

But she couldn't get real food.

"Do you know what I mean, Captain Carson?" She looked across the table at her guests.

The ugly troll who'd alighted from the lifeboat with the fabulously beautiful woman and the mysterious girl looked up from his plate in bewilderment.

The luxurious layout was surely wasted on troglodytes like him, Claudia was thinking.

"I agree, never thought I'd eat from a Salacian plate." He tapped it to elicit a dainty ping. "Fabulous dinnerware. But you're referring to aliens, aren't you? Like the microscopic life on Chiron—living in the liminal zone between the hot molten core and the near absolute zero of cold, open space."

Perhaps he just *looks* like a cave dweller, she thought. "As one example, yes. And then we have the ancient race that left behind that little bauble you brought with you."

The silence was profound.

Claudia might have smiled. She was bemused that they hadn't expected her to know about it. She knew everything that happened on Chiron. "Believe me, Captain Jack, my interest is only academic. But for edification purpose, I would like to see it, as I imagine Sammy might also."

Her son looked up suddenly at hearing his name, his head swiveling around. He and the mysterious girl had been having a private giggle over some adult inanity.

He's been isolated from his peers far too long, Claudia thought, knowing he'd soon need to look into universities. Just she and her son on Chiron, it was a special occasional when they had guests such as these.

The ugly man put the cube on the table.

Some trick of light caused it to fade from her vision when she wasn't looking at it directly. If she hadn't told him to put it there, she wouldn't have seen it. As if it occupied an entirely different dimension.

"This is a ghost cube, isn't it?" she asked.

The exchange of looks between the trio confirmed that it was.

"A Gaussian Holistic Oscillating Subliminal Tesseract," Claudia said. "Worth more than Chiron in its entire. And a star if it were orbiting one. The species who manufactured it gone without a trace—or at least no trace but this. As if they occupied an entirely different dimension." She turned her gaze to the woman, briefly groping for her name. "Cherise, you've seen it at work, when you three were escaping the Imperial compound on Alpha Tuscana—" she smiled at their gasps, again bemused that they didn't expect her to know such things—"What's your impression?"

"Just that it represents a level to technology we'll never likely achieve, Professor."

Not an intellectual giant, Claudia thought. She looked over at the girl, Misty.

Unfathomable, that one, the Professor knew. There was some quality about her that—like the cube itself—was just outside the range of human receptivity or comprehension.

But then we're all a bit beyond comprehension, aren't we? Professor Kinkaid thought idly.

"You have an Empire that wishes you dead and thinks it may have annihilated you," she said, addressing all three of them, "And a device whose capabilities make it among the most valuable of alien artifacts. Where will you go, my ineluctable guests?"

She watched them glance amongst themselves, as though deciding which of them would speak. As if she hadn't listened in on their conversation and knew the substance of their decision already.

Earlier, she'd escorted Captain Jack to the cavern where she kept all her vessels.

Ice crystalized on every surface like lichen. The air was thin due to absorption and leakage. Their breath fogged in front of them like the finest of powdery snow, but the floor was warm beneath their feet, huge pumps circulating magma-heated water throughout the rooms in her underground compound. Here at five miles beneath Chiron's ice-entombed surface, it was still cold enough to freeze everything instantly. The liminal zone—that place in the planet crust where basic proteins might form, warmed naturally by the magma but not too hot to boil water—was easily five miles below them. Few creatures lived outside the liminal zone.

"Here's the ship I can loan you," she'd told him, showing him the two-person sport yacht she'd bought right before she'd become pregnant with Sammy. She'd used it half a dozen times since, and had been meaning to sell it for years, but somehow hadn't gotten around to it.

His eyes went wide as he'd gazed upon it. "But that's a Quasar."

One of the most expensive brands, built for speed and able to outrun any Imperial patrol no matter what its load.

She'd held up her hand to stop any protest. If he weren't so ugly, she'd have demanded sex from him in payment, and considered it anyway in spite of his repulsive physiognomy. Mating practices on outlying colonies where men predominated had given women substantial bargaining power. It's been too long since I've had a man, Claudia thought. "Just remember that I helped you. If you're able at some point to pay me for it, or return it, that would be even better." She'd smiled at his continued objections.

Now, over dinner, she watched her three guests closely. She knew they'd considered the far side of the Galactic Bar, and she knew they weren't going there. She also knew they were unlikely to tell her. Perhaps it was better she didn't know.

"Perhaps, it's better you don't know," Misty said nonchalantly.

Claudia gazed placidly at the girl, who grazed placidly on her dressed-up mush. "And why would that be?"

"You know why," the girl said slyly, a gleam in her eye. "You don't own your own rogue planet by being ignorant."

Claudia chucked, surprised at the girl's depth. There was a fine sophistication to Misty's face, a translucence to her checks, a patrician authority to her nose, and a knowing mischief in her eyes. "Perhaps I do know why. You might consider searching for the origins of your little toy." She noticed it was already gone from the table. Prudent, she thought.

"You said there isn't a trace of them left," Cherise said.

"A trace that we have eyes to see or instruments to measure," Claudia added, smiling. "But you have in your possession an instrument that half-exist in other dimensions."

"You're suggesting that we try to enter those dimensions?" the woman asked.

Claudia raised her initial estimate of the woman, too. All three of them more intelligent than she'd expected. "The Empire would certainly find it difficult to pursue you, wouldn't it?"

* * *

The Emperor Phaeton Torgas looked down into the chamber and smiled at the guest adjacent to him. "It does appear you were successful in annihilating this scavenger, Detective Brewster," he murmured, pitching his voice so that only she could hear.

As if his every word weren't instantly seized upon, analyzed ad infinitum, and sieved for the slightest nuance.

But at least his other guests weren't privy to his remarks.

The arena was small, an intimate affair constructed for the Emperor's entertainment. The field itself was a cube—not ironically—which looked impervious from the inside, its inner surfaces mirrored. Around its four sides were seats, cascading theater-style from a round, raised circumference. The field might be viewed from any angle, above or below in addition to all four sides. From the outside, the field looked to be completely open, as the polarized glasma permitted light to pass through from only one direction—from inside to out.

No light passed from outside to in.

In each corner of the cube was a glowb, lighting the interior and its contents. Live plays, musical concerts, duels to the death, and orgies of every stripe had been preformed for the Emperor's edification and entertainment on multiple occasions, but the subject of this evening's show hadn't been arranged for the Emperor.

It had been arranged for his guest.

And inside the cube was Captain Caeneus Lang, erstwhile commander of the Imperial compound on Alpha Tuscana. He still wore his uniform, but all the elements of insignia—epaulets, chevrons, decorations, and medals—had been ripped from the fabric, raveled edges outlining slightly darker fabric spared exposure by the appliques sewed directly on the uniform.

"It has come to attention that certain spectacles are a predilection of yours, Detective. I bring you one such spectacle, in honor of your accomplishment."

"Your August Highness, you do me too much honor." The big woman with the bulldog face inclined her head his direction. "I did what any humble Imperial servant would do."

Someone's been coaching her, Phaeton thought, his Prime Minister the likely culprit. The Emperor did not look in Custos Messium's direction, the other man in attendance and sitting smugly back in the shadows almost directly across from the Emperor.

Present also were the Admiral, Sophocles Camelus, a childhood friend of the Emperor, if friends could be had by such, and a bevy of the Emperor's consorts, who in his opinion needed regular reminders of what he was capable of.

Phaeton smiled.

Of all the human expressions, the smile was the least honest. A frown was rarely mistaken for much else, universally represented displeasure or discomfort, and never masked a person's true feelings. A smile often indicated amusement or pleasure, but just as often indicated something far different. A smile might represent a decision, particularly one with unpleasant consequences, a task undertaken in the face of obstacles or repercussions. A smile might simply be an ambiguous expression, sowing confusion and uncertainty. Or a smile might be dissimulation, utter obfuscation, a feint meant to mislead the observer.

A smile could dissemble fear, hatred, malice, avarice, or any among the litany of human excesses. In particular, a smile was the mask worn in the theater of human drama, a character whose true face remained hidden in the play of life, an anonymous actor whose true motives remained murky, and whom audiences continued to wonder about after the curtain fell and the theater emptied, a character whom audiences still imagined upon the stage long after the last bow had been taken.

Audiences will wonder about me long after I've taken my last bow, Emperor Phaeton thought, smiling.

He held up his cloaked fist, a gold-embroidered silk kerchief covering over his hand and the object in it, his scepter.

Both the symbol and the source of his power, his scepter held in the center of a circlet a two-inch silvery cube, slightly beveled along its edges, a plain and unassuming cube, but one whose looks—quite analogous to a smile—were often deceiving.

If a person noticed it at all.

Scepter in fist, a cloak over it, the Emperor ordered the event to begin.

A woman rose from the audience, long robes cascading to the floor. She descended the tiers like a wraith, smoothly, without the suggestion of legs. She stopped at the arena wall, and a portal formed in the side of the cube.

She stepped into the transparent cube, and the portal collapsed behind her. "I am Justice Minister Janis Astraea.

"Captain Caeneus Lang, you have been condemned to death for dereliction of duty. As arbiter of innocence and purity, I do hereby proclaim that your death will cleanse us of the smirch that your deeds have left on our souls. Only your death will balance the scales. So it shall be, so it is done."

The portal opened behind her, and she backed from the arena.

"So this is it? Nothing else?" Lang asked the reflective walls, his own image mirrored back to him on all sides, ad infinitum, his own words echoing back to him from all sides, until distance itself distorted the sight and sound beyond recognition, a transmogrified representation of a life lived well, a life ended badly.

"No hearing, no court martial, not even an opportunity for me to face my accusers? What monumental cowardice! Hide behind your mirrors! Hide behind your sterile glasma walls! My death cleanses you of nothing, I tell you! Your failures are writ large by my death. You will suffer the torments..."

The Emperor yawned, not deigning to give succor by responding to the increasing vitriol. "It has always been a subject of some interest, Detective Brewster, how people choose to die. Don't you think?"

"I've not had the pleasure to study such, your August Highness," she replied. "I'm honored to have that opportunity."

"Do you prefer spams, Detective?" The Emperor flicked a gaze at the prisoner.

Waves of muscle contractions washed over the Captain, stopping the obloquy. He flopped across the floor like a fish.

"Perhaps contusion," the Emperor murmured.

Visible skin sprouted violet-red abrasions, and the Captain tore at his clothes, a half-strangled scream gargling from his throat.

"Ataxia?"

Captain Lang stood with an ungainly wobble and ambulated puppet-like around the cube, his movements jerky and disjointed, his speech garbled and slurred beyond intelligibility.

"Or no muscle tone at all?"

The man in the cube collapsed in a heap, like a rag doll. Moisture spread at his crotch as his bladder emptied. His face was lump of clay, his eyes looking different directions.

"Or simply pain?"

The Captain went rigid and screamed, leaped to his feet, and ran in tight circles, as though to escape the inescapable, his face a rictus of agony.

"Well, Detective Brewster?"

Captain Caeneus Lang dropped to the floor, his face beaded in sweat, his lungs gulping huge volumes of air.

"Pardon, your August Highness, I must have missed the question."

Just as you missed your target, the Emperor thought. Even the finest of tools needed refinement. "How would you prefer to see Captain Lang die?"

"Pardon, your August Highness, but my wishes in this circumstance are immaterial. I would defer to you, Lord."

He considered annihilating her for the breach in address. How dare she refer to me with lowly "Lord," he thought. But he needed her and that galled him all the more. He reminded himself he was sharpening this instrument, not breaking it. "It appears your interest lies in inflicting the indignity yourself. Very well, Detective Brewster, perhaps on another occasion you might do me the service of showing me how you work." The Emperor flicked an eyelash toward the prisoner, never taking his eyes off Brewster.

In the arena, the Captain in the torn and soiled uniform began melting from the feet up, puddles of ooze forming around the stumps he stood on, their length lessening even as he watched, the molecular cohesion of his flesh releasing and turning into the ninety-percent fluid that it always had been.

"Know, Detective Brewster," Emperor Phaeton said, watching as horror crept onto her face, her eyes riveted to the spectacle of someone melting away right in front of her, "know that this miscreant, the scavenger Jack Carson, escaped your bungled attack on the freight tractor. Know, Detective Brewster, that I require you to eliminate him. Know, Detective Brewster, the fate that awaits you if you fail."

A bubbling puddle of plasma was all that remained on the area floor.

Chapter 14

Jack felt the barely-tamed power of the Quasar under his hands as he guided the yacht delicately up through the narrow shaft toward the planet surface.

"Good luck, Jack," Professor Claudia Kinkaid had told them just before they'd boarded, a hint of mischief in her eyes.

Cherise had suggested how Jack might compensate their host for her untoward generosity.

Misty nudged Cherise. "Jack didn't sleep much last night."

"When you get older," the woman told the girl, "you'll find that there are things more restful than sleep." And she winked.

Misty laughed and threw a grin at Jack.

Who tried to ignore them both. Having spent nearly all his formative years in a brothel, he wasn't embarrassed by nocturnal machinations. He simply didn't want to discuss it. "It was very thoughtful of you," he told Cherise, knowing he had thought of it, too.

But he was male, so of course he hadn't mentioned it.

The Quasar interior was mahogany inlay and satin fabric. The seats were form-fitting and articulated to each person's frame, the buttock and upper thigh areas riddled with vibrating nodules for comfort and massage. The controls were tactile-response glasma, mounted at the ends of his armrests, his hands fitting inside them like gloves, a backup set of manual controls in front of the copilot's chaise. The visual display was semicircular seamless glasma whose edges included a shrunken view of the ship's stern. The engines were turbo interpellant vectoring fusion thrusters, whose hydrogen conversion to lithium produced temperatures nearly equal to those of a solar surface.

They ascended a narrow shaft toward the planet surface, its frequent turns preventing rubble from pouring into the compound located ten miles below, an occasional maintenance bot slipping into a side crevice to let them pass. The shaft walls glittered with frozen particles, all gasses instantly crystallizing, and only methane able to maintain any liquidity in the near absolute-Kelvin temperatures around them.

A sensor blared when they got too close to the shaft wall, and Jack guided the craft back toward the center. The journey was mostly just tedious, as long as their pace was slow. If they'd tried to hurry, it might be hazardous, but the shaft itself had to be wide enough at all points for the largest of Professor Kinkaid's supply ferries, a craft easily thrice the Quasar's bore.

The shaft expanded into a canyon, a deep rift in the planet surface whose jagged sides were coated with diamonds of ice.

The cube sat on the Quasar dash, just within Jack's reach, to one side of the controls.

Cherise could easily reach it as well, equidistant. "Where are we going?

"He's going to throw the cube away."

Jack glanced over his shoulder at Misty. It didn't surprise him that she knew. He wasn't subtle and he'd never learned to hide his feelings. He was guileless and lacked the finesse to obfuscate his intentions.

"You can't do that, Jack," Misty said. Her voice carried that resigned ennui of a person who argued in spite of the futility.

"I am anyway," he said, determined.

"Oh, Jack," Cherise said, biting her lip and looking away.

"It wants you to Emperor," Misty said, her voice higher, her tone imperative.

"Well, it forgot to ask me what I want!" he snarled. His voice boomed around the cabin as though amplified by a megaphone. He instantly regretted raising his voice when he saw Misty blink away tears. He saw Cherise wince, too.

She took his hand. "I'm glad you don't want to be Emperor. You wouldn't be the sweet gentle man I love."

He melted inside a little, knowing how disappointed she must be at his relinquishing all that wealth and power. He'd never wanted it anyway, at least not for himself. Until Cherise had mentioned it, he'd forgotten the late night longings he'd once articulated to an orphan girl who like him yearned only for the comfort of a home and a family to call her own. And perhaps to help others in similar circumstances find the same.

It hadn't been a lot to ask of the universe, but the pitch black emptiness of space had turned its cold shoulder to him and left him to fend for himself.

Oh, he'd tried to make a home and a family three different times, but each time, those homes and wives had had demands which he'd found impossible to fulfill, priorities at odds with his own, conflicts he lacked the skills to resolve. Most the marriages had ended in acrimonious divorce, two of three wives begrudging him the time away from home to earn a living the only way he knew how. Often, he'd found the homes empty of the warmth and welcome he so badly needed, welcoming he'd only found twice in his life, once when he was very young, in the arms of Cherise, and once when he was somewhat older, with Daria.

Warmth he had somehow found again when he'd returned to Cherise on Alpha Tuscana.

He looked over his shoulder toward Misty, grateful she'd brought him on this journey, grateful she'd insisted he bring her to Torgas Prime. "Thank you," he said, quietly.

"Thank you, Jack," Misty said.

Jack nodded, blinking away the blurriness in his eyes. He hoped she wouldn't miss him when she was princess.

"I'll miss you when I'm princess."

Do I have a megaphone in my head that shouts out all my thought? he wondered.

"You have a megaphone on your face that shouts out all your thoughts," Misty said, giggling.

Another reason he could never be Emperor. No dissimulation, not a shred of disingenuousness. A person as open-faced as he was could be manipulated easily, forged to the will of those more crafty and less scrupled.

"Can I come to visit?"

Misty nodded, smiling. "I still think you're being unwise. There's a reason the cube chose you to be Emperor, and you're not as easily swayed as you think."

"With all due respect, Princess Misty, I'd say it's rather difficult for a nine-year-old to imagine the degree of duplicity or the depth of depravity among those who crave power."

"Maybe," she said. "With all due respect, Emperor Jack, I'd say it's rather difficult for a man accustomed to abandonment and rejection to embrace the purity and innocence inside his own soul, particularly one who's had so few chances to express that."

He didn't believe her for a moment, looking at her for the least sign of mockery.

The classic lines of her face held the sincerity of ancient philosophers.

"Somehow," Cherise said, "you've managed to become a decent person in spite of insurmountable obstacles and a complete absence of allies."

I'm such a scoundrel, he told himself, not believing either of them, incredulity of his face.

"What's the matter with him?" Misty asked.

"An incurable case of self-deception, perhaps." Cherise reached across the console and brought his hand to her lips. "If only you could see yourself through another's eyes."

He snorted dismissively and turned his attention to the controls.

The cube on the console showed his ugly mug on its sides.

"Vulpecula Salacia," Jack said.

"Setting course for Vulpecula Salacia," the ship responded. "Course plotted. Engage?"

"Engage."

* * *

"What's down there?" Cherise asked.

"You'll see." Jack requested permission to land from the Spaceport Authority.

Below them, hot rings of fire encircled lush, green continents and rimmed blue-gray seas as shiny as mirrors. The vegetation on Vulpecula Salacia III had adapted to the volcanic climate in a way rarely seen elsewhere. Chemolithotrophs had developed the ability to siphon sulfur and its poisonous variants—the sulfetes, sulfites, and sulfodes—and had proliferated on the highly volcanic planet, turning an otherwise unlivable hellhole into a tropical paradise.

The stench of rotten eggs pervaded the place.

Across the eons, the fine particulate filtering ability of the chemolithotrophs had left behind large deposits of silicates, and where those deposits had escaped metamorphic pressures, beds of clay had accreted, clay so fine and pure that it could be fired in layers thin enough to be transparent. Impervious to heat, these ceramics were utilized throughout the Empire for a variety of industrial purposes. Tableware from Vulpecula Salacia was in such high demand that it could hardly be obtained, but once it was obtained, it lasted forever, never chipping, breaking, nor succumbing to temperature stresses, the repeated heating and cooling that eventually led to the weakening of most materials.

Navigational beacons guided the Quasar to a greenbelt forty degrees north of the equator, a region Jack knew to be almost unbearably humid and tropical. Along the coastlines of this continent, volcanos belched ceaselessly, but their ash plumes fell almost immediately to the ground, intact. Airborne chemolithotrophs—themselves as heat-resistant as the ceramics manufactured in such abundance here—

bound with the volcanic ejecta almost immediately upon its departure from the vents.

The Quasar dropped like a stone between turgid fountains of glowing ash and rock, plasmas of fire dancing around them like demons. Jack couldn't imagine trying to navigate between the multiple volcano plumes, the ship's course plotted and controlled from the ground, a course that changed as necessary, as the plumes themselves changed with prevailing winds.

"You should see this place at night," Jack told the other two.

Both of them wide-eyed and sweating, they looked as if they had no interest at all in seeing it during the day.

Their landing pad, one amongst thousands, was a small square of tarmac barely larger than the ship's footprint. Jack was somewhat surprised that the authorities let anyone land, some planets requiring everyone to dock their vehicles at orbital stations and use shuttles to get groundside. Vulpecula Salacia had less habitable land than most planets with livable climes.

Jack looked among the yachts around the Quasar. Bentleys, Jaguars, Porsches—a veritable concours d'Elegance of vehicles. The glitterati in Maseratis flocked here for both the fine ceramics and the tropical delights, volcanic tourism in vogue.

Exactly what Jack was looking for.

* * *

Their hotel suite was a significant distance to the north at the peak of the continent where three tectonic planets collided, where a chemolithotroph-enhanced jungle thrust its greedy leaves high to grasp the last bit of sun and sulfur-laden air, where stasis fields stabilized soaring hotel towers, built above a mantle so unstable that earthquakes scaling ten plus on the Pictor scale were a daily occurrence, and where volcanic plumes hurled their hellish vomit skywards on three sides. The skies were so full of soot they could not be navigated with any known craft.

One cone stood silent, not even smoke issuing from its caldera.

Their tram rocketed into the city on a stasis-field suspended tube, the ground too unstable for a road, the air too thick with particulates for a hover craft.

The moment Jack disembarked from the tram, the tectonic activity was unmistakable. The ground shook under his feet constantly, a dull, teeth-rattling rumble.

"You'll get accustomed to it," their taxi driver said, loading their bags onto an odd-looking ground vehicle. Sporting four large, round, rubber tori, two on each pair of axles, a noisy, smelly engine rumbled fitfully and spewed noxious, oily, gray smoke. The vehicle looked too fragile to get them anywhere. Further, the roads leading away from the tram station looked like puzzles that had once been assembled but then had been thrown haphazardly back in the box, many of the pieces canted out of place at various angles.

The vehicle took the puzzle-piece roads with surprising equanimity, the large balloon-like tori climbing right over chunks of displaced roadway.

It pulled to a stop under their hotel, a massive column of steel and glass whose base was linked to the ground only by conduits of coolant necessary to keep its occupants in comfort. The structure did not actually touch the ground, suspended by stasis fields a few hundred feet above the jungle canopy. Even here, this far north, the humidity was oppressive, and the pervasive smell of rotten eggs permeated everything.

"Who farted?" Misty asked.

"The planet itself," Jack replied, smiling, the smell worse here than at the spaceport. Soon they and their luggage were climbing up the hotel side in a glasma-enclosed platform, belching volcanoes occupying all one hundred eight degrees of their view. One cone stood silent.

"We came here to see those?" Misty looked bewildered.

"Sort of," Jack said. "You'll see."

Cherise glanced askance at him, also looking bewildered.

* * *

Cerasma tubes formed a perimeter just inside the ring of volcanoes. Made of the same heat-impervious ceramic for which Vulpecula Salacia was famous, the cerasma tubes carried ferries full tourists to and around the volcanoes, the four-hundred mile tour itself taking an entire day, at minimum. Side tours at the largest volcanos might themselves take an entire day, spider webs of smaller, walking tubes catacombing the three largest volcanoes among the twenty-five that ringed this northern cape.

Jack followed one plume, tracing it from its caldera, where the ejecta column launched into the sky, where it plateaued and began to spread, then narrowed again as it turned white, as though cooling somewhat, then formed a tail which dropped from the plateau to the jungle below, the tail like a chute or a hose, propelled side to side by the force of what it ejected, leaving everything in its wake coated with a fine grit of ash, nutrient rich and ready for absorption, a constant cloud of it billowing around the point of impact, miles away from the caldera that had spewed it into the sky.

"The cerasma wall is just a quarter-inch thick," their guide was telling them as their ferry trundled along, taking them toward the first of the six volcanoes on their itinerary today.

Nervous tourists clad with cameras and already sporting Vulpecula memorabilia glanced apprehensively amongst themselves, wondering if such an insubstantial barrier were adequate to protect them.

"When we get closer to the columns of ejecta, additional outer cerasma tubes will be added, and special cooling systems designed for these extreme environs will help to keep us comfortable in spite of the thousand-degree-plus temperatures just inches away."

A brisk wind funneled through the open-top ferry, as much to oxygenate as to ventilate, Jack able to see several similar ferries as intervals both ahead and behind them.

Ahead, through the cerasma distortion, Jack saw the dormant cone he'd seen on arrival.

"We have a special treat today for everyone," their guide said. "One of our cinder cones has gone silent, and has just today been deemed safe by park management for tours. Already, cerasma tubes are being lowered into place, and we'll have the opportunity to walk down into a caldera."

"You mean nothing between us and that?!" Misty asked, pointing to the ejecta column adjacent to their trolley.

Jack squinted toward the pulsating pillar of molten mush belching into the sky. At least a quarter mile away, the width alone was overwhelming to apprehend, and Jack hadn't even looked up to see the plume traveling miles into the sky.

Near the column was a mist that seemed to form right at the base, where the ejecta left its funnel, a mist that was sucked immediately into the vortex created by the high-speed ejecta rocketing skyward.

"To the ferry's right is the spout whose geologic age makes it a comparative youngster. Pliny the Younger we call it, for its similarity to the eldest cone in this chain. The light fog that you see gathering at the vortex where the ejecta leaves the spout isn't a fog at all, folks, but a colony of chemolithotrophs, those microscopic creatures who metabolize the sulphs and make Vulpecula Salacia livable for us. In that colony alone are an estimated one quadrillion chemolithotrophs, whose life cycle still is not completely understood, but whose breeding depends on the chemicals first released there, at the vortex of cinder cone and ejecta, a class of molecules called sulfodes."

"Are you on vacation?" a woman of advanced years asked Cherise from across the aisle. Beside her was a man of similar years, one of his eyes having that permanent droopy wetness indicative of declining health.

Cherise nodded and introduced herself.

"So nice to see a family on vacation," she said. "We have two children about your age, both with families." She turned her adorning eyes on Misty. "And I have a granddaughter about your age. You're what? Nine or ten years old?"

Misty nodded bashfully.

"You've got a face of a princess."

"I am a princess," she said.

Jack nearly panicked, looking around for anyone who might have overheard. Imperial spies could be anywhere. He was hoping that as public a place as the volcanoes of Vulpecula Salacia was the absolute last place they would think of looking for him.

Cherise had put a hand on Misty's arm.

"So cute, your daughter," the old woman said, "reminds me of my own at that age." Then she said in a loud stage whisper, "They all should think they're princesses, shouldn't they?"

Misty glanced between them, looking either amused of offended or trying to decide which, while Jack sighed in relief.

He knew what she wanted to say, which was, "And I would be princess if Jack would just agree to be Emperor, humph!"

"And I would be princess if –"

Jack shushed her. "Not here, not now."

She looked crushed. "All right." She bit her lower lip and dropped her gaze to her lap.

He really disliked rebuffing her, and could see her feelings were hurt. Pulling her to him, he put his arm around her. Her head buried in his shoulder, they watched the passing cinder cone giants, their tour guide droning on about chemolithotrophs.

"Such a cute family," the old woman murmured from across the aisle.

* * *

Just after lunch, they arrived at the quiescent cinder cone, the one that had ceased erupting five days before. Seismic readings indicated no imminent eruptions, according to their tour guide, "and therefore it's completely safe."

As safe as an Emperor who sees treachery in every nuance, Jack thought.

Lunch had been cacophonous affair at a pavilion suspended between two belching calderas. Volcano-fried steak and volcano-grilled potatoes had been served, unique only in that they'd been cooked in the heat belching forth from the planetary core and seasoned with sulfur. "Fine source of minerals," the menu had proclaimed.

Misty had been delighted.

Watching her now, as their ferry docked at an unloading platform across from another tour just departing, Jack wondered how she'd respond. He'd found himself intrigued and delighted with her responses thus far, her awe and excitement infectious.

At one cone, the cerasma tube approached an ejecta column within fifty yards, the column a solid wall of volcanic blow—lava, steam, smoke, ash, and magma—rushing upward at unbelievable speed. Three layers of cerasma protected them from the heat, as high as 2900 degrees Fahrenheit (higher than that would vaporize the rock, their guide told them). Between them and the pyroclastic column hovered a cloud of chemolithotrophs.

Misty had seemed fascinated with the concept that a creature could not only survive in such an environment, but thrive. In addition, their ability to wrestle such incomprehensible power as contained in a volcanic plume, and tame the wild magma to their own purpose amazed her. All by a creature who at the individual level could not be seen by the unaided human eye. It defied comprehension.

Jack admired the girl. She had seemed to rebound almost instantly from his earlier rebuke. He wished he had that kind of resilience. Even at her age, Jack had found himself deep in despair for days on end after some slight, even ones he'd later discovered he'd imagined. Predisposed already to dwelling on a topic, Jack had been frequently called morose by the adults around him. It was only much later, after he'd run away from the brothel and got himself a berth on a garbage scow that he'd learned it might have saved him from a lifetime of employment as an escort. His irredeemably ugly face wasn't necessarily a deterrent to his entering the trade, as sometimes a sunny disposition might overcome a lack of physical attractiveness. But the combination of a sour disposition and an ugly face had practically guaranteed he wouldn't be considered for the pleasure trades. Madame Mariposa had attempted on a few occasions to cajole a smile from him, but had been so remarkably unsuccessful that she'd quickly relegated him to kitchen and grounds-keeping duties.

Misty was quite the opposite.

"What?" she'd said, looking abashed, a fry perched at the tips of her fingers, about to be plunged into her mouth. "What did I do now?"

He'd smiled and shaken his head. "Nothing except be yourself. I want you to know how much I admire the joy you find in almost everything around you."

She'd giggled and smiled. "I can't wait to get down into a caldera. Our guide did say we'd be going into one, didn't she?"

Jack'd nodded. "I'm excited too." He hadn't let himself think why.

Hand in hand with Misty, Cherise a few steps behind them, Jack walked down the long, sloping cerasma tube toward the sere landscape of the recently-quiescent volcano.

"As you'll see, even in this harsh environment," their guide said, "sprouts are already growing from an area that just days ago was a pyroclastic flow."

A thin green coat of fuzz covered the blasted ground, which Jack had thought a byproduct of the sulfodes.

The tube brought them to a platform which arced out over the vent, a waist-high railing separating the tourists from a plunge into the abyss. Around them, cameras whirred and clicked, Jack feeling somewhat naked without this standard tourist accessory.

The three of them walked out to the end, a point directly above the bubbling cauldron of newly-quiescent lava. The roiling surface looking anything but quiescent.

Cherise and Misty to his left, Jack leaned over the railing.

"Hey, not too far," Cherise said.

Jack grinned at her, the hot, viscous mud burbling discontentedly below them. "How hot do you think that is?"

"Hot enough to melt anything we know about," Misty said, eyes fixed to the turbulent liquid rock some eighty feet below.

"Anything?" he asked.

"Anything," she replied, nodding emphatically.

He reached into his pocket, pulled out the cube, and hurled it into the lava, where it disappeared with a small splash.

Vertigo seized Jack, reality warping around his head. He grasped the railing and thrust himself back, nausea roiling his lunch.

Cherise gasped.

He glanced at her, was surprised to find her gaze on the lava below, where the cube had disappeared, a look of shock and dismay on her face.

Where'd Misty go? he wondered.

"I'm right here," she said, stepping from behind him, her hand on the small of his back. "Are you all right?" Her face was turned up toward his, full of concern.

"You do look a little green," Cherise said, her face full of wonder. "I'm flabbergasted you did that, Jack, and I'm proud of you." She stepped to his side and kissed his cheek, Misty pressed between them.

Jack held onto them, looking at the increasingly active surface below them, shocked at what he'd just done, but knowing he'd planned it. He supposed the duality of mind necessary to plan such an act and to keep it secret even from himself was a skill he'd honed after years of being addicted to the smoke. One part of his brain had constantly planned his next episode of smoke-drenched delirium, while the rest of his brain had gone about his usual daily activities.

"What's the matter? Why are you crying?"

Soft sobs shook him, and he didn't know why. He felt as if he'd thrown away his dreams. He hadn't really hoped to become Emperor, had he? How ludicrous. Loser Jack Carson, orphaned who knows when, reared in a brothel, runaway on a garbage scow, triple divorced and quadruple bankrupt, and more petty offenses on his record than excrement had maggots, Jack couldn't imagine what he'd been thinking. He'd done the Empire a favor to spare it his stewardship!

So why was he crying?

"Evacuate! Evacuate!" their guide yelled. The mountain rumbled ominously below them. "Seismic readings are spiking! She's about to blow! Evacuate! Evacuate!"

Jack pushed Cherise and Misty ahead of him, and the three of them ran for the tube. They hadn't felt the rumbling, the platform suspended about the caldera by a stasis field. It sure didn't look stable, Jack thought. The smell of the sulfur became an overpowering stench, one that clotted the nostrils.

Halfway to the tube, running as fast as he could, he realized he couldn't breathe.

Misty and Cherise both had their hands to their throats.

Weariness washed over Jack. It wasn't just sulfur fumes, it was also carbon monoxide!

All three of them stumbled fifty feet from safety.

We'll never make it, Jack thought, his vision clouding. Inanely, he wished he'd never thrown the cube away. He pushed the thought aside and held onto Cherise and Misty, darkness closing in on him. The only two people who'd ever loved him ... it seemed right and good that he should die with them.

A cloud enveloped them, the mist so thick that it soaked their clothes, and Jack snapped his eyes open, suddenly alert again. He could breathe, although it felt humid.

"Come on," he said, peering through the mist. He pulled the other two to their feet and urged them on. He couldn't see the tube entrance but he knew it was there.

They stumbled along the platform, the side railings keeping them from plummeting into the percolating brew below.

"There they are," Jack heard, and hands grabbed them. And pulled them forward. Jack stumbled and fell onto a smooth-as-glass surface.

They'd made it! The cerasma cold on his cheek, Jack watched licks of lava lurch from the pool below. The tube itself began to move, retracting from the caldera.

A surge of lava leaped upward and engulfed the platform that the tourists had just vacated. Slugs of slag crumbled into the hungry maw.

The last of the mist dissipated from around him. The three of them were surrounded by other members of their tour, including the nice elderly couple.

"You made it!" the old woman beamed. "I can't believe you made it! We thought for sure you were gone, and then those chemo things swarmed around you. It's a miracle!"

The Mist! Must have been the chemolithotrophs, Jack thought, the flying bacteria able to breakdown the lava and release the oxygen.

He checked Cherise and Misty, saw that they were all right.

Winded and scared, but all right.

"Let's get you to a hospital, just in case," their guide insisted.

At first, Jack objected, but then he relented. "But we go together, all three of us."

He held onto Misty and Cherise all the way to the infirmary.

Chapter 15

"She saw it with her own eyes, your August Highness!" Prime Minister Custos Messium bowed his head to hide his disquietude. "And surveillance cameras also verified he threw something into the caldera, an object very nearly what you described." What other proof does he want that it was destroyed, its very cinders? he wondered.

The Emperor had grown increasingly paranoid of late.

"Your August Highness," Custos said, "perhaps I may better assist if I knew your concern in more detail." He gave a small bow, as the Emperor had been more fickle of late, more arbitrary.

"No, you may not ask. Spies and cameras are sometimes unreliable. I want proof! Bring be its very cinders if you can!"

Custos glanced at the scepter. He'd long known that it was the source of the Emperor's power—the power to see anything anywhere in the universe, and the power to influence people to his causes, even against their will.

What he hadn't known was that another just like it existed, had been found on the planet Canis Dogma Five, the former Capital of the Circian Empire, whose fall had preceded the rise of the Torgassan Empire by some fifteen hundred years.

Had been found by a luckless scavenger who couldn't maintain a marriage, keep himself out of hock, or even keep ahead of the law. A feckless fool who'd duped an antiquities dealer for five million galacti with the sale of a plain, reflective cube of alien manufacture. The same feckless fool who'd bilked all the major casinos on the Vega Strip and had finally stolen nearly seventy million galacti from the Ballsy Palace Casino. The same fool who'd somehow eluded capture on Alpha Tuscana, actually escaping a high-security Imperial compound.

The same feckless fool who'd just been seen hurling that cube into the caldera of an active volcano.

And if one other exists, Prime Minister Custos Messium thought, then perhaps there's a third or even a fourth. It had long been a mystery how the Circians had held the entire galaxy under their sway for almost two millennia while the Torgassans had been unable to extend their influence beyond the galactic bar. Only a quarter the size of its predecessor, the Torgassan Empire constantly chafed that they seemed doomed to the shadows of the once-great Empire that had gone before.

Salt on the wound. A decubitus of the soul.

And now to find out there'd been another cube all along.

Dismayed, Custos was careful to keep the emotion off his face. "One slight difficulty with the latter request, your August Highness. The volcano which had been dormant for five days began erupting again, and in fact, almost killed this scavenger and his family. Not possible to recover the ashes of this artifact, sorry to say."

"Well then, we don't know it's destroyed, do we?"

It was not the royal "we." He specifically means me, Custos knew. "No, your August Highness," he replied dryly, "we don't."

He didn't begrudge the Emperor his stubborn refusal to believe that the scavenger had destroyed the cube, after all—

"There was that antiquities dealer, who was convinced this scavenger somehow spirited it away from him from under his very nose," the Emperor said.

Custos had long since grown accustomed to the Emperor's filching his every thought. The Prime Minister was mystified he hadn't been eliminated long ago, some of those thoughts bordering on perfidy. But he hadn't navigated the Imperial whim across forty years and two successive Emperors because he was blindly loyal.

He'd done it because he was effective.

"If I may suggest, your August Highness?"

The Emperor looked up suddenly, as thought he'd been deep in thought. "What is it, Lord Messium?"

"Whatever the events on Vulpecula Salacia, whether he destroyed the cube or not, it would behoove us to insure he did not employ some fantastical prestidigitation, as it appears he did on Alpha Tuscana. And the Vega Strip. And Denebi III. In fact, we would be prudent to insure that this scavenger never finds another cube again, your August Highness."

"We would be prudent, yes," the Emperor said. "Make it so."

Custos smiled, knowing that this kind of efficacy was precisely what the Emperor desired of him.

About to bow and take his leave, Prime Minister Custos Messium paused, feeling his palmcom vibrate in his pocket.

It wouldn't vibrate during an audience with the Emperor unless it were really important. He read the message and smiled. "Good news, your August Highness. Our recently acquired source confirms events on Vulpecula Salacia."

"The source you told me about just yesterday?"

"Indeed, your August Highness, the one whose veracity is unassailable."

Tension visibly left the Emperor, and a slight smile emerged. "Well, then, perhaps that final step won't be necessary."

"Perhaps, your August Highness." Custos said. But rather than taking his leave, he waited.

Knowing he was clear about what needed to happen.

"You still think it prudent, however."

"I do, your August Highness," Custos said, bowing and backing from the chamber.

* * *

Brewster stared at Prime Minister Custos Messium and knew what she was being ordered to do.

Scott Michael Decker

She also knew what it meant for her.

Detective Monique Brewster wasn't under any illusion that this hadn't been coming. The moment she'd been summoned to the Imperial Capital, Torgas Prime, she'd known that this was her fate. To some extent, she welcomed it. The worst part was not knowing when the Imperial ax would fall, not having the wherewithal to gauge how much longer she would be of use to the Imperium.

It was all she'd ever asked for—to be of use.

But this—being under the direct orders of the Prime Minister—was far more use than she could ever have hoped for. A life well-lived was a useful one, she'd always believed, and the Imperial Bureaucracy, like every government before it, sought at all costs to preserve itself primarily, and secondarily to provide for the needs of its citizens.

Which was why Brewster knew that she'd be eliminated the moment she'd eliminated the scavenger. Her killing him made her a liability to the government, a liability that had to be eliminated.

"What about the recently acquired source?" she asked. If it were disclosed how Brewster had leveraged the source, the headlines might not reflect well on the Imperium.

"Yes, well, it would be the most efficient disposal," the Prime Minister said dryly, coughing once.

Brewster wished he'd just say it. She knew she was out of her league, that the subtleties of communication at these rarified levels of the bureaucracy left her gasping for meaning, the air that they breathed composed exclusively of plausible deniability.

Brewster breathed concrete, pure and simple. Tell me what to do and get out of my way while I do it, she thought, disinclined to use nuance and even less receptive to it.

He wants the inside source eliminated, she divined.

And if he didn't, he could always deny he'd told her that.

"What about the other one?" Blunt, like a bludgeon, Brewster knew she made the Prime Minister squirm. She wasn't some bureaucrat he could consign to the bowels of a distant archive housed several thousand feet beneath an inhospitable planet surface, as much a symbolic as a literal burial. No, she was dangerous, and he knew it. She knew he knew it and knew he'd see to her elimination once she'd completed the job.

"Other one?" Messium asked, looking mystified for a moment. "Oh, yes, the innocent one. Well, as they say, innocence exculpates."

"Huh?" Blunt described Monique in many ways, her vocabulary among them.

"The answer was no," the Prime Minister said, looking around as though for the door.

She could take a hint. "Very well, Lord Minister. I'll have your results soon." She wanted to summarize what was instructed, but sensed he'd have none of it. Precisely the specificity he wanted to avoid. They were, after all, at the Hall of Justice on Torgas Prime. The Capital.

She nodded and bowed to him, and watched him leave.

The interview room was pleasant if spare, vague pastels to the furniture which might match any other furniture vaguely pastel in color. A serving cart to one side, two pitchers on it, cups, implements, condiments. Four chairs around a low table.

She pulled the stiff blue suit away from her neck, hating having to wear it. An escort would arrive momentarily to guide her from the building.

An escort had greeted her when she arrived. The escort had brought her here and asked her to wait for her host, no indication given that the escort knew who she was meeting with.

The blue suit, the escorts, the waiting, all part of the machinery. Not that she couldn't have left the building the same way she'd come in, but that a visitor wandering a secure building was both compromising and in bad taste.

It wasn't that she didn't understand, which others might suspect from her stoic demeanor and blunt persona. She just didn't have any use for it. She'd have gone berserk long ago if she'd had to work in such an environment, needing her feet on the ground and her hands on a suspect. A suspect's neck, if possible.

There was a certain thrill and satisfaction in both.

The escort was the same person who'd brought her into the building, a young man whose eyes saw everything and whose face gave away nothing.

"This way, please." He wasn't incordial, impolite, or insouciant, but simply uncommunicative. As he guided her from the building, down seventeen floors, past ten checkpoints, across three foyers, and through a gigantic waiting room—government buildings all had to have waiting rooms—he didn't inquire as to her business nor even how it had gone, he didn't ask after her wellbeing or as to the weather, and he made no mention of the uprisings in progress at two places on the periphery.

"Wait here, please," "Through here, please," "Step up to the scanner, please," "Speak your name slowly and clearly, please." Instructions precise but pleasant. Having hints of an oft-repeated tone but tinged with a consideration that his escortee had likely never heard them before. Not a hint that what he was doing was boring, superfluous, or unnecessary in any way.

Until they reached the main lobby, a four-story, glass-walled, marble-floored mausoleum intended concurrently to crush any vestige of human spirit and declare the absolute hegemony of the Torgassan Imperiosity. Diamond slabs of marble tessellated the floor in all directions, interrupted by but a single pillar. Diamond sheets of mirror tessellated the ceiling similarly. A central pillar of elevators was all that interrupted these parallel planes of impersonality.

"Have arrangements for all your comforts been made for your evening on Torgas Prime?" the escort asked quietly over his shoulder.

It was the longest sequence of words she'd heard from him, ascending or descending. She was caught off guard by their profusion. Then she assembled their meaning, and she was shocked. "Only the early evening. Later comforts are still lacking."

He extended a comcube. "Completely discreet, of course."

She took it, grateful. "Of course. Obliged."

"My pleasure." No hint of it in his voice, just simple information.

She looked around the dolorous lobby, at the numerous bureaucrats going multiple directions. It was unlikely that anyone had overheard, and would have been quite difficult to monitor, the cavern an echo chamber. Intentionally so.

They were the last words he spoke to her before she left the building.

She didn't ask if he'd been prompted to offer, and she wondered who'd originated the idea.

Probably the Prime Minister Custos Messium himself.

The more she thought about it, the more convinced she was that he had.

* * *

"More them likely, it was the chemolithotrophs that saved you," the doctor said.

Jack, Misty, and Cherise exchanged glances, none of them having realized how close to death they'd come.

"The volcanic gasses are noxious, certainly, but it's specifically the carbon monoxide that's lethal. It's colorless and odorless. It binds with the available oxygen in the air until there's nothing to breathe. For a person in an enclosed environment, such as a room, an increasing lassitude sets in, followed by somnolence, and then sleep, quickly followed by unconsciousness and death. Fortunately, calderas emit other gasses along with carbon monoxide, alerting you to their presence. What drew the chemolithotrophs was the presence of sulfodes."

The doctor shook her head. "We get one or two cases similar to yours nearly every time a volcano goes dormant. I've been trying to get the tour companies to put in gas detection sensors for years. You'll find you're a bit logy for a few days while the residues dissipate, but there'll be no lasting effects. If you have continued fatigue for longer than a week, please see your physicians. Enjoy the rest of your stay." The doctor shook hands with each of them and left the room, consulting her palmcom before she'd reached the door.

Jack looked over at Misty, then at Cherise. The room was crowded with three hospital beds, but they'd insisted. "I guess I could have done that while you weren't there," Jack told them.

"Why are you saying that?" Misty asked. "You think the cube caused the volcano to erupt?"

Jack nodded, frowning. "I put you both in danger, and that was wrong of me." He pulled at his hospital gown and smirked, wondering where his clothes were.

"Doesn't seem like it could do that," Cherise said.

"Besides," Misty said, "you didn't even know the other part of your brain was going to do that until right then."

He smiled, finding comfort in the fact that she knew him so well. He located his clothes. "I'm getting dressed. I'd like to get out of here." He pulled his wraparound curtain closed.

From beyond came the sounds of their getting dressed. "Where are we going, Jack?"

He was still thinking when they'd finished dressing and had signed all the hospital discharge papers, collected all their belongings, and were out the door.

He was silent all the way to the hotel, the night sky pale with the light of both erupting volcanos and the plant's lunary, an orb half the size of Vulpecula Salacia itself, which contributed to the instability of the planet's crust.

"You just want to go, don't you?" Cherise asked, looking around their hotel suite.

Jack nodded.

The tube-shuttle ride across the moon-lit planet was roller-coaster past hundreds of volcano spouts, liquid fire pouring from each like hoses.

"Where are we going?" Misty asked.

Jack frowned and shook his head. "Someplace we can hide, while we get you ready for your Imperial presentation."

"And what then, Jack?" Misty asked. "What will you do?"

He looked over at her, having heard the catch in her voice. It was a long ride to the spaceport near the equator.

She was blinking tears from her eyes.

Jack blinked them from his own. "I don't know, Misty. All I do know is that you and Cherise are the only family I've ever known, and I'll feel terribly sad when I leave you on Torgas."

She came over and sat beside him and put her head against his shoulder. "I'll miss you terribly, too."

Jack saw Cherise wiping a tear from her eye.

"You wouldn't consider a position in my administration, would you?"

He chuckled and shook his head. "Chief Sanitation Engineer? I don't think so."

"Not even Chief Garbage Collector?" Cherise asked.

They all three shared a laugh, and Jack bent to kiss the girl's hair.

"What if I wanted you to be my regent?" Misty asked.

Jack liked how close she was, the warmth and glow of her fine-boned face near his, the twinkle in her eye like magic fairy dust on his soul. "Regent? You mean rule the Empire for you until you're old enough?"

Misty nodded.

"I remember a boy I knew when I was young," Cherise said, "who talked for long hours deep into the night how he dreamed one day of all the things he would do when he became Emperor, of the great navies he would muster and the huge battles he'd fight as he spread his influence to the far corners of the galaxy, of the distant places he'd explore and the great engines of manufacturing he'd build, and how he'd provide every family with enough to eat and every child with all the clothes he or she wanted and a safe place to live and a family to live with.

"I remember a boy who wept with the determination to give to everyone all those important things that had been missing from his life, and from mine.

"I remember that boy," Cherise said, "and how much I loved him, for his generosity, for his compassion, and for his determination. I loved him then and I love him now for the wonderful person he is. I'm glad you threw away that cube, Jack, so that we can be together, just us, ourselves. It wouldn't have been the same if you'd been Emperor. Thank you, Jack."

The multiple, erupting volcanoes were blurred by the memories of deprivation that spilled down Jack's cheeks. He held Cherise to him for the rest of the ride, Misty snuggled between them.

He'd remembered to com ahead, so the Quasar was fueled and ready for departure. Jack paid the dock fees and loaded their luggage, and then they boarded.

On the dash sat the cube.

All he could do was stare at it. Over and over in his mind, he played the scene back to himself, suddenly reaching into his pocket, grabbing the cube, and hurling it into the caldera, where it splashed into the lava, a lick of molten goop arcing up at the impact. Jack could feel Misty's and Cherise's gazes upon him.

He couldn't comprehend its being here.

The human mind was flexible if nothing else, in both active and reactive ways. Even when confronted with enormities that appeared beyond apprehension, such as an erupting volcano, its ejecta column but inches away, or the universe in its sixteen-billion-year entirety, more galaxies in the universe than the stars in the Milky Way, the mind somehow found a way to accept and to cope.

But not with this. How am I supposed to understand this? Jack wondered.

You're not, said that other part of his mind, the one that had plotted his getting rid of it, the one that arranged for his smokeouts without his knowing it, the one that operated just below the level of consciousness, occasionally poking its little self up above the blue event horizon of awareness to alert him to the nasty things it had been up to. His savior and his nemesis.

Don't even try, that other part of his mind told him. Don't let it bother you. It's not worth it.

He reached for the com and requested permission to lift off.

Cherise and Misty scrambled for their seats as Jack stepped through the preflight checklist.

The cube stared at them, quiescent.

Just like the volcano, Jack thought.

Permission was granted and Jack launched the Quasar.

"Uh, Jack?" Misty asked.

He looked over his shoulder at her, her seat behind and in between his and Cherise's. "Yes?"

"Where are we going?"

He smiled. "You know where. You know me far too well, Misty. You tell me where we're going."

"The Imperial Capital, Torgas Prime."

"And why is that, Princess Misty?"

"Not because you promised to take me there!" She stuck out her lower lip. "What you're thinking is, 'If I can't throw it away, maybe I can give it away—to the Emperor himself.' "

* * *

Brewster felt the gush inside her and a spasm seized her too. She threw her head back in ecstasy and slammed slammed slammed her hips into his, pulled back a ham-sized hand, and with her next spasm, brought it across like the bludgeon it was, and smashed his face.

He went limp at the dull pop from his neck.

Which excited her more and she continued to buck above him until her spasms subsided, and she fell across the corpse, her breathing rough from exertion.

Beside the bed, her palmcom went off.

A message alerting her that her quarry had left Vulpecula Salacia.

She was off the bed and into her clothes with nary a thought. She took the stairs five at a time and had hailed a taxi for the spaceport, excitement of different kind now pumping through her veins.

Chapter 16

The scene filled his sight and the voice rang in his ears.

He was in a cavern, and a man stood before him, dressed in sequined silks of multiple colors, upon his head a slim, simple circlet and in one hand a silvery, two-inch cube.

"I am Lochium Circi the Ninth, Emperor of Circi, a civilization that once reached to the outer arms of the galaxy." Behind the figure was a small table, on it a vial filled with orange fluid, and a large stone slab set a foot off the ground. "Welcome to my final resting place, Traveler. You have now been selected for a sacred duty. You see me now because you have been chosen.

"With this cube," Lochium Circi the Ninth said gravely, holding up the silvery, two-inch cube, "the Circians spread their influence throughout the galaxy."

A remote rumble shook the chamber, and dust drifted down from the ceiling. "And now our influence is dying. Barbarians bombard Canis Dogma Five into oblivion as I speak.

"You, Traveler, have now been chosen to become the next Emperor of the Circian Empire, with all the privileges, responsibilities, and obligations thereto implied, and to bring together again all the remnants of our once-great Empire under the auspices of one government, to live peacefully until the end of time under you and your successors.

"The cube has chosen you, Traveler, because you are worthy and noble and pure. May the stars light your path with brilliance."

* * *

Jack stared out the viewport of the Quantum as though he might discern their destination from the void around it. In the copilot's chair sat Misty, sleeping fitfully, and behind them both, snoring softly, was Cherise.

He shook his head, still disbelieving. Every fiber of his being screamed at him that this was a mistake, that he should turn the ship around and head the other direction and put as much distance between them and their destination as he could.

The cube had told him he would be the Emperor, an idea still as incomprehensible as it was ludicrous. An idea that fit him with the comfort of an iron fist—shoved into his back passage.

An idea that hadn't changed from the moment he'd first touched the cube some three months ago. The one reason he'd not gone about living his desultory life was Misty's insisting he take her to Torgas Prime so she could be princess.

And not just any princess, but Princess Misty Circi.

The Circians hadn't ruled in two millennia. By what logic or right or heavenly mandate did she think she could just go to Torgas and depose Emperor Phaeton from a throne that his family had occupied for five hundred years?

Because the cube had told Jack he'd be Emperor? And that he would naturally adopt her and make her his princess?

Jack glanced over at Misty.

The relaxed pose softened the classic lines of her face. The imperious manner was nowhere in evidence as she slept.

He looked at the cube on the console, where he habitually placed it when piloting a vessel.

The dull silvery cube stared back at him, quiescent.

It had exhorted him to become Emperor through the recording of the last Circian Emperor, Lochium the Ninth. Then it had stymied his every effort to rid himself of it.

As had the girl.

He looked at her again, unable to fathom the faith she had placed in him.

He looked at the cube again, unable to fathom the faith it had placed in him.

The feeling of déjà vu seized him, and Jack didn't know why. A shiver shook him from tailbone to neck, and his skin crawled.

He sighed and put his head down.

All of it had seemed so farcical—or would have if his life hadn't been in danger. The Imperial patrols he'd evaded, the gaming gangsters he'd escaped from, the Imperial compound he'd slipped out of, the freighter that'd been blown from under his feet, the volcano that had nearly annihilated him.

All of it farcical. And yet entirely consistent.

Jack's life had been anything but consistent. Orphaned at an early age, taken in at a brothel, running away on a garbage scow at age twelve, working his way into the ownership of his own Scavenger vessel, marrying three times disastrously, bankrupted four times, and arrested more than both combined.

If there were some theme or meaning to the chaos he called his life, it might be noted as defiance. Defiance of his origins in coming so far, defiance of convention in living at the edge of the law, defiance of the perpetual beating that life seemed to inflict on him.

No matter how many times life had knocked him down, he'd always rolled to his feet and danced away to live another day, his spirit undaunted.

He glanced over at Misty, who in that way at least reminded him of himself. Whatever had come their way, she'd remained undaunted in her quest to reach Torgas Prime. Her grandiose delusion of becoming Princess aside, she was a lot like him.

Behind Jack, Cherise stirred.

He was glad he'd returned to the Southern Birds on Alpha Tuscana and found her. The dreams they'd shared as youths had helped him to see now that his life did have a pattern and a purpose, that he could be a part of something greater than himself, that his latent dream of making the universe a better place for those less fortunate had not been just a dream.

Misty and Cherise were with him for a reason.

Jack wiped away a tear of gratitude, something deep inside healing just a little at the thought of their devotion. Incredibly, they believed in him.

He didn't know how it'd happened, and he couldn't say why—but they did. And he could accept it. He might not believe in himself, but he could accept the fact that they did.

And somehow, so did the cube.

Which was why he was flying a course toward Torgas Prime, and not running as fast as he could the other direction.

Afraid?

Of course.

But facing his fear, as he'd always done, confronting his challenges.

Jack thought it bizarre that not long ago he'd considered his life an abysmal failure, and the path he'd taken through it to be strewn with the detritus of its hurricane, a swath of destruction that was as irreparable as it was inevitable.

Somehow, he'd learned otherwise.

Playing his trump against the casino and repaying his ex-wife the money he'd lost, and then giving back to the antiquities dealer, Delphin, the five million he'd inadvertently swindled from him. Not irreparable at all.

And certainly not inevitable.

"When I'm Emperor," he'd once said to Cherise when he was but nine years old.

Little had he known he'd been given the opportunity.

He stared at the cube. "But you knew, didn't you?"

The cube stared back at him, silent.

* * *

Returning to the spaceport on Tertius Diamond, Jack got out of the flitter taxi and stepped toward the terminal entrance.

And froze.

Brewster stood just inside, saw him, and came his way.

Jack didn't need to turn and look. He was already surrounded.

"No use in running, Jack," Brewster said, her bulldog face watchful. She stood two inches taller than he and outweighed him by at least fifty pounds. "Where's the cube?"

"Hole it, Brewster."

She signaled, and officers converged, pinning Jack's arms. Swiftly, they cuffed and searched him and found nothing. A Crown Dick flitter replaced the taxi, stripped of markings but sprouting so many antennas that it was unmistakably an undercover law enforcement vehicle.

They bundled him into the back seat, Brewster getting into the front. She half-turned as the vehicle took off. "Where's the cube, Jack?" Her voice was muffled through the glasma partition.

He laughed at her. "Really? As if anyone in his right mind doesn't know how I've tried to get rid of it?"

"Then you won't hesitate to hand it over, will you?"

"I'd be delighted to give it to Emperor Torgas, his August Highness, himself."

Brewster laughed at him. "Really? As if any ruler in his right mind would allow you on the same planet?"

"Seems we're at an impasse," Jack told her. "But we still want the same thing. Certainly gives a person something to think about, doesn't it? On, and I assume you have Cherise in custody?"

Brewster's sharp look indicated that very fact.

"You won't ever capture Princess Misty Circi, Brewster, so stop trying," he said, knowing that the source of the Detective's concern.

"So even if we do capture her, it'll be because she wants to be captured?"

"The answers to how many engineers it takes to change a light bulb," Jack quipped. "How many times do we have to play this game, Brewster? You know you can't win."

She stared at him through the plasma partition.

He pulled his hand from behind his back and held up the restraints between two fingers. He'd ghosted them into thinking they'd closed the restraints. "You can't win, Brewster." He ghosted the driver and sent the flitter off the road and into a culvert. The vehicle landed on its passenger side, trapping Brewster. His door—never fully closed—flew open, and Jack leaped out.

The multiple vehicles from their escort pulled to a stop on the road above.

Jack ghosted himself off their visual cortices and climbed back up to the road. One of the escorts vehicles—identical to the one that Jack had just wrecked—stood idling, its driver door wide open, its driver attempting to free Brewster from the wrecked vehicle.

Very kind of them, he thought, climbing in and taking off.

No one saw him leave.

He ghosted the Quasar on the tarmac. A bevy of Imperial Secret Service beefs stood around it, a bright orange boot fixed to one of its landing struts. They all stood in defensive postures, crouched and weapons drawn, looking as if they expected attack from any quarter. An unmarked Crown Dick buzzed overhead.

He ghosted the mind of the squad commander, and learned they'd taken Cherise under heavy guard to the local detention center, these Imperial compounds ubiquitous throughout the Torgassan Empire. When I'm Emperor, I'll get rid of them entirely, Jack thought, forgetting momentarily he didn't want to be Emperor.

At the compound just outside the city boundary, Jack parked his blatant undercover Crown Dick and got out.

It looked like an Imperial compound. The usual triple-layer cyclone fencing with barbed wire curls coifing its crown, the watchtowers every two hundred feet, the pole-mounted cameras as thick as a forest, and the elaborate checkpoints both inside and outside the gate, the low-brow building whose bulk was underground.

Knowing the compound similar if not identical to that on Alpha Tuscana, Jack walked in past the slack-jawed guards staring dumbly at their frantically beeping alarms. He located Cherise on level six, below ground. Ghosting a guard on that level, Jack puppeted her to open Cherise's cell and escort her up.

Jack met them in the foyer, the multiple glasma barriers between the elevator and the entrance now flung wide open in spite of the strobes and klaxons declaring their protest.

"Oh, Jack," Cherise said, throwing her arms around him.

"Are you all right? Did they hurt you?" He knew Brewster capable of torture. A single glimpse into her mind had shown him that.

"No. I'm fine. What about Misty? They kept badgering me about her. I thought she was right beside me when they converged on the Quasar, but then she was gone."

"Well, I suspect she'll be joining us soon. Come on."

They walked out of the compound together through the lights and the noise. Cherise giggled at the guards staring insensate at their berserking devices. "I'm surprised they aren't drooling," she said.

"I could throw that in just for fun," Jack said, grinning.

En route, a multivehicle motorcade of Crown Dicks roared past them the other direction, toward the compound, all their lights blazing and sirens blaring, Bulldog Brewster clutching the controls of the lead vehicle, her face fierce and determined.

Jack watched in his rearview as chaos erupted behind them, Brewster belatedly recognizing Jack in his Crown Dick. A pile up ensued as Brewster braked and all the vehicles following her swerved to avoid her.

Flying the flitter back to the spaceport, Jack ghosted the squad surrounding the Quasar. He had them remove the bright orange boot from the landing strut and attach it to one of their own vehicles.

Jack pulled onto the tarmac, activating the Quasar remotely with his palmcom, and parked the Dick as close as he could, the Quasar surrounded by other similarly unmarked Crown Dicks.

He and Cherise threaded their way through them and the several-dozen Imperial officers staring dumbly at them. The Quasar hummed in anticipation of takeoff.

Misty was already buckled into the copilot's chair. "I was wondering where you'd got off to," she said.

Jack put in a request to lift off and went through his checklist.

The ghosted space traffic controller gave Jack the go-ahead in a voice that was almost robotic.

A single Crown Dick pulled up just as the Quasar lifted off. Brewster fired a blasma cannon in their direction but her shots went wide, the Quasar already in the stratosphere.

"I think we'll be seeing more of her," Misty said, grimacing.

"Much to our dismay," Jack replied, nodding.

Chapter 17

The acquisition of the Circian Crown Jewels seemed to trigger a cascade of support. Coms poured in from across the Alpha Sector, each one with an offer of resource or materials.

"We need a cruise ship," Misty insisted. "No self-respecting princess would arrive on Torgas Prime in anything less pretentious."

Sorting through the offers, Jack found one from the Vice President of Heiress Cruise Lines, Johanna Phoenicia.

"I've got the perfect suggestion," she stated over the com. "If you're willing to work with a few negative connotations." She explained that their cruise liners were named after members of the English Royal Family from old Earth, but as they'd begun to exhaust this theme, they'd had to expand this to any ruler of England. "By virtue of its being our least popular cruise liner, it also happens to be available, and at a fraction of the usual cost."

"The Oliver Cromwell?" Misty replied indignantly. "Wasn't he some usurper?"

Jack tried to explain that there really wasn't another cruise liner of such proportions available anywhere on such short notice.

"I want the Queen Victoria!" she demanded.

Not available for another ten years.

"How about the Queen Elizabeth I?"

Extremely popular, not for another fifteen.

"And the King Henry the Eighth?"

Fully booked by philandering fraternities for the next five years.

"All right, then, but at least paint over the name."

Jack sighed, one logistical nightmare resolved. And in leasing the Oliver Cromwell from Heiress Cruise Lines, Jack was spared the onerous task of finding a crew for it.

But it was one chore on an exhaustive list of logistical tasks that Jack had no patience for and no experience in. There was the honor guard—which needed uniforms, weapons, a commander, a Royal Crest. There was the coterie of servants: chauffeurs, kneemen, legwomen, coiffeuses, coutures, stockinglasses, chaperones, equestrians, scullery maids, enderlasses, chimney sweeps, fishmongers, nannies, tinkers, tailors, soldiers, spies, nincompoops, dunces, jesters, and jokers.

"Of course, I need all that staff. A princess needs to be prepared for anything!" Misty said when Jack complained.

"But they won't all fit on the cruise liner!" he told her sarcastically. When filled, the cruise liner with its full contingent of passengers and staff would hold nearly a million people. Of course they'd all fit, but he just wanted to see her reaction.

"Then they'll just have to follow in the lifeboats," Misty declared.

The other worry constantly on Jack's mind was Brewster. When was the next attack coming? When would she try next? What would she try next? How could she not be aware of the flurry of activity taking place in orbit of Alpha Tuscana as the Imperial Menagerie of Princess Misty Circi painstakingly assembled itself?

Fortunately, the Oliver Cromwell was an optimal place to assemble such a menagerie, its numerous decks and multiple bulkheads creating easily compartmentalized societies within the hull. The expenses mounted horrifically, one of but a billion worries that Jack had to contend with, one that seemed magically to take care of itself. Nearly a week passed before Jack realized that Cherise had invited Daria aboard to handle the financial logistics of the enterprise.

The cruise liner fully stocked and all the personnel aboard, Jack commanded that the ship prepare for launch.

"Hey, wait a minute," Misty said. "You didn't ask my permission."

Jack thought ruefully how he'd run afoul of the law more times than he'd been divorced or gone bankrupt combined, but he hadn't ever really violated the law intentionally, nor ever contemplated doing so—one of the hazards of living in a law-obsessed society. Upon hearing that from Misty, however, he found himself plotting her murder.

I'll think about that later, he told himself, and promptly asked her permission.

"Granted." She grinned at him, fetching in her diamond tiara and sequined royal dress. "Now, what about you?"

"Me?" Jack asked. He'd had not a spare moment to think across the last month, and in the circumstances, he couldn't fathom what she was talking about.

"You'll accompany me when I land on Torgas Prime and escort me to the palace for the formal Imperial introduction, right, Jack?"

"I, uh, guess. I thought I was just taking you there."

"And you'd abandon me on the palace doorstep, like some orphan?" Tears welled up in her eyes.

"Well, I hadn't quite thought it through." In fact, he'd been plotting his thorough obliteration in some unseemly smoke shop somewhere far away from Torgas Prime. And what about the cube's exhortation that you become Emperor? Jack asked himself. Don't be ridiculous, he told himself. It's undignified to consider such an irrelevant idea. "If you insist, your August Highness," Jack said.

She fled, wailing disconsolately.

"What did I say?" Jack asked Cherise.

"It's what you didn't say," she told him. "Now, go find her, apologize, and tell her you'd be deeply honored to escort her to the palace and present her to the Emperor, that you can think of no higher honor than being asked by her August Highness to perform this sacred task."

This, Jack knew, was his blind spot, that place in his character that seemed to be absent, a hole in his soul that no charm school could fill, a gap that could not be remedied.

He found her and apologized and swore his fealty and begged her forgiveness for his thoughtless remarks from both knees.

In the end, she begrudgingly accepted his apology and acceded that without him, she was a waif without standing or status, and she was grateful for all he'd done, and she'd soon release him from her service once the Imperial introduction had been made.

"You're sure you don't want to be Emperor?"

Jack nodded and frowned. "I'm sure." As much as he might have pined away in his youth about his beggarly circumstances, Jack was so thoroughly unfit for such authority as to provoke more laughter than Misty's declaring she was a princess.

"Well, we have to make you something if you're going to escort me to the palace and introduce me to the Emperor."

"Captain Jack will do," he said.

"No, it won't, not grandiose enough." The she grinned at him. "How about Paladin?"

"Never heard of it."

"It means Champion, particularly in battle."

"Princess Misty Circi, arriving aboard the Usurper Oliver Cromwell, introduced to the Imperial Court by her Paladin Jack." He shook his head at her. "Guaranteed to get me killed."

"They wouldn't dare."

"What's the Emperor going to do, step off the throne and invite you to take it?"

"Of course not, Jack. You're so silly. But we have to give you a title, and Paladin it is."

* * *

"Your August Highness," Admiral Sophocles Camelus said, his tone grave, "the upstart Princess Misty Circi informs us that she is now en route with her Paladin, Captain Jack Carson. Her curseliner, the Oliver Cromwell, landed moments ago."

Emperor Phaeton Torgas looked around the room. "Curseliner?"

"Er, uh, sorry, your August Highness. My apologies for the typo."

"Does anyone here doubt she comes to claim my throne?" the Emperor asked.

No one spoke. They had been debating the issue for weeks while the cruise liner with the ironic name was being prepared openly in orbit above Alpha Tuscana. While there was general disbelief amongst them that an unarmed and unescorted cruise liner could do a smidgen of damage to Torgas Prime in a direct frontal assault, not a one of them doubted what the arrival of a rival princess meant for Torgassan rule.

Phaeton looked among his advisors, the Ministers of his various cabinets, among them the Prime Minister Custos Messium, the Chief Justice Minister, Janis Astrea, Admiral Camelus, and the Emperor's daughter, Princess Andromeda Torgas, the heir to all his domains.

"There is only one way to deal with upstarts like her! Slaughter the bitch!"

Everyone turned toward Andromeda.

Phaeton held up his hand at the multiple objections, nearly everyone aghast at the brutality of annihilating an unarmed cruise liner. Even Admiral Camelus had been shaking his head. Phaeton had noticed however that Prime Minister Custos Messium had been notably silent. "Lord Messium," Phaeton said, "your silence speaks volumes. Do share your thoughts with us."

The tall aesthete looked among his peers, then bowed to the Emperor. "It should be as her August Highness says," Messium said. "If it can be done."

"What do you mean, 'if it can be done'?" Andromeda said immediately, venom-like rebuke in her voice.

The thin face turned slowly her direction, "I mean, your August Highness, that all previous attempts to kill or capture this purported Princess and her Paladin Jack Carson have failed miserably. Yes, I agree that an immediate assault upon the cruise liner Oliver Cromwell needs to be mounted, *and* we need to be prepared for its failure."

"Our Armada will not fail!" Admiral Camelus declaimed. "Not like your sniveling clandestine agents!"

The Prime Minister sneered at the Admiral. "When the Armada fails, you'll find out how effective my clandestine agents are!"

"Stop it, both of you," Phaeton said, wanting to egg them both on to mutual blows, neither one much to his liking. They'd both been inherited from his father and both reminded him of rotten, hard-boiled eggs. "So, Prime Minister, what will we do in the unlikely event of a failure?"

"Your August Highness," Admiral Camelus interjected, "we won't fail."

Phaeton tried to contain his annoyance. "I'm sure you won't, Admiral." He turned to Messium. "But if that should happen, what then?"

"Why then, your August Highness, then we invite her August Highness Princess Misty Circi—"

"Don't call her that!" Andromeda shouted, launching herself from her chair at the Prime Minister.

"Hold!" Phaeton said.

Andromeda's dagger was inches from Messium's heart.

The Prime Minister hadn't flinched. "We invite her to Torgas Prime," he finished, as though he hadn't been interrupted.

"Next time, Messium," Phaeton said, "I'll consider it treason and I'll kill you first. Daughter, put away the knife."

Slowly, she retracted it, murder never leaving her face.

Phaeton wondered what he'd have done if she had disobeyed him. Probably thanked her for ridding him of the snake. "Invite her here to do what?"

"Forgive me, your August Highness, for not being clear. We invite her to the Palace." Messium picked a speck of invisible dust from his sleeve. "We then have multiple means at our disposal with which to attend to hers."

Phaeton made a distasteful face, as though he disliked having to take out the trash. "And an upstart who has eluded both capture and frontal naval assault will be so easy to dispose of?"

"By no means, no, your August Highness," Messium said. "She and her Paladin Jack will prove as slippery as rotting fish. But at least we'll have them in our net."

* * *

The bridge aboard the Oliver Cromwell was brazen.

Polished brass flooring reflected sepia-toned images. Polished brass ceilings reflected those reflections. Polished-brass cloth upholstered chaise lounges sitting at polished-brass control consoles. Viewports lined with polished brass showed a view out the bow. A polished-brass serving cart held polished-brass pitchers and polished-brass goblets.

Two navigators sat forward of the Captain's chaise, while behind it sat the operations engineer and the environmental engineer, respectively. The Captain's chaise swiveled on its maglev in all directions, a palmcom mounted at the end of one brass-cloth armrest.

"Bring the helm round to point two-seven-five degrees at warp point-five," Jack said.

Both navigators repeated the course instructions.

"Engage," Jack ordered.

"Course engaged," both navigators said simultaneously. Ships the size of the Oliver Cromwell were required to have two human navigators in addition to their multiple redundant computer navigational systems, each rechecking the calculations and measurements for safety.

They had just steered clear of local traffic in the Southern Birds constellation and had entered the interstellar traffic lanes on the Imperial Highway, that conduit of space traffic for all travelers coming to and from the Imperial Capital, Torgas Prime.

A vessel so large as the Oliver Cromwell could not exceed warp two, even if it were able to achieve such a speed. Even completely empty, Jack doubted it could get to warp one-point-five. With Princess Misty Circi's entire retinue, and its full complement of crew, the Oliver

Cromwell was only at a quarter capacity, only five of its twenty pods occupied.

Jack looked almost regal in his white spats and brass tacks. Why these were traditional Captain's wear was beyond him. He felt ridiculous wearing such archaic clothing. Just gimme a pair a plain formalls, he thought. Furthermore, his hair had been coiffed to the style most recently to rage through the Capital Ignorati, a halo of curls not too terribly dissimilar to the halo of platinum encircling the top of the Imperial scepter.

He might have found it ironic had he known that in that platinum circlet was mounted a cube identical to the one in his pocket.

The short, sharp whistle of the Boson's Mate signaled the entry of the Captain onto the bridge.

Captain Jack Carson stood and saluted, Captain Seamus Starswinger having relinquished his duties temporarily to Jack for the launch. He gave the oncoming Captain a status report and then stepped aside as the other man took command of the bridge.

The Boson's Mate blew another short trill as Jack stepped off the bridge.

Cherise was waiting for him in the Captain's lounge. "You look wonderful," she said, giving him a hug. Behind her, the monitors showed the bridge real-time, Captain Seamus Starswinger doing a status check of all systems.

"Thank you. A brilliant idea to broadcast our journey, by the way." He smiled at her.

An unarmed cruise liner approaching Torgas Prime carrying her August Highness Princess Misty Circi was a momentous event, but one broadcast to a watching Empire was pivotal.

Like him, Cherise was dressed in the latest fashion, her couture assembled in consultation with five designers frequently seen among the Capital Ignorati, her hair coifed more elaborately if similarly to his, a veritable penumbra of a lion's mane.

"You look fabulous," he said.

"The companion to the Lord High Paladin Jack Carson must be properly attired and groomed, no?"

"As the Lady High Duenna to the August Highness Princess Misty Circi, you'll have to be more than properly attired and groomed. You'll have to be properly behaved as well."

"Then you'll be lonely and sad," Cherise objected, pouting.

Jack giggled. "There'll be time." He looked into her eyes and saw eternity.

"We're sitting ducks," Misty said, bursting into the lounge. She stopped short as seeing them in an embrace. "Bad timing, looks like."

Jack let go of Cherise. "You have a talent for that."

"I do, don't I?" She grinned. "We should have an armed escort, at least. Not that the Emperor would try to do anything, but what about pirates?"

"Don't worry, Misty," Jack said, "Nothing will happen to us."

Chapter 18

"Attack!" Admiral Camelus ordered.

Armed with a blasma pistol, Prime Minister Custos Messium watched from the rear of the bridge, intent on the viewscreens and the single undefended cruise liner, the Oliver Cromwell, that cruised obliviously toward Torgas Prime.

They were aboard the Torgas Armada Flagship, Lepanto, named after a naval battle between ocean-going vessels back on Earth in the Christian Era year 1571. The Lepanto was a small city unto itself, its capacity equal to that of its prey, the Oliver Cromwell. Unlike its prey, the Lepanto bristled with guns of all sizes. And if she fired all weapons on one side, she could have launched herself into a spin.

The armada that Admiral Camelus had just ordered to attack was comprised of twenty fighter carriers with each three hundred fighters, fifty destroyers, thirty battleships, forty-five battle cruisers, two hundred scouts, and five hundred patrol cruisers, as well as over a thousand logistical supply ships. Such an armada was only deployed in the event of a direct threat upon the Imperial Capital, Torgas Prime.

Before the attack, Admiral Camelus had addressed the entire fleet over secured comchannels. "My fellow Torgassans, sailors, gunners, pilots, and crew, we are about to embark upon an assault on an enemy far more powerful than any we've ever faced. The cruise liner Oliver Cromwell may look like a helpless beached whale, but it is precisely that supposed vulnerability that makes this ship and its occupants so dangerous. You may have heard rumors that aboard the Oliver Cromwell is a nine-year-old princess. She claims to be Princess Misty Circi. Yes, Circi, a name once heralded as great, a family who once ruled the galaxy two thousand years ago. These upstarts who have commandeered this name for its gravitas would have you believe that she approaches Torgas Prime on a mission of peace. Usurpation is her only goal, the usurpation of Imperial power from his August Highness Emperor Phaeton Torgas. Therefore, we will withhold no weapon, will leave no gun unmanned, and will bombarded this cursed vessel the Oliver Cromwell with the utmost fusillade of blows until our magazines are emptied. Once you begin firing, you are not to stop until nothing is left of this cruise liner but its detritus. Nothing! Keep firing until it's gone!

"My fellow Torgassans, sailors, gunners, pilots, and crew, go forth and destroy!"

Prime Minister Custos Messium had listened with cynicism. He'd heard a thousand rousing speeches in his lifetime, and the Admiral's wasn't terribly different. He'd come aboard the flagship Lepanto with his bulldog assassin, Detective Monique "The Bruiser" Brewster to insure with his own eyes that the upstart Princess Misty Circi and her Paladin, the scavenger Jack Carson, were obliterated once and for all. Like Admiral Camelus, Prime Minister Messium did not underestimate the threat posed by this pair.

And even though the nine-year-old girl proclaimed herself princess and seemed the more prominent threat, it was Jack Carson, the scavenger of ill repute, with three divorces, four bankruptcies, and more arrests than both combined, who posed the most danger.

How had he acquired a cube? Custos had asked himself a thousand times. How do we get it from him or obliterate him or both?

"You know this assault will fail," Brewster had told him yesterday as the Armada had converged on the cruise liner.

"Eh? You speak treason." He stared at her, alarmed.

"Is it treason to prepare for all possibilities?" She stared back at him, calm.

He was glad they were alone. He'd have had to kill her if anyone had overheard. "No, no, of course not, but you can't be so sure that it will fail."

"The Junkman has eluded me three times. Me, Detective Monique Brewster. No one's ever eluded me once. What makes you think some bludgeon-minded dolt like Admiral Camelus will be any more success-ful against the Junkman? Sheer force of arms?" Brewster snorted.

She even sounded like a bulldog, Custos thought, careful not to let the thoughts reach his face. Although he was taller than her by an inch or so, she outweighed him nearly two-to-one. Prime Minister Custos Messium was very thin.

"So you must be prepared," Custos had told her.

"I am," she'd told him. "While you're on the bridge, watching the charade, I'll be in my Viper in launch bay two thirty-seven, waiting until it's clearly a debacle."

Watching from the rear of the bridge while Admiral Camelus launched the attack, Prime Minister Custos Messium feared Brewster was right.

On screen, phalanxes of ships launched volleys of laser, phaser, and blasma bolts, sunlight cannons, uberlight torpedoes, pseudolight mortars, and epithets in all the vernaculars. The side of the Oliver Cromwell erupted with constellations of light, each pinprick of light a huge gout of flame.

The deck shook under Custos in time with the blows. How odd, he thought, the flagship Lepanto not among the attacking ships.

The armada surrounding the cruise liner continued to pummel the helpless ship. The deck under the Prime Minister's feet continued to shake.

"Lord Admiral, we're under attack!"

Custos realized what was happening, remembered the Admiral's ex-hortation to keep firing, and left the bridge at a dead run.

Behind him, he heard, "Our own armada is bombarding us!"

Chaos erupted, the deck under him lurched as the gravgens failed momentarily, the lights died, and emergency lighting kicked in, klaxons blared, sailors scrambled up and down corridors, and Custos headed for the nearest escape pod.

Brewster was right, he thought, hoping she'd been able to launch successfully. How Princess Circi and Paladin Jack had done it, Custos didn't know. Somehow they'd deceived the entire armada into thinking that the flagship Lepanto was the cruise liner Oliver Cromwell.

The Prime Minister struggled along the corridor, battling the flickering gravity and a steady stream of sailor going the other direction. The deck under his feet bucked and slewed in the continuing bombardment, and he crawled the last fifty feet to the escape pod hatch.

"This one's mine, mate!" the terrified sailor inside said.

Custos pulled the blasma pistol from his belt and blew the sailor's head off.

Getting the body out became much easier when the gravgens failed completely. Now covered with blood, Custos sealed the pod and strapped himself in before hitting the launch sequence. He prayed his escape pod was somehow missed in the all-out assault. The pod launched, shooting him into space and safely beyond the offensive line of attacking Imperial vessels.

* * *

Brewster checked her anchors once again and looked past the Viper toward the stern of the Oliver Cromwell.

Just visible astern was the flaming wreckage of the Imperial Flagship Lepanto. Tiny streaks continued to spear the already battered and blistered flagship, the Imperial armada as yet unaware they were bombarding their own ship, and not the cruise liner.

She had launched at the first sign of trouble and had escaped the offensive perimeter, had guessed—and found—the cruise liner a parsec away, placidly continuing on its leisurely course toward Torgas Prime as though nothing usual had just occurred not far astern.

Brewster had then matched pace with the Oliver Cromwell in her Viper and had brought it in for a smooth and undetected landing on the larger vessel's underbelly.

Her airshell crackling at having to repel the vacuum around her, Brewster searched the hull for a maintenance hatch. Before leaving Torgas Prime, she'd obtained the Cromwell's blueprints and access codes through Imperial intelligence, an oxymoron and conundrum simultaneously.

Armed with the ability to access any part of the huge cruise liner, Brewster found a hatch and opened it with an access code, carrying on her back all the tools she needed to sabotage the vessel, her palmcom easily storing the Cromwell's schematics.

Inside the hatch, she paused to reconnoiter.

The trilithium core was only two bulkheads over. She couldn't have asked for a more propitious landing. I'll be in and out of here in less than an hour, Brewster thought. She dropped from the access tube into a corridor.

Empty.

As she'd thought, the crew whittled down to its skeleton, their passenger manifest limited to the "Princess" and her entourage, which though vast was barely a quarter of the cruise liner's capacity.

Brewster strode brazenly down the corridor toward engineering, wearing a nondescript uniform similar to those worn by Heiress Cruise Lines crew members.

The hatch to the engine room was locked and coded.

Brewster held her palmcom to the reader, and both beeped. The hatch swung aside.

A Boson looked up from a control panel that took half the room.

Brewster blasma'd him, and the figure crumpled. She dragged the body out of sight and made her way into the engine core, ignoring the warning signs, overriding the "No access permitted" locks.

She hoisted the pack from her back and set it on the floor. Above her pulsed the trilithium drive, a fusion reactor that forced three molecules of hydrogen into one molecule of lithium and harnessed the energy thereby released.

She got the timer and pushed the pack up against the cerasma barrier, that clear layer of heat- and impact-resistant material between her and obliteration. She could barely look at the turbid nuclear soup just beyond the cerasma containment vessel.

Brewster smiled and backed out of the fusion chamber, then made a hasty retreat to the access tube where she'd entered.

Detaching the anchors and boarding the Viper, Detective Monique Brewster navigated away and put as much distance between her ship and the Oliver Cromwell.

Her palmcom beeped to inform her of the impending detonation, and she dimmed her vids in anticipation.

"Three," it told her, "two, one, now."

At first, nothing happened. The Oliver Cromwell looked unchanged. Then a ripple moved across it from amidships toward bow and stern, bright cracks spreading across the hull like hot flowing lava underneath the brittle shell of cooler, hardened rock. Then an explosion engulfed the Oliver Cromwell, and the blast sent debris in all directions, flaming shards spreading out in a small nova with the shockwave. They're dead! she thought.

The shockwave jolted Brewster as though waking her from a dream, and she watched helplessly as her obliterated Viper disintegrated before her eyes, illuminating the hull of the Oliver Cromwell under her with its explosion.

Panicking, Brewster looked around. Then she started pounding on the hull. "No! No! NO!" she screamed each time she struck the cruise liner's intact hull.

A figure appeared nearby, a blasma gun aimed at her. The one-armed man whose left shoulder and face had been half-blasted away at some point in the past grinned at her. "Jack said I'd find you here, Detective Brewster. I'm Ignatius Argonavis, Ig for short. You can come with me peacefully, or you can die. Which is it?"

* * *

Emperor Phaeton Torgas stared morosely at his minister of interior affairs. "Destroyed? The flagship itself? By our own armada?"

"How could that happen?!" Andromeda demanded, leaping to her feet. "We just saw the cruise liner being destroyed!"

The Emperor and his daughter had just watched the vid feeds of the battle and had seen the Oliver Cromwell disintegrate under a barrage so intense that Phaeton had for the tiniest period of measurable time felt pity for its occupants.

But it had passed quickly.

Relieved, he had been grateful to be spared the guilt.

And now, and few minutes later, he was being told otherwise. "Minister," he said, "explain yourself!"

The interior minister, newly appointed to her position after being abruptly vacated by its previous incumbent, abruptly vacated her bowels and began to weep. "Please don't kill me like you did my predecessor, please, your August Highness!"

"Tell me what happened! Stars above, just say it!"

"That's just it! We don't know. One minute, they launched the attack, and the next, the cruise liner was a parsec away, intact! And the armada flagship Lepanto had been obliterated! By our own armada!" She broke down in tears and threw herself on the floor at his feet.

Andromeda held her nose in disgust. "Get her out of here!"

The Emperor waved at the servants to do this daughter's bidding, the overpowering stench of voided bowel nearly causing his eyes to water.

"Incoming com from Prime Minister Custos Messium, your August Highness."

Servants cleared away the interior minister and her mess, and a vidscreen descended from the ceiling.

"Your August Highness," Custos said, his thin, ghostly face gigantic. "Forgive me. I should have anticipated the subterfuge. Brewster warned me something would happen. You were right from the very beginning, your August Highness. This scavenger is more of a threat to your rule than all your enemies combined."

"So it's true then, Lord Minister."

"Yes, your August Highness."

"But we just saw the cruise liner go up in flames!" Andromeda protested. "How can this be?"

"Forgive me, your August Highness," Messium said, his face drawn and sure, "but he has in his possession something that until a few months ago we thought was unique. He has a cube."

Andromeda's gaze went to the scepter in the father's hand.

Emperor Phaeton nodded to her to try to dispel the disbelief in her gaze. "Yes, daughter, one of these. A Gaussian Holistic Oscillating Subliminal Tesseract—a ghost cube."

She recoiled in shock and horror. "What are you going to do, Father? You have to stop them!"

He frowned. "Since we can't stop them from coming here, we go the next step better." Then he brightened and smiled. "Prime Minister Custos Messium, would you do the honors of inviting Princess Misty Circi and her Paladin, Captain Jack Carson, to attend upon the Imperial Court here on Torgas Prime?"

Chapter 19

"Jack, it's a trap!"

He glanced over at Misty, Cherise looking drawn and pale. They had just receiving a com from the Prime Minister Custos Messium, in which he had invited them to Torgas Prime to meet with his August Highness Emperor Phaeton Torgas at the palace itself.

Jack smiled. "Of course it's a trap."

"And knowing it's a trap," Misty said, also smiling. "You'll know exactly what to do about it."

Two days ago, he'd have panicked and whined and hemmed and hawed and found some excuse to turn tail the other direction and find the nearest smokeshop.

But after diverting an armada into attacking its own flagship and deceiving Brewster into blowing up her own Viper, Jack felt confident he could do anything.

At the approach of the armada, he'd noticed the similarity in size between the Oliver Cromwell and Lepanto. The rest had been easy, it seemed, his ability to maintain the illusion with one part of his mind undistracted by events swirling around him aboard the Cromwell.

And during the bombardment of the flagship, Brewster's viper had come shooting out a launch bay and had veered toward the Cromwell with unerring accuracy. How she'd found them, Jack didn't know, but with a little concentration, he'd altered her reality just enough for her to think she was destroying the cruise liner. Brewster now occupied a makeshift brig down in the bilges.

The thought of walking into the palace on Torgas Prime—and into a trap—didn't bother him much. He felt he could handle whatever the Emperor might have lying in wait for them.

* * *

An Empire watched, nervously quiescent at this self-proclaimed princess who'd evaded two attempts to stop her cruise liner and who now approached the Imperial Capital, presumed usurper but virtually unarmed and defenseless.

The paparazzi printed stories about the princess and her cortege faster than the Treasury presses printed money. Wild and lurid—and wildly inaccurate—descriptions of Misty's life on Canis Dogma Five, of Jack's and Cherise's lives on Alpha Tuscana, of Jack's adventures roaming the galaxy in search of salvage, of Jack's nasty divorces and despicable bankruptcies and innumerable arrests by the Imperial patrol, rippled across the airwaves by the hour, providing the cruise liner with a little comic relief if not much in the way of accurate information.

In the five days from the armada attack gone awry and their arrival at Torgas Prime, fictionalized dramas about the three of them had become the main fare of evening vidcom entertainment, but by far the most popular and successful shows were the sitcoms about Jack. Which he might have found funny if they hadn't been so accurate.

"It's almost as if they were looking over your shoulder," Misty told him after seeing an episode of "Gambler Jack, Card Shark."

The cruise liner settled into orbit above Torgas Prime, a bright green-and-blue tropical world without ice caps, circling a young blue primary. A smaller secondary star, a red dwarf, orbited the primary far beyond the habitable zone, tracing its lurid arc across Torgas Prime's night sky for fifteen years at a time, and adding a purplish tint to the daytime sky the other fifteen years.

The attacking armada had turned into both an escort for the Oliver Cromwell and a funeral procession for all the lives lost aboard the flagship Lepanto.

On the day after the attack, Misty had dressed in her royal couture, a dainty tiara upon her fashionably-coiffed hair, a few choice selections from the Circi Crown Jewels adorning her person, and had addressed the Empire. "Citizens of Torgas, I am Princess Misty Circi, and I bring to you my condolences over the loss of your fellow citizens in the wreckage of the flagship Lepanto. I feel greatly aggrieved at your loss, and while nothing can compensate for the deaths of your sons, daughters, sisters, brothers, fathers, and mothers, please know that I share in your loss and pray for their salvation in the next realm." She'd then bowed her head and had shed a single tear.

The Emperor had followed moments later to address the Empire from the palace, his manner grave. He too had expressed his condolences but in comparison to the broadcast but moments before, he had come off as insincere and shallow, frustrated and awkward. Princess Andromeda sitting just to his left had looked homicidal.

It had been that vision, the face of a princess contemplating murder, that had most disturbed Jack right up to the time of their arrival in orbit above the Torgassan Capital.

Their ground transportation was a limoshuttle from the Emperor's fleet—not the Imperial limo, reserved for the Emperor himself, but the next best thing: Princess Andromeda's limo. The sequined limo with its diamond-encrusted exhaust flukes, platinum wings, and gold-thread upholstery seemed appropriately lavish for an arriving princess. Jack found it ironic that an arriving, usurping princess would descend from orbit in the incumbent princess's limoshuttle.

They landed on the tarmac just beyond the terminal, the Prime Minister Custos Messium prominently visible above the other cabinet minister assembled to welcome the arriving guests, his white hair and conspicuous height emphasizing his gaunt, familiar features.

Epaulets of gold, cufflink diamonds, and rainbows of insignia accenting his uniform, Jack marched off the boarding ramp and stopped at its base, saluted the gathered government officials, and then stood at attention beside the ramp while a band struck up the Torgassan Imperial Anthem.

We should have composed our own, Jack thought, as Misty emerged from the limoshuttle.

"Her August Highness, Princess Misty Circi of Canis Dogma Five," Jack intoned in his most sonorous voice.

The assembled diplomats bowed, Custos at their head going to one knee.

Misty descended the ramp, resplendent in her evening gown, her dogstone bracelets and necklace glittering in the afternoon light of the young blue primary, her Duenna Cherise carrying her silken, sequined train.

Prime Minister Messium stood to greet her, kissing her outstretched hand as she curtseyed. He looked twice as tall as she, a contrast exacerbated by his rail-thin form.

Her smile was perfect as she accepted his obeisance and greeting.

"On behalf of his August Highness the Emperor Phaeton Torgas, and his daughter her August Highness the Princess Andromeda Torgas," Custos said, pausing dramatically, "a thousand welcomes." His smile was perfectly mischievous. "Enjoy your stay, your Highness."

A small gasp among the audience was quickly stifled, his addressing her as simply, "Highness" and not "August Highness" clearly denying her status equal to that of Emperor Torgas and Princess Andromeda.

"Thank you, Lord Minister Messium," she replied, a mere flicker in her gaze indicating she'd noticed anything.

It was exactly such subtleties that would have been lost on Jack three months ago, when he'd first laid his hands on the cube. It was exactly such subtleties that reverberated in his consciousness since.

Now wait a minute, he told himself. Covert hostilities had been a daily feature of his for as long as he could remember, and such slights had frequently burned in his thoughts deep into the night, inflicting their shame and humiliation long after the person had administered the slight and left Jack's presence.

"Your flitter awaits this way, your Highness." Messium gestured at the bunting- and banner-bedecked walkway, a plush red carpet so thick it was almost a berm leading through the terminal to the waiting flitter beyond. Messium bowed again, and stepped aside.

Misty nodded. "Thank you, Lord Minister Messium, you're more than kind." She stepped along the plush walkway.

Messium fell into step behind her, right next to Jack.

"Lord Paladin, I presume?"

"Lord Minister Messium, a pleasure," Jack replied.

The two men nodded to each other without breaking stride. "A pleasant trip, Lord Paladin?"

"Quite, Lord Minister, barring a mishap or two." He glanced over his shoulder. "I've brought you a present."

Ignatius Argonavis and his charge, the hulking bulk known as Detective Monique "The Bruiser" Brewster, were just exiting the limoshuttle behind them.

"Very kind of you, Lord Paladin," Minister Messium said, his smile perfect but his gaze giving away his fury. "May my personnel take custody?"

"She's not a bother, Lord Prime Minister," Jack said, loud enough for the Imperial flunkies around them to hear.

"Oh, but I wouldn't presume to bother you with her keeping any further, Lord Paladin."

"She's collateral against your good behavior, Lord Prime Minister." Jack smiled.

The pale skin turned beet-red, then subsided. "As you wish, Lord Paladin."

Misty in the meantime was smiling and waving to the crowd as bouquets flew overhead and landed on the carpet, marigolds and roses, chrysanthemums and camellias, daisies and lilies. Servants gathered the bouquets, their scent quickly overpowering the stench of betrayal coming off the Prime Minister.

"What do you and the little usurper want?" Messium asked.

Jack admired the man's steel, remembering that the Prime Minister was on his second Emperor, having served Phaeton's father and having survived the transition. Both considerable accomplishments. "Time will clarify all, Lord Minister," he said cryptically. Not that he hoped to compete in cryptics with one so experienced, but simply that the die had been cast and all the galaxy awaited their fall.

The open-top limoflitter was equipped with a place for the honoree to stand. Jack sat on one side, Misty standing a few feet forward of him, while Custos Messium sat on the other side, level with him. Several other vehicles would load with the remaining personnel of Misty's retinue and follow at their leisure.

Sitting behind Misty, Jack realized just how slight she was, how vulnerable and ethereal, small even for a nine-year-old girl. Sharp, savvy, and smart, but an insubstantial nine nevertheless.

The wide boulevard between spaceport and palace was crammed on each side with spectators all the way to the palace. A vertical city, antigravs suspending its insubstantial arches, colonnades, skywalks, and crosspaths, the Capital was a chaotic vertigo of intricate architecture. At night, it was purported to look like a swarm of fireflies. On every available surface, faces looked down upon the flittercade, the tiny form of Princess Misty looking up and smiling and waving. Building sides were plastered with close-ups of her face, with occasional momentary cutaways to Messium or Jack.

For all the waving the crowd did back, it was remarkably silent.

"Are they always so lacking exuberance?" Jack asked.

"My question is their question. The uncertainty ties their tongues."

As it certainly should, Jack thought. He held his smile fixed to his face and continued to wave, but inside was an insidious anxiety. What did he and the little usurper want?

At that moment, Jack couldn't have answered.

She was adamant she was the Princess, and the Emperor might confer that status upon her and legitimate it as only an Emperor could. But what about Jack?

Jack Carson, orphan adopted into the bosom of a brothel, runaway
it age twelve, pilot of his own Salvager by twenty two, thrice divorced
and quadruple bankrupt, more arrests than both combined, the finder
of an alien artifact that exhorted him to be Emperor.

What did he want?

At the moment, Jack couldn't have answered.

He sighed under his smile and looked at the crush of humanity
around him, their anxieties infectious. By what right or mandate did
he have to insinuate himself between them and their security?

By the word of a feisty, nine-year-old girl?

Nearly as ludicrous as Jack's becoming Emperor.

The journey finally ended at the palace entrance.

The vertiginous city restrained its impulse to soar the closer it got
to the palace, and the infrastructure abutting the Emperor's home assumed an obsequious note one would expect from anyone approaching his August Highness.

The palace itself was fortress and home, administration center and
cultural beacon, the sprawling complex four small cities within a city.
At its center was a throne room for his August Highness Emperor
Phaeton Torgas, a towering rotunda of glasma and steel, atop the rotunda a replica of the platinum circlet at the head of the Imperial
scepter.

Inside it a cube.

The limoflitter pulled up to the gate, which swung wide onto a cir-
cular drive, a fountain dancing in the middle.

A band struck up the Imperial Anthem as Misty stepped down from
the flitterlimo and was greeted by a woman who introduced herself
as the interior minister. A small knot of civilians stood nearby, their
presence a puzzle to Jack.

After he was introduced to her, a pleasant smile possessed her face.
"Oh, *you're* Jack. I was wondering who these people were asking for.
Seems you have visitors already."

The small knot of civilians rushed at him.

"You, Jack Carson, are hereby served a summons to appear—"

"You owe your ex-wife Felicity Carson—"

"Payments of your salvage vessel are five months—"

"The department of revenue recovery on Denebi III—"

"You're under arrest for failure to appear—"

"Hey!" Misty shouted, louder than them all. "You'll just have to wait!" she said, hand on her hip. "How can a princess be presented to the Emperor without her Paladin?"

The solicitors looked amongst themselves, befuddled.

"Upon my word, you may serve your summonses once the ceremony is over." Misty looked among them. "You have my oath. I, Princess Misty Circi, do hereby swear to make Jack Carson available to you to serve your various legal citations at the conclusion of today's ceremony." She looked at them one by one until she had them cowed. "Thank you." She turned to him and bellowed, "Stars above, Jack, couldn't you have taken care of all that before we got here?"

He followed her abashedly, falling into step beside the Prime Minister again.

"Sounds like a heap of trouble," Messium murmured, his tone not unsympathetic.

"Seems to follow me," Jack muttered.

Their procession threaded between two lines of an honor guard, saluting soldiers in dress spats and white gloves, and then they were in the palace.

The first thing Jack noticed was the silence. It seemed to enfold them like a tomb. Much of it to increase discretion, nearly every surface was designed to absorb sound. Their progress was deathly silent.

The second thing Jack noticed was the subtle opulence. Silk wallpapers whose fabric itself was embossed with its own pattern, gold filigree threading through carpet and drape, elaborate trim embedded with silver thread, portraiture framed with intricate trim, lighting that appeared source-less, as though seeping from the walls and ceilings through osmosis. An opulence intended not to overwhelm but to assert itself subliminally.

The subliminal opulence obscured the third observation from Jack for the first few minutes: That their course was a windy one, meant to confuse and befuddle, intended to be irretraceable.

Oddly, he had no impression at all that they were being watched. Footservants stood sentinel at every corridor intersection, their faces impassive, their gazes unwavering and obsequious, dropping to a knee at the Princess's passing. Wait staff were everywhere, yet unobtrusive as furniture, their genuflections as silent as ghosts. Jack knew that there had to be cameras everywhere and multiple monitoring stations actively tracking their progress through the labyrinthine palace, but Jack found no evidence of either, neither visual nor intuitive.

Then their procession entered a long corridor; at its end a terrible long distance away were a pair of double doors. The corridor itself grew gradually taller and wider, but all in such perfect proportion that the doors to the throne room at its expansive other end were impossibly small—much too small for a human being and probably too small for a mouse.

The Lilliputian guards besides these doors lent the corridor its only perspective. Above these doors was that platinum circlet again, in relief, the cube at its center. This emblem dwarfed all else. This, too, all intended to impress.

Jack felt as he strode the long, expansive corridor that he was gradually shrinking, being diminutized to the size of the Lilliputian guards.

Whatever spirit or pride or stature that a person possessed before entering this corridor was slowly worn away until the spark of one's spirit was compressed to a pinprick. Not until you are completely humble may you attend upon his August Highness the Emperor Phaeton Torgas.

Their party stopped at the double doors, and Jack stepped forward. "Her August Highness Princess Misty Circi of Canis Dogma Five."

The guards all bowed and the doors opened wide.

Onto a corridor whose foreshortened dimensions mirrored the corridor behind them, as short as the other corridor was long, at the far end a throne that looked gigantic, and upon that throne a man, alone.

Robust and ramrod straight, he held a scepter capped with a platinum circlet, a plain silver cube suspended inside it.

Jack stepped forward five paces and knelt to touch his head to the floor, then he stepped one pace to the side. "Her August Highness Princess Misty Circi of Canis Dogma Five."

Misty entered the chamber, her robes resplendent, the full complement of Crown Jewels making her look oddly lighter despite their nearly fifty pounds of heft. She stepped forward effortlessly, elegantly, and bowed, knee to carpet.

"Pathetic," the Emperor said. "You and your newt-faced Paladin," he added, the sneer in his voice matching the contempt on his face.

Jack would have hurt his neck had he looked, per protocol keeping his gaze on the ground at Misty's feet.

Misty laughed lightly, then ceased abruptly. "Then why not kill us outright?" She smiled slyly. "Because you can't. Really, Emp, you must know you're defeated. You must! And yet you've brought your entire cabinet to witness your last attempt to hold onto power, and put your daughter behind you to kill us in case you fail somehow." Misty spread her hands.

The wall retracted to expose on either side several rows of chairs, bureaucrats of all shapes and sizes—but predominantly round and fat—occupying them all.

"And failing that," she added, "you then put your own personal assassin in charge of our escort, the redoubtable Prime Minister Lord Custos Messium.

"All in vain, of course, your August Highness. So your calling us pathetic is like a red dwarf calling a blue-white supergiant a dim bulb. Really, Emp, you're supposed to be the brightest bulb in the chandelier, or at least in the galaxy. What happened?"

The Emperor's hand on the scepter clenched and unclenched, the knuckles white. A muscle rippled in his jaw and a vein wriggled at his temple. His eyebrows seamed to grow together of form a single line of hair.

"We're not a threat to you, Emp," Misty said, an impish smile on her face. "So why the attack on our ship? Pity Admiral Camelus didn't survive. The real tragedy was the five thousand sailors who died alongside him. His own armada killing him did you the favor of ridding you of his incompetence."

"You insufferable little witch!" Torgas exploded, leaping to his feet. He looked ready to hurl the scepter at her.

"Pipe down!" she said, and pushed an open hand at him.

He was hurled back into his throne, the front two legs coming off the dais momentarily.

"You'll probably want your bulldog back at some point." Misty gestured over her shoulder.

Ignatius Argonavis guided his prisoner forward.

Detective Monique "The Bruiser" Brewster looked two sizes smaller right then, as she was turned over to the palace guards.

"Detective Brewster's many attempts to capture or kill us failed miserably, of course. Including her last attempt, in which she tried to breach the cerasma containment vessel of the trilithium reactor aboard the Oliver Cromwell." Misty grinned. "And blew up her own Viper instead."

Then Misty backed to the side by a pace. "And finally we arrive at the most insidious betrayal of all." She looked at Cherise, kneeling just two paces behind her.

Jack stared aghast at his friend.

Cherise began to weep, her face crumpling. "Oh, Jack, I'm so sorry! They threatened to kill everyone at the Southern Birds if I didn't spy on you."

He watched as though through a sterile glasma pane as she crumbled, begging his forgiveness and weeping disconsolately.

"Worse yet, Emperor," Misty continued, "you have two more attempts up your sleeve to avoid your fate, but both will prove futile."

"Salacious succubus!" he screamed. "Want do you want?!"

"One would think at nine years old that I'm much too young to know what you mean. But duck, weave, squirm, and dance, Emp, because none of it will avert the fate that is already written on the stars for you and your Empire."

"What do you want!?" he screamed again, his face red and bulging, his neck tendons straining as though he struggled against some invisible restraint.

"Ah yes, the central question. Well, since you put it bluntly, I'll answer it bluntly. We want you gone.

"Abdicated, overthrown, assassinated, suicided. Whatever means you'd prefer, Emperor. Pretty simple, isn't it? Your Empire is finished."

Princess Andromeda stepped from a hidden doorway behind the throne and blasted Misty with a blasma pistol.

The girl crumpled to the floor, and chaos erupted.

"No!" Jack leaped to her side and held her. "No!" and began to weep.

"Jack," she rasped, a trickle of blood seeping from one corner of her mouth. "Jack, listen."

He suppressed his sobs, seeing she was fading fast. The blast had struck her in the abdomen, eviscerating her.

"Jack, it's up to you now. You can do it. You must take the Emperor's cube from him."

"Misty!? No, don't ... " He could see her eyes were glazing.

"It's all been for you, Jack." She coughed up a gout of blood. "All for you. Everything I've done. To help you gain the confidence you needed. Jack, look at me."

He blinked away his tears.

Her gaze seemed to clear for a moment. "You have all the resources you'll ever need inside you. You always have. You just needed to be shown. I'll be with you from beyond, Jack. Rule justly and well, Emperor Jack."

And she died.

The bolt seemed to take a long time to reach him.

Jack knew what it was before it struck, but he seemed helpless to prepare. Misty had just died in his arms. What could possibly be more important than that? Couldn't they see he was devastated and disconsolate?

As the bolt struck him, Jack apprehended its nature and its source and its essence in ways that had eluded him since he'd placed his hands on the alien ghost cube three months before.

Yes, the power behind the Emperor's blow might have killed him.

And as much as Jack might have liked to prepare for the blow in the eternity between Phaeton Torgas's launching the attack and the blast actually striking him, there really wasn't any way to prepare.

Not for this.

The Milky Way reeled below him, the local galaxy group not far behind.

The alien race that had manufactured the cubes weren't extinct, per se. Neither did they exist any longer, either. Not in the dimensions accessible to the Human Race, anyway. And as might be expected, the ethnocentric blindness of humanity had masked its ability to grasp the incorporeal planes of existence all around them, those places of being impossible to measure, observe, or even know.

When this blow of ethereal energy from the Emperor's ghost cube struck Jack, it did kill him, in one manner of speaking. It displaced his soul long enough from his body to launch it on a journey through time.

I always thought that time was static, Jack thought, as the universe shrank before him.

The idea came to him in words because language was how Jack integrated the reality. But he realized that the alien presence who'd imparted the idea hadn't communicated in words.

The universe shrank to a single point in time.

Jack was the point in time.

Jack was god.

Again, the words, but transmitted along some medium that defied the limitations of language. He was omnipotent, omniscient, omnitemporal.

And still unalterably, ineluctably, insufferably human.

He slammed back into his body and channeled the blow into an alternate universe. He might have encapsulated himself and let the energy wash past him, but everyone behind him would have been obliterated.

Phaeton struck again and Jack opened a door to elsewhere between them.

Andromeda fired her blasma pistol at him, but its energy was a glow globe to her father's supernova.

Jack was no longer in its path when the blast struck. He lifted the blasma pistol from her hand. "You won't need that."

Her open hand whistled through air through the space where his face had been.

The momentary distraction allowed the Emperor's next bolt to land.

Jack had a choice, and he thought long over the dilemma.

Let the real-time energy destroy the molecules of the body that his spirit had occupied for thirty-two years, or save his body by deflecting it, killing Andromeda with the eddy?

He ached at Misty's death, she who had been all but a daughter to him, and he hesitated to inflict similar suffering on Phaeton Torgas, who for all his Imperial pretensions was also another human being. Me or Princess Andromeda? Jack wondered for a short eternity.

And even though Jack now knew he would survive the destruction of that collection of molecules which had housed his spirit so faithfully, he elected to preserve it, even though that meant Andromeda would die in the backwash of the blast.

The universe had its own immutable laws of action and consequence. Time started again, and her body liquefied and splashed the floor behind him.

"No!" the Emperor wailed, reaching a hand her way.

Jack lifted the scepter from his other hand as Torgas lunged toward her remains.

The robust man who'd ruled an Empire shrank as he crumpled where his daughter had fallen, where nothing remained but a liquid muck, vaporized by the blast.

Jack sighed and stepped to Misty's body, tears filling his eyes. "Here, help me out," he told Cherise.

The woman he'd loved when young and had lost and regained and lost again stared at him through fearful eyes, tears streaking her cheeks, and knelt beside him.

He brushed away her tears. "They'll never be able to hurt you again, Cherise."

Together, they lifted Misty's body and placed it at the foot of the throne. Together, they knelt and bowed.

"Princess Misty Circi of Canis Dogma Five, I hereby posthumously name you inheritor of all my domains, and honorary Empress Misty the First, may you rule wisely and well."

Jack held the ghost cube he'd found on Canis Dogma Five in one hand and the ghost cube he'd taken from Emporia Phaeton Torgas in the other , and he launched himself into time and space to search for Misty's soul.

But it was nowhere, and nowhen, to be found.

She was irrevocably, irretrievably gone.

Emperor Jack wept inconsolably.

Epilogue

"Jack, you won't believe this."

He glanced over at Cherise from his favorite spot on the balcony of their suite high in the palace. Below, the vertigo Capital city sparkled, never sleeping.

The glow of her palmcom lit her face from beyond the rounded bulge of her abdomen. They'd married soon after his coronation, and now she was six months pregnant.

Jack's first year as Emperor was drawing to a close. He couldn't remember feeling so tired. The moment he'd taken the throne, every long-simmering dispute, every suppressed grudge, all the local conflicts, and every politician or military leader who'd pined for that next rung of the power ladder, had erupted in rebellion. Many had harbored long-standing resentments at having been subdued under the Torgassans, but some simply sought to expand their spheres of influence.

"Every single vid—and the Torgassans had a lot of surveillance vid—is lacking the one person it should have."

He frowned in her direction. "Huh?"

Nearly every rebel had backed down after a personal visit from Jack. With the two ghost cubes, Jack was able to suspend the constraints of time and distance and place himself where and when he needed to be. Sensing he might alter the universe in terrible ways if he were to reverse time at all, he chose only to suspend it for short periods. But when confronted with an Emperor they couldn't kill, or one who might catch them in compromising circumstances, most rebels hesitated in the headlong rush to war.

"I've been reviewing all the surveillance vids from the time you found the cube on Canis Dogma Five," Cherise said.

Jack nodded. "What prompted that?"

The few rebels who'd continued to defy Imperial rule after such a visit frequently found their adherents scattering inexplicably. Jack would simply ghost those adherents with an aversion to their intransigent leader. Without fellow insurgents to carry out orders, most rebels found their rebellions fizzling quickly.

"Do you remember," Cherise said, "how Misty would mysteriously appear different places? Didn't you tell me you'd tried to leave her behind on at least three occasions? And when we escaped from Brewster at the compound on Alpha Tuscana, somehow she not only spirited herself out of the facility, but also located us at the freighter in spite of having no way to know where we'd gone."

Jack nodded, remembering all that, missing her still. They'd held a quiet funeral service for Misty, ensconcing her ashes in a lonely crypt behind the Southern Birds, the erstwhile brothel now an orphanage. And every time Jack visited some obstreperous rebel whose intransigence seemed insurmountable, Jack would bring to mind what Misty had told him.

"You have all the resources you'll ever need inside you."

He smiled at the memory.

"So I started looking at all the vid to see if I could figure out how she was doing it."

Jack looked over at Cherise when she didn't continue. The ghost cube was in his pocket, slightly warm. The other cube, nestled in a platinum circlet atop the Imperial scepter, remained in the throne room and was used primarily for ceremonial occasions.

There were only three rebel leaders who were so fanatical in their opposition to Imperial Rule that Jack had to do more than visit or ghost their adherents. When he ghosted each of those three rebels, he discovered that each was in one way or another so severely imbalanced that they shouldn't have been granted any influence whatsoever. And no amount of cube-induced influence was going to deflect them from their goals. He'd killed them, much to his dismay. Looking back on his first year as Emperor, their executions were what he regretted most.

"Also, I've been thinking how she always knew what was on your mind, how she'd say things that you'd just thought of."

Misty would have handled those three rebels differently, Jack was sure. "So what did you find?"

Cherise shook her head at him. "So you *were* paying attention. I got the distract impression you hadn't heard a word I said."

"Oh I heard it all." Then he grinned at her sheepishly. "I just didn't listen."

"I thought as much." Cherise sighed. "Whatever will I do with you, Jack?"

He shrugged. "Love me forever and hate me occasionally."

They shared a laugh and Cherise shook her head. "I certainly will." She ran her hands across her abdomen. "Do you think she'll be like her namesake?"

"Misty?" Jack shook his head. "I don't know. I hope she's her own person, more than anything."

Cherise nodded. "Me too. So, what I found isn't nearly as important as what I didn't find."

"Didn't find?"

"Jack, in every single vid of you, there isn't a trace of Misty."

He'd known that that's what she was going to say. By tacit agreement, Jack never ghosted Cherise and never had. Still, he'd known.

And he didn't believe it, not wanting to believe it.

"What about the Imperial compound on Alpha Tuscana?"

Cherise shook her head. "That place has more cameras than a porcupine has quills, and she doesn't show up once in their vids."

"But dozens of people saw her on the vid monitors."

"And even now they swear she was there, Jack. The investigation of our escape is rife with descriptions of what she did, what she wore, what she said. But not a bit of it is on video or audio."

Jack stared at Cherise, his mind stumbling toward meaning, his disbelief refusing to yield.

"One final question, Jack."

"Uh huh?"

"In the moments before you put your hand on the cube for the very first time on Canis Dogma Five, did you have any hint that anyone was nearby—any hint at all?"

In his memory, Jack retraced his route from the Scavenger into the relatively intact apartment building and up two floors. Although the memory was hazy, he did remember distinctly having an awareness of feeling totally alone. "No one," he told Cherise. "In fact, I remember wondering where she'd come from."

"That's what I thought." Cherise sighed and shook her head. "Jack, do you remember how old you were the first time you told me you wanted to be Emperor, just so you could give every child a home?"

"I was nine. I'd just turned nine, in fact."

Cherise took his hand in hers. "Jack, I don't think Misty was real. I think she was a projection, a manifestation of that horribly traumatized nine-year-old boy who was determined to see that no one else had to endure what he'd endured."

"What do you mean, 'a projection'?"

"The cube, Jack, a Gaussian Holistic Oscillating Subliminal Tesseract. It integrated your sublimated desires and tesseracted them into the persona we came to know as Misty."

Jack stared at her. "How do you know that?"

"I *don't* know, Jack. It's just a guess. But it's the only one that makes any sense. It's why she doesn't appear on any of the surveillance vids. It's why you couldn't leave her behind. It's why she always knew what you were thinking."

Jack pulled the cube from his pocket. The cube he'd found on Canis Dogma Five, the one that had belonged to Emperor Lochium Circi, the Ninth and Last, rested in his hand, quiescent. Its silvery, reflective sides were quiet and contemplative.

"That's not possible," Jack said. He blinked away his tears, missing her still. He knew with dead certainty that Princess Misty Circi from Canis Dogma Five had not only been real, but had changed the course of history. "Misty was as real as you or me," he told Cherise.

Emperor Jack looked at the cube in his hand. "Isn't that right?" he asked it. "Misty *was* real, wasn't she?"

The cube stared back at him, silent.

* * *

Dear reader,

We hope you enjoyed reading *Cube Rube*. Please take a moment to leave a review, even if it's a short one. Your opinion is important to us.

Discover more books by Scott Michael Decker at https://www.nextchapter.pub/authors/scott-michael-decker-novelist-sacramento-us

Want to know when one of our books is free or discounted? Join the newsletter at http://eepurl.com/bqqB3H

Best regards,
Scott Michael Decker and the Next Chapter Team

About the Author

Scott Michael Decker, MSW, is an author by avocation and a social worker by trade. He is the author of twenty-plus novels in the Science Fiction and Fantasy genres, dabbling among the sub-genres of space opera, biopunk, spy-fi, and sword and sorcery. His biggest fantasy is wishing he were published. His fifteen years of experience working with high-risk populations is relieved only by his incisive humor. Formerly interested in engineering, he's now tilting at the windmills he once aspired to build. Asked about the MSW after his name, the author is adamant it stands for Masters in Social Work, and not "Municipal Solid Waste," which he spreads pretty thick as well. His favorite quote goes, "Scott is a social work novelist, who never had time for a life" (apologies to Billy Joel). He lives and dreams happily with his wife near Sacramento, California.

Where to Find/How to Contact the Author

Websites:
http://ScottMichaelDecker.com/
https://twitter.com/smdmsw
https://www.facebook.com/AuthorSmdMsw

Cube Rube
ISBN: 978-4-86747-584-3

Published by
Next Chapter
1-60-20 Minami-Otsuka
170-0005 Toshima-Ku, Tokyo
+818035793528
21th May 2021

Lightning Source UK Ltd.
Milton Keynes UK
UKHW011835100621
385314UK00001B/128